A GREEN DRAGON SLEEPING

A Green Dragon Sleeping

EMMA CHARLES

To Barbara Louise,
baby sister and biggest cheerleader

Chapter 1

Softly at first, then more clearly, music from the open windows reached into all the nooks and crannies of the *Hotel L'Esperance* gardens. Moonlight, loosed as clouds broke and drifted apart, bleached the colors from orchids and bougainvillea and threw sharp shadows across the garden paths. From the heart of those shadows a small sound like the keening sigh of the wind escaped. The music twirled languidly, carelessly about the night, setting leaves and blossoms alike to motion. Setting, it seemed, the very shadows to motion as one detached itself from the night and stepped into the light.

"Step. Step. Encore... encore. Gracefully! Gracefully!" The music guided Samille's steps through the remembered commands, leading her into that lovely dreamless state of being where everything faded about her. As the music quickened, she followed suit, oblivious for once to the heady fragrance of roses massed in the gardens. Grace and strength marked the long, lean lines of her and her every gesture, every movement with a yearning, desperate pleasure in a world set beyond the night by the strains of Tchaikovsky.

Large, roughened hands closed about her waist and mouth simultaneously. With an instinct born of long years in the city, Samille went limp in her attacker's grasp as he drew her back into the shadows. The grip on her mouth relaxed infinitesimally. She bit down hard.

"Ah-h-h!" The exclamation ended abruptly as a sudden jolt sent both Samille and the man who held her sprawling into a bush. Striking the ground square on her face, Samille rolled, the wind knocked from her lungs. Violent thrashings of the bushes reached her, followed by cries of consternation and dismay as other voices arrived at the scene.

Careful hands lifted her. Opening her eyes, Samille found herself face to face with the strong features of a European male. She cringed involuntarily.

"Sh-h, little ballerina! Can you stand?" Her rescuer's voice, unexpectedly gentle, shook from the unaccustomed exertion.

"Are you hurt?" Still she did not speak, but warily watched his face and those of the men beyond him as he helped her stand. He was at least a head taller than her own slightly above average height. Breathing more easily herself, she tensed beneath his touch as he turned her face into the light. A sharp exclamation escaped him.

"Here, you, hold the light closer. The child's bleeding." Impatiently, he gestured to the others, releasing her as he did so. On the instant, Samille took one long step back onto the shadows, stooped, grasped a handful of stones, then ducked into the bushes and flung her pebbles towards the street.

"What? She's gone! Run, you fools! She's hurt!" Savagely, the European man shoved the man in front of him towards the street and ran himself.

Samille bit her lip and counted to one hundred. When the men did not return, she grimaced and worked her way cautiously to the garden wall. In the densest patch of darkness she knew—oh how well she knew—the strong vines of a creeper would take her slight weight with ease. She slipped noiselessly over the wall and into the alley that ran behind the gardens of the *Hotel L'Esperance*. She was adept at disappearing into the night, a skill that kept her from harm on her erratic midnight excursions. Not only did the more lawless elements of the populace rule the night, but! Samille lurched against a doorway and froze. That sound! The soft pad, pad, pad of a cat leaping past her. It was only a large, rangy tomcat on the prowl for his supper. She took her hand from her heart and forced her body to move on. More than a hundred people in a year, as careless as she herself, lost their lives to tigers which frequently prowled the city environs at night. Never again would she yield to temptation! Too many menaces haunted the nights of Singapore—the Lion City!

Later, curled on the clean straw pallet of her bed, Samille saw again those strong-willed features and heard her rescuer's voice. And now, once the shock had subsided, she'd time enough to realize—an American! Better still that she'd sense enough to hold her tongue. 'Little ballerina!' Foolish dancer, she chided herself. To forget her safety to such an extent had almost proven her downfall.

But, the music! How she remembered! Another time, another world so lost to her now it might all have been a dream... Paris .... Madame Roussin in her fringed black shawl, leaning heavily upon her mahogany cane as the young girls pirouetted before her. M. Blouet, as always, impassive at the piano and Mama.... Mama's face glowing with happiness, reflected from the mirror as Samille twirled and leapt in her turn. And now, now, she told herself harshly, it was time to sleep. Time to forget. Morning would come all too soon as it was. 'Little ballerina'.... laughter and affection warming Mama's voice....

Old Yen-shu looked once at her bruised face and scolded her in a burst of shrill Chinese. Tiny, wizened, ancient, he was a druggist in Singapore's Chinatown district. Eight years ago, so Yen-shu told the story, he and his Malay wife, Sakai, had opened their shop one morning to discover a quivering bunch of rags asleep in their doorway. Childless since the loss of their own young son and infant daughter to cholera, they took in the dirty, mute orphan and gave her a pallet in their storeroom and food in exchange for her labor.

At first she swept out the shop every morning and evening and helped Sakai prepare meals. Gradually, in a combination of pantomime and a flood of Chinese, Yen-shu taught her to help in the preparation of his various herbal concoctions. She ground, chopped, and pulverized roots, dried leaves, and other substances under the watchful eye of the shopkeeper. Other times she ran errands for her master—checking the arrival of junks in the harbor and the loading and unloading of other sailing vessels in the Roads, all of which brought cargoes from China, the East Indies, and the Malay peninsula. Sometimes she went to market for packets of spices or rice or tea. Then there were the occasions when she accompanied Yen-shu to visit those wealthy individuals whose patronage was so valued the old man could not afford to offend by sending a mere messenger to deliver a carefully prepared ointment or balm.

Included among this latter category of customers was Wei-chu Chuang, Yen-shu's cousin—a powerful merchant who moved in the higher circles of life in Singapore, often entertaining English guests at his bungalow on the Serangoon Road on the outskirts of Singapore. On these particular trips, Samille remained with Sakai at the shop. Nor did Yen-shu ever send her to Wei-chu's prosperous shop at the corner of Bonham Street and Boat Quay near the Elgin Bridge within the heart of the city.

Yen-shu long ago abandoned his attempts to teach the girl-child so fortuitously acquired to speak Chinese, or to speak at all, for she would not, remaining stubbornly silent.

"Sparrow-dancer," he named her, telling Sakai "child hop like bird, here, there, hop hop—dance all day!"

Keenly observant, however, he noticed the quickness with which she learned the tasks he set her and the fact she understood English. British and American sailors now and again came to the druggist's, some seeking toothache powders or aphrodisiacs or acupuncture treatments for headache. On one such occasion two sailors from a British naval vessel came in together. While Yen-shu sought a freshly arrived consignment of ginseng in his storeroom, the red-haired younger man complained to his mate of having trouble falling asleep. When Yen-shu returned to the counter, he found Samille busy with mortar and pestle, grinding the leaves for a gentle soporific tea. As the first man paid for his ginseng preparation, he gestured to his companion.

"Listen, Yen-shu, got anything to help a mate get some sleep?"

With a sharp glance at Samille, old Yen-shu calmly took the neatly tied packet of tea from her and explained its use to the greatly appreciative red-haired sailor. From that moment on, the pantomime ceased. Yen-shu addressed her in his careful English. He never tried to make her speak, although Samille knew on more than one night he had slipped into the storeroom and waked her from nightmares in which she cried out, giving her tea to drink and leaving a single candle to burn until she slept again. He never referred to these nocturnal episodes in the light of day, never questioned her nor ever told her what she might have said in her dreams. She never remembered, herself, what the dreams were about.

As the years passed, these nightly terrors came less and less frequently. The fear behind them, however, kept her mute until by now, in the year of 1896, she was long accepted by the community as Yen-shu's idiot shop-assistant. Quick on her feet, the Sparrow sometimes did small favors for other shopkeepers who gave her fruit or rice cakes or an occasional cuff on the ear for her trouble.

Lately, though, Yen-shu grew increasingly worried over her future. By rights she should have long been married by the age of seventeen, but her foreignness precluded an arranged marriage with any of the Chinese relatives of Yen-shu. He was himself in slight disfavor owing to his Malay wife and his lack of a proper Chinese son, even though his age and apothecary skills lent him a certain status.

In her trousers, tunic, and coolie hat, Samille often passed as a boy through the streets of Singapore. Tall and thin as she was, however, she was as distressed as Yen-shu at the inevitable curves and other changes in her body's development from child to young woman. She moved with a rhythmic, natural grace, as if in her silence she was constantly attuned to some inner music. More than once in recent months she uncomfortably found the speculative glances of male customers upon her.

Deep in her heart she began to be afraid. She knew absolutely that Yen-shu would never sell her as a concubine. To Wei-chu, for example. Nor would he ever sell her services to the parade of foreign sailors who streamed into and out of Singapore day and night. She harbored an abiding affection for the old man, who had never beaten her, but had shown her only kindness. He wished, she knew, to return to China and the village of his birth some-day. That day would most likely come when Sakai passed away. Samille understood she could not go with him, and to be truthful with herself, nor did she wish to go.

No matter how she turned it about in her mind, she saw only one or two possible ends for her once old Yen-shu returned to his homeland. Some merchant would claim her as his woman and keep her until he grew tired of her, or she could sell herself on the streets. There was a third possibility—no! To allow her mind to even think along those lines was to invite the gates of despair and terror to swing wide again.

It was to escape such fear-seeded thoughts that Samille sometimes slipped from the storeroom at night and crawled over the wall into the garden at the *Hotel L'Esperance* when some member of the British community held a musical evening. Such were usually touted in ad-vance in the local papers. She sought out copies of the *Straits Times* and read these voraciously, keeping herself abreast of local events as well as those affecting the world at large. Yen-shu, when he discovered her at this, took to leaving the newspapers on the counter—ostensibly for wrapping goods in, but, she noticed, he was careful never to take them until she finished with them.

Through her reading of the paper, slowly the germ of an idea came to her. Haunting the harbor in her little free time, Samille began to take note of the comings and go-ings of British and American merchant ships. She eaves-dropped, unnoticed in the market, in the gardens, in the temples, to casual conversations between British wives. Now, after the nearly disastrous night behind her and with Yen-shu's distress so plainly before her all day long, she resolved to ease the old man's burden.

She waited until after their evening meal, when Sakai retired for the night. Yen-shu sat at his calligraphy, engrossed in the swift, soft strokes of wet brush on paper.

"Yen-shu." Softly, so Sakai would not awaken, she spoke for the first time. Kneeling across from him, hands clasped respectfully, she poured out her plan to her tiny, aged master. The light from the oil lamp reflected in his brilliant black eyes, glinted from his greying queue and his long thin beard. Methodically, his brush swept across the paper, never hesitating.

"I am going to leave Singapore when you are ready to return to China, Master. I will ask the religious sisters to help me find employment as a companion to some British merchant's or soldier's wife returning to England, where I will be able to seek a position. I'm strong and I learn quickly.

"I've heard the women talking sometimes. They say help in their homes is hard to find. So you see, Yen-shu, it will be all right when you go."

Anxiously, a little breathlessly, Samille waited. It was a good plan, she thought. Why did he not answer? At last the old man lifted his brush from the final stroke. He did not look at her as he cleaned his brush.

"Sparrow-dancer, my heart is troubled and I cannot think. Go you must, but—to speak! There are ears in Singapura—the City of Lions—which would hear and stir the green dragon that lies sleeping." His voice trailed off, almost as if he had forgotten her presence and spoke to himself. Samille barely caught his words. He gathered his brushes together, picked up his tray, and rose.

"I will speak for the sparrow. Yes. When you are ready, Sparrow, let me be your voice." Yen-shu looked directly at her then, for the first time in the whole odd interchange. His dark eyes held a strange, touching mixture of affection, sorrow, and concern, but surely not—lurking in their depths—fear?

Much later, still sleepless, Samille recalled those eyes and could not decide if his fear was for her, for himself, or for them both. What could Yen-shu know? Had she cried aloud in her nightmares something lost to the light of day? Or, was there another reason the old man had kept her all these years? Ashamed of such thoughts, she shivered beneath her blanket and waited once more for the first straggling rays of light to breach the single, high window of the storeroom.

Waiting out the inevitable day's rain next morning, Samille clutched her packets to her chest and let her mind wander. The music of Tchaikovsky spilled from memory. She closed her eyes, swaying as her body remembered and responded to that rich, inner melody.

Across the street, a tall, slender American, sandy-haired and lightly tanned, took refuge from the downpour in another shop doorway, a newspaper tucked under his arm. His fine, straight hair lifted in the breeze and one hand absently touched his neatly trimmed, dark-blond mustache as he stepped back a pace to avoid a portly Indian matron intent upon her chattering offspring and a bolt of saffron-colored cloth slipping from her grasp. She caught it just before it struck the street, and catching a pair of azure blue eyes upon her—alight with amusement and interest, laughed out loud. He joined her, his laugh deep and rich.

She passed on and he rested lightly on the balls of his feet, rocking gently back and forth, caught up in the swirl of unfamiliar sights and sounds. The tapestry of daily life in the Singapore bazaar reflected her role as an entrépot. British, French, Danish, Norwegian, Belgian, Prussian, Dutch, Portuguese, and American sailors and merchants mingled with Chinese and Indian merchants, tin miners, rickshaw drivers, and Malay laborers. Stalls selling coal, sari material, gold jewelry, and live birds crowded the crooked streets. Lantern makers, letter writers, tobacco sellers, and moneychangers thronged shoulder to shoulder on each side of the street. Satay vendors hawked their mouthwatering wares—bamboo skewers of chicken or other meat cooked over charcoal braziers and served with a sweet, peanut-cocoanut milk sauce.

Like an oasis of calmness, he casually surveyed the gaudy, restless scene. Then, the startling blue eyes beneath their fair lashes focused abruptly. Benjamin T. Greaves pursed his lips soundlessly and stepped from the protective shelter of a chemist's shop.

The girl stood across the street, the bruises on her face livid against the finely-drawn pallor of her skin, withdrawn into her thoughts as she waited for the downpour to lift, but restive in her waiting. For it was her movements that caught his eye. The pointing of her foot, the ceaseless, natural repetition of the basic balletic positions. How came this street urchin by such knowledge?

A rickshaw shot out of a narrow alley. Benjamin leapt to safety, crashing heavily against a bone-thin flower-seller, who righted him, dusted him off, and sent a string of curses after the hapless rickshaw driver. Thanking the man profusely, Benjamin tried to back away. From the corner of his eye he caught her movements as she darted agilely down the street, away from him.

Samille hurried now the rain had ended. Sakai was ill again this morning, wracked by a cough that would not leave her. Yen-shu, his face creased with fatigue and worry, would be dividing his time between the shop and his wife. Old Yen-shu dearly loved his Malay wife. Still slender, Sakai's tired features held a hint of a serene, exotic beauty that—with her sweet, even-tempered nature—had so entranced the young Chinese émigré he had risked the anger of his family to marry her. Nor had he put her aside, later, when she bore him no more children after the loss of their son and baby daughter. Nor, even later, when young Chinese brides were permitted to come to Singapore from their home villages. Now, having delivered her packets of Tiger's balm and herbal oils to Lin-yi, a clerk in the ship chandlery store, she hastened back to spell her master in the storefront.

Samille tied a clean apron about her waist and set about tidying the shelves during a lull in business. A small mirror, bartered by some tramp steamer's hand for a dragon bone concoction, hung crookedly on the wall behind her. Samille straightened it as she was wont to do most mornings, and paused a moment, grimacing at the bruises on her cheek. Black hair, shiny and clean, glinted with sapphire highlights where the light touched it. Long, thick, and straight, it fell to her waist when unbound. She never wore it thus, but rather plaited it French-style as her mother had done before her in a single long strand. Surprising green eyes, always watchful, concealed all expression, all emotion, all thought from the outside world. So well had she, in fact, blended into this world that sometimes, as now, it came as a shock to her that she was not Chinese. But although a faintly exotic tilt was evident about her eyes, the porcelain white skin molded features essentially Western in origin. Delicate features, an oval face with high cheekbones—the bruises shocking even as they faded, and a sweetly curving mouth that rarely betrayed itself with a trembling vulnerability, as now, were usually well-hidden beneath the coolie hat she wore on her jaunts away from the shop. Her neck, long and slender like her hands and feet, rose from well-muscled, thin shoulders. Beneath her tunic the swell of small firm breasts was muted by the enveloping apron she wore. Samille sighed. She could not wish she were not a woman, but life would have been ever so much easier if she had been born a male.

Resolutely she scrunched her fine, winged brows as she made a face at herself in the mirror and thrust a duster at her image. There had not been many occasions for laughter in her life, but she could usually laugh at herself when self-pity threatened. No need to remind herself *why* she must remain dead to her other life. One final swipe with the duster and! Samille's eyes widened. In the mirror before her, quizzical blue eyes met her own. She whirled about, dropping the duster in her haste.

Benjamin put out his hand and gently turned her cheek to the light.

"That's an ugly bruise you have there, little ballerina. I'm happy to see you made it home safely." A corner of his mouth quirked into a grin and the blue eyes sparkled with humor. "What a fine trick you pulled on me—a nice thank-you after I chucked myself into a bush for your sake." He paused, but the girl before him stared unblinkingly at him, unspeaking, then picked up a small bell on the counter and rang it sharply.

"I see, you don't speak English, do you? Of course not, how simple of me. And yet," his eyes narrowed thoughtfully and his hand came up as if he intended to touch her again. She shrank back a step. "And yet, there's European blood in your veins, unless I'm badly mistaken. Let me tell you, my charming friend, Benjamin T. Greaves is rarely wrong about anything that matters."

The calm assurance and curiosity in his voice overwhelmed her. Samille fought to keep her face blank, so he would not guess she understood him. What was keeping Yen-shu? She rang the bell again, deliberately, slowly, so this man—this Benjamin T. Greaves—would not sense her panic.

The curtain twitched to her left. Yen-shu took one look at her tightly clenched fists and faced the newcomer, bowing his head.

"How may I be of assistance, young sir? My assistant, she not speak."

Benjamin acknowledged Yen-shu with a nod and drew a card from a case. "My name is Benjamin T. Greaves. I'm a reporter for Nathanial Hawkins of the *Straits Times*."

"Yen-shu Wu, at your service, Mr. Greaves."

Nods were again exchanged and Benjamin began to look slightly amused, as if he were prepared to play any game and outlast the other players to get what he wanted. He was direct about what that was.

"I happened to be at the *Hotel L'Esperance* the other night where I met this young lady under rather peculiar circumstances. She was attacked by a brute in the gardens and I was able to be of assistance. Before I could be certain of her well-being, however, she disappeared. But, before this incident occurred, I witnessed an extraordinary performance. Imagine my surprise, Mr. Wu, to see what I took to be a Chinese street urchin performing classic Western ballet movements.

"Of course, now I can see she is not Chinese after all. I would like very much to interview her, sir, with your permission, because I am convinced a most interesting human interest story lies behind this young woman. Our readers would be most enthralled. Will you make her understand what it is I ask?"

In spite of her resolve, Samille felt her rigid self-control crumbling. A newspaper reporter! Her story splashed across the front pages of the *Straits Times* and picked up by who knew how many other papers here and abroad—as far as England or America, for all she knew. It would be the end. She would not be able to save him! A hiccupping, wheezing sound escaped her. She turned large, frightened eyes from Benjamin to Yen-shu and clutched at the old man's sleeve. Shaking her head violently from side to side, she felt breathless and a dreadful wheezing erupted from her like some wounded, whimpering animal. The world faded before her, then a dull thud reached her and a peculiarly distant voice barked in her ear.

"That stool—quickly!"

Strong hands lowered her to the stool and thrust her head roughly between her knees.

"Breathe, girl! Breathe!"

Two, three deep breaths and the world righted itself before her. The wheezing stopped. Samille covered her face with her hands. Beside her, Benjamin spoke harshly to Yen-shu.

"For the love of God, Mr. Wu, what set her off? What's frightened the poor child out of her wits? Who is she? What's wrong?"

Yen-shu stroked her bent head gently.

"Sparrow-dancer come to us when she tiny girl-child, Mr. Greaves. She like many orphans on streets of Singapore." Samille felt, rather than saw, his shrug. Many bastard children were abandoned on the streets of Singapore, surviving as best they could by scavenging, stealing, and prostituting themselves. Fortune had more than favored her when she stumbled that night into the old druggist's doorway out of a hundred similar doorways in Chinatown.

"She never speak. But," with a quick glance at her still-bowed head, "she come long time ago—long time when many foreign people sick and die in Singapore. Choking sickness kill many, many people then."

A breath of relief and gratitude swept her. Old Yen-shu was as quick-witted as ever. Samille darted a cautious look at Benjamin Greaves.

"So, you believe her parents were foreigners who died in a cholera epidemic several years ago? I'm certain the *Times* morgue will have papers going back that far. If we can find her name, sir, she may have family living still who would take her in."

Did she imagine it, or did his persuasive, concerned voice check even as another spasm of panic crossed her face? At her side, Yen-shu replied with a quiet dignity.

"I take her in, Mr. Greaves. My wife and I give her home, care for her. Sparrow-dancer happy here. But, I will ask her if she want you to do this." He turned to Samille and spoke to her in Chinese.

Samille clutched at Yen-shu and shook her head no vigorously. The shop bell tinkled as the door was pushed open. Chin hui, Wei-chu's cousin and right-hand man, entered and bowed perfunctorily. The tension in the narrow shop heightened perceptibly.

Yen-shu bowed and briefly addressed Chin hui in Chinese. Chin hui listened impassively, his cold, hard glance missing nothing—not the American behind the counter, or Samille, head bowed, between Benjamin and Yen-shu. He made a short, sharp reply. Yen-shu bowed again and turned to reach a neatly tied package down from the shelves. This he placed on the counter with a quick comment for Chin hui.

Wei-chu's messenger stared again at the tableau before him, picked up the package, sent a rain of Chinese at Yen-shu, then bowed mockingly and left the storefront. A grimace twisted his lips in a parody of humor.

"Well?" Benjamin asked, his voice terse, worried. A little shiver of relief swept Samille. So she had not imagined a confrontation had occurred.

"The Crab, he sharp-clawed. He tell me next time beat girl where her customers no see." Contempt filled the old man's voice.

"What?!" Benjamin, incredulous this time.

"Oh yes, Mr. Greaves. If Sparrow-dancer with some other... master, she worth much money."

Had she only conjured up the slight hesitation in Yen-shu's words? The two men stood before her now, Samille thought, as if they had forgotten her presence.

"I never sell her, Mr. Greaves. But, she pretty young woman. I old, old man. One day Sparrow-dancer be alone."

"I see." Benjamin whistled soundlessly between his teeth. "What do you propose we do about her?" He jerked a glance at Samille. "What other skills has she?" He scratched his chin absentmindedly. "Being mute would be a bit off-putting for most folks."

Samille flushed. How dared he? Speaking of her as if she were no more than a sack of rice in yesterday's market! But, she checked her rising anger with difficulty. Had a hint of challenge tinged the look he threw her? If he thought to goad her into some uncontrolled reaction, he would find himself quite mistaken. The stakes were much too high, the cost too dear if she failed now.

She rose deliberately from the stool, retrieving the feather duster as she did so. Avoiding Benjamin's questioning gaze, she turned away, replacing the stool in its usual position, and resumed her dusting. The silence drew out behind her. She stretched to reach a higher shelf and out of the corner of her eye saw Benjamin shrug, hoist himself lightly to the counter and vault nimbly to the other side, where he turned back to Yen-shu.

"Your sparrow has twice refused my help, Mr. Wu. I won't force myself upon her, but I trust you will not forget me nor hesitate to call upon me if I can be of any assistance whatsoever in the future. Just because I work for a newspaper at present," he drawled, "doesn't mean everything I know is for public consumption.

"Good-day to you, Mr. Wu. And you, Sparrow—if you should ever—" he caught himself up short and ended surprisingly, softly, "someday I'd like to see you dance again in a moonlit garden."

The shop bell rang violently, once. Samille heard the soft shuffle of old Yen-shu's slippers on the wooden floor and the quick rustle of fabric as the curtain fell into place. Her shoulders sagged and she leaned her forehead against a shelf. *If you should ever*—the words rang in her mind again. How long would she wonder what he might have said? In her misery and fear, she slipped a finger carefully under the mandarin collar of her tunic, under the near invisible gold thread about her neck and lifted the necklace from its hiding place. Her hand closed about the warm jade tablet, and in spite of herself, in spite of the fact she would never see the self-assured Benjamin T. Greaves again, an answering warmth glowed within her. He wanted to see her dance again!

Chapter 2

Samille shifted her bundle and sighed. Fat old Li Po, the letter writer, had promised her a few coins to deliver a letter to his younger brother. This brother had made arrangements to sail home to China with a returning merchant, whose large junk lay into harbor near the Borneo Company's wharf. Li Po had, naturally, neglected to tell her he was also sending a bundle of assorted odds and ends to his brother. Still, she was always glad of an excuse to visit the harbor. Having eventually discharged her errand without mishap, for she knew the younger brother by sight, Samille sauntered slowly along the Roads. So many vessels clogged the harbor, it was next to impossible to see the horizon. Cloughton's Dock held a small Swedish brig taking on fuel and water. Farther on, a large barque stood in at Jardine's Wharf, discharging coal and loading for Bombay. The Bengal lancers who manned the barque worked quickly and efficiently.

British merchant steamers crowded close in, some making the run between Calcutta and Hong Kong and others running up the Malay Peninsula to Siam. Two one-hundred-fifty-ton American steamers were taking on new cargo and passengers—from the looks of things on their way to Shanghai. Samille suppressed a shudder as she looked at the long, five-oared Malay sampans congregated together. Navvies loitered on a pair of French gunboats that were on their way to Saigon and had stopped to take on supplies. The *Hydaspe*, a French mail boat, was also in port—one of the *Messageries Imperiales* which plied between Singapore and Batavia on the island of Java, connecting with the mail steamer from Europe.

The *Enterprise* and *Fair Malacca*, two small, Singapore-built steamers, were packed with passengers readying themselves for a return trip to Malacca. A whole fleet of the fifty-five-ton ships regularly steamed between the two ports. Three flagships were snugly berthed in Dalhousie Pier, one just arrived from England to relieve another on its way home, and a third British ship from India, since Singapore was on the India Station. The newly arrived *Princess Royal* had two decks and carried a complement of seventy-three guns.

This she knew from reading the *Straits Times*. She paused reflectively. If one ship was on its way home after its tour in Singapore, then the officers' wives would also be making ready for the voyage. Surely, among them one would have need of a female companion or helper. Perhaps she should speak to Yen-shu. It was possible the good women of the American Methodist Episcopal Mission would assist him in finding her a position among the returnees.

A curious sense of longing filled her and she blinked back long-unaccustomed tears. England would be all new to her—tied to no one and nothing in her past. She could vanish into some great house and live her life in relative obscurity, dividing the year between London and the country or the seashore. She could speak her language again. She would have a small wage and save for music. There would be real music, live dance to watch. But, most of all, it would be safe. Yes, tonight she would speak to Yen-shu. It was time.

Samille squared her shoulders and walked briskly away from the Roads. Sakai was free from her cough today, but even so, she should be there to help. The streets were crowded this morning, and it would grow worse, she knew, in the afternoon. The mass of jostling, crowding people made her uneasy. All too frequently, street fights broke out between the secret societies which plagued Singapore. The Klings or red and white flag societies of Hindus and Mohamedans clashed with regular ferocity. Religious processions like the Mohurrum had long since been banned because of repeated disturbances between such groups.

Fat old Li Po, for example, belonged to one of the numerous Chinese tong societies. It was rumored, too, that Yen-shu's powerful cousin Wei-chu was a leader of the Ghi Tok tong. She had glimpsed Wei-chu, always at a distance, and felt certain the rumors were correct. On the surface he moved easily and confidently through Singapore society, but dangerous currents seemed to eddy about him, hinting of darker, unplumbed depths.

As her fingers grasped the hidden necklace she wore, her roving glance was arrested. Penang, a Malay-Chinese dwarf, was standing before a stall of gaudy scarves. Momentarily indecisive, Samille hesitated then set out after Penang as the dwarf moved away from the stall. Penang wove purposefully, skillfully, through the crowded streets. Samille followed, hurrying a little breathlessly to keep her quarry in sight as Penang, with a confidence that spoke of long-familiarity, left the streets behind and negotiated the maze of shack-lined canals teeming with the poorer segments of Singapore society.

Here she would have ended, beside these canals or dead within one, if not for Yen-shu. And there, in her split-second lack of concentration, she'd lost sight of Penang. Silently fuming, Samille squinted back the way she'd come, then again before her. Penang stood before a shack, grinning impudently as she ducked inside. Samille's rare grin briefly saluted Penang as she followed the dwarf inside.

The single dark room of the shack was lit by a smoking group of candles. Several people sat on the mat flooring, neither speaking among themselves nor looking up as she knelt behind them. In front of them, a hook-nosed Malay *dalang,* a shaman, unwrapped a series of long, clacking figures. Penang leaned across and whispered throatily at Samille's side.

"See, he chooses the princess. She will speak for you, my sad-eyed friend."

One by one the figures were revealed as a set of flat, painted puppets moving upon long, slender sticks. Samille's eyes shifted from the figures to the wall. A figure was raised, its shadow striking the wall. Another shadow appeared and the *dalang* began to speak. She felt herself drawn into the proceedings, fascinated as always by the subtleties of the shadow play. The audience watched not the painted figures as one would do in a European pantomime, but the story unfolding in the shadows thrown upon the wall. The complexities of meaning and hidden depths to the art intrigued her.

Penang had first brought her several years ago. She'd met Penang when the dwarf came to Yen-shu's shop. Perhaps the scampering, quick-witted woman had felt a kindred sense of isolation with the young mute girl who assisted the apothecary, for she returned at irregular intervals to bring a bit of ribbon or a sweet. Once, spying Samille on the streets as she ran an errand for her master, Penang had treated her to a crisp satay skewer from a crony's street corner brazier, then took the young girl by the arm and propelled her along to the *dalang's* hut. At first, Samille had been bewildered and frightened, but once inside, with Penang whispering in her ear, the drama of the shadow play caught her rapt attention and she relaxed.

"See how the princess glides serenely on her way, but beyond, other figures gather. Evil goes before her and trails her."

Samille suppressed a shudder as the shadows coalesced, save for the sharp, clear image of the princess.

"She is a shadow-dancer, afraid, my princess, of facing the light. But she cannot hide from the past nor her destiny." Penang's disembodied voice materialized in her ear as if the very spirits narrated the scene before her. The sibilant whisper unnerved her. Always it seemed when Penang brought her the *dalang* foresaw her future—or perhaps this was only Penang's vivid imagination. She shivered again as the shadow figures grew menacingly larger, looming over the solitary princess who danced carelessly along her way.

"But, see!" Penang's sharp exclamation startled her, "see, comes another figure. And another. Through one comes the other, and they become two pieces in the pattern of her dance. See how the evil recedes! She moves alone and yet, no longer alone. The direction of her dance has changed—she is less frightened, more aware of danger, more aware of herself.

"See how they turn, now, in unison and face the darker prince and his minions. They shriek, but they are strong, my princess. The dark prince retreats; beware his return. See, he and his companions regroup beneath a green dragon sleeping! Beware the wrath of the ancestors and gods if ever the dragon wakes!"

Outside once again, the light blinded her. Samille blinked. Penang came out behind her. Her friend looked old and worried today. On impulse Samille bent and hugged her fiercely. If Yen-shu helped her, she might never see her one friend again. She walked rapidly away, feeling a curious sense of time shifting back into place, as if her future had indeed been unfolding before her. A stray thought struggled to reach the fore of her attention, some scrap of memory trying to force itself to be recalled.

Samille shook her head as she rapidly traversed the canals. It was only a tale—a puppet's tale to amuse small children or superstitious villagers. Now, she scanned the streets before her with dismay. Only a few shoppers lingered now. Her earlier uneasiness returned full-force. Even the rickshaw drivers who usually cadged a few moments' rest in shaded doorways were nowhere to be seen. Trouble was brewing. It was time to get off the streets and take cover, but she was so close now, to Chinatown. With any luck at all, she'd make it through the bazaar before the seething violence erupted.

A blood-curdling yell broke from her left. White-turbaned Hindus spilled into the street. Quickly retreating, Samille saw a few other individuals scattering in search of shelter. Running feet pounded behind her. Then, before her! A silent, grim mob of Malays swarmed from their hiding places. Rice knives glittered in the sun. Sweat beaded on her forehead. Dimly, she was aware of the onrush of fierce, twisted faces and the fact she was no longer moving. The melee would trample her and she could not move. The flashing rice knives mesmerized her. Like the shadow-dancer, she thought incoherently—careless once too often! Her knees buckled. Her mouth opened, but her scream was lost in the confusion about her.

Shaken, she fought the panic which engulfed her and struggled to focus. A taut featured face loomed before her—piercing blue eyes deepened in concern. Benjamin! Strong arms came about her and she clung desperately to him. From everywhere about the two of them came the sounds of fighting. Sweat-soaked, panting men pushed and shoved above them, all around them. Silhouetted against the sky, a rice knife arched downward. A cry rang out. Crouching, Benjamin half-ran, half-pulled her out of the street into an alley.

The rice knife glinting red in the sun! Samille buried her face in Benjamin's shirt, burrowing her way to safety, to oblivion—away from memory. She whimpered, sliding headlong into a past too long thrust from her conscious mind—headlong into a terror that broke free and raged before a frightened child.

Finding himself on a deserted street, Benjamin heard the battle sounds faint behind them. Sparrow-dancer—light as a bundle of rags—cowered against him, trembling like a hurt bird in the cold. Strange whimpering cries escaped her. There—he recognized the nearest corner. Yen-shu's apothecary shop should be just along the way. He thrust through the door unceremoniously with his burden. Old Mr. Wu gaped at them, startled from his papers.

"She's in shock, Yen-shu. Have you blankets, hot tea?"

Yen-shu raised his voice and called to someone in his native tongue, pulling back the curtain and motioning Benjamin to follow. Inside, he indicated a doorway on his left. A tiny Indonesian woman appeared. Yen-shu spoke quickly, decisively, over her soft exclamations.

Benjamin attempted to lay his bundle on the pallet, but the sparrow would not loosen her hold. He lowered himself and wrapped the single blanket about her, stroking the dark head and murmuring soothingly. The old woman entered, carrying a small tray with a pot of fragrant steaming tea. She poured a cup and handed it to her husband. Yen-shu knelt beside him and together they tried to get the girl to take some. Still, they could not loosen her hold. Her face mirrored an absolute, implacable terror.

Behind them, the old woman took up her tray and began to cry quietly. A spasm of coughing shook her. Yen-shu half-rose, clearly torn between his charges.

"See to your wife, Yen-shu. I'll stay with your sparrow and give her tea when she's calmer."

Yen-shu bowed quickly and helped his wife from the room. Several times severe spasms of coughing interrupted their progress, but at last Benjamin heard movements overhead, and the muted, hoarse coughing of the old woman. In his arms the girl's ragged breathing slowed, becoming more regular. Gently he pushed the black silken fall of hair from her wet face where it escaped her braid. Awkwardly tilting her face up, he held the cup to her lips. This time her mouth opened slightly and she swallowed several small sips before turning her face away. Putting the cup down, Benjamin eased her body carefully onto the pallet and tucked the blanket closely about her.

"Poor Sparrow-dancer," he murmured as she tensed restlessly beneath the blanket.

"Sh-h-h!" The green eyes shot open, and he realized they stared not at him, but rather through him to something he could not see.

"Sh-h-h, Samille. Quiet, darling. We must be very quiet and not wake Papa." She lay quietly for a few moments and in the interlude he managed to get more of the hot, sweet tea into her.

"Mama?" The barest whisper reached his ears. "Mama, mama, I'm afraid! Where's Papa? Who is that man, Mama?"

"Sh-h-h. Yes?" Benjamin leaned closer. It was as if he listened to a conversation between two people.

"Yes, I told you. I'll leave tonight. No. No, be sensible, Kwang-ju, I give you my word. My daughter and I, and my husband goes free.... promised me, no harm will come to my Samille nor to my husband. Tell him, I embark immediately." A long interval of silence ensued. Benjamin thought perhaps the girl slept, but then she stirred fitfully.

"Samille, darling, you've been very brave. I'm so proud of you. I know you can't understand all of this, my sweet, but try. There are some wicked men who want something they think I have." Surprisingly, the voice raised a tone in indignation.

"No, darling, I don't understand that part at all. I don't know what they want, nor why they think I have something that must belong to them, but I hope to explain clearly to them. So, we must go to them, darling, and tell them they are mistaken. Then Papa will be safe and we can go home to Paris.

"We are going on a boat, Samille, for a long trip. Please don't talk to anyone. Who? Mr. McNamara? Yes, he does seem to be a nice man. Yes, dear, you may wish him a good-morning if he speaks to you and I am near." Again, she lay still for long moments, then her breathing grew rapid, her body agitated.

"No! Mama, no!" Forcefully, it was the voice of a determined child. "Mama, I won't leave you! No, no! Mr. McNamara! Mama!" Her voice rose in a frenzy of terror. "Don't touch my mama!" She lurched up from her pallet and screamed, screamed again, her hands covering her eyes. Benjamin cradled her in his arms and fought her to stillness, until she sobbed brokenly against him, the words barely coherent.

"They held her down.... I could not help her... could not... save her.... Dragged her and the other women to the deck. Screams everywhere... bodies....

"Malay sailors mutinied.... threw them one by one into the sea... Mama couldn't swim.... caught a piece of driftwood....

"'*Save my child! For God's sake!*' I heard her pleading, her voice raised above the melee. A Bengal lascar held me. He put me down... the Malays set upon him, knives gleaming. He picked me up and let me fall.

"Mama... Mama tried to reach me.... I felt her grasp... her touch... then I went under. Something, someone pulled me to the surface. Mama was gone...."

Her hoarse whisper faltered horribly on a fresh torrent of sobs. A lifetime of pent-up grief and horror shook her. Benjamin pressed her to him fiercely, as if he could will the pictures away from her mind. At last her breathing rose and fell more regularly. Sheer exhaustion mercifully claimed her. For a few more minutes he held her to him, before carefully he eased her onto the pallet and straightened the blanket over her.

In the storefront, Yen-shu anxiously awaited him.

"She's asleep. Yen-shu, who is she? What do you know of her?" Roughly, his own voice shook from weariness.

"I tell you all I know, Mr. Greaves. Sparrow come to us as a child. When little girl, she cry out in nightmare for her mama, but she all alone."

"And the story of sickness," Benjamin probed gently, "was just a fiction? Why, Yen-shu?"

The old man's shoulders sagged, and then he lifted a face full of dignity and sorrow to the young man.

"Sparrow frightened by you, by your words. I want to help. She special girl-child for Sakai and for me, too. Now, what do you do, Mr. Greaves?"

Benjamin contemplated the tiny, elderly man, and a wry grin briefly lit his eyes.

"I'm a newspaperman at the moment, Yen-shu, and I smell a story here. Not," he checked the old man's attempt to speak, "not necessarily for publication, mind you. But you must see, Old One, she has no future here. Perhaps she has family...." his voice trailed off. The blue eyes grew cold and smoky. He spoke again, very softly.

"Her mother died a terrible death, Yen-shu. I intend to find those responsible. Someone lured her to her death. One day they will pay."

Samille slept for well into the next day, waking late in the afternoon to fresh bouts of tears. At last, by the evening she was able to face Yen-shu and Sakai, who brought her a bit of fish and rice. It was her favorite dish, and for their sakes, she made an effort to eat all that was put before her. The tea, hot and sweet, comforted her and eased the dull aching of her head. She slept the night through and well into the following morning. Sakai fussed about her, however, so she rested the remainder of that day as well, reading the accumulated *Straits Times* and trying to think clearly what she should do next. Of Benjamin T. Greaves, there was no sign. What to do about him? Samille sighed. It did no good to harangue herself for her own carelessness. Much better to disappear quietly and quickly. No matter whether the tenacious Benjamin returned or not, she would be long gone from Singapore and whatever trouble stirred within the confines of the city that had been her home for so long.

In the morning, then, she would ask Yen-shu to go with her to the mission. The British warship had not yet steamed from port, according to yesterday's paper. Someone would surely welcome her help with small children or a wife who was a poor traveler. With a feeling of resolution, she tucked her chin into the hollow of her shoulder and let sleep steal over her.

Morning came and with it the sounds of Sakai coughing. Distressed, Samille rose at once, made her toilet, re-braided her hair and put on her spare set of drawers and tunic. If she could not ask Yen-shu to leave his ailing wife, she could relieve him in the shop. Even as she fortified herself with tea and rice, the shop bell rang and a voice called out from the front of the shop. Ducking around the curtain, she found Chin hui restlessly prowling before the counter. Catching sight of her, he stopped and watched her as she located the already prepared package in its customary place on the shelves. Her skin crawled as his eyes bored into her back. Samille turned and laid his order on the counter. To her surprise and discomfort Chin hui made no move to take the packet, but continued to stare at her before finally picking up the bell and clanging it sharply for Yen-shu.

The latter came almost at once, his face grave and impassive. He spoke to Chin hui, clearly questioning him as he indicated the packet. Impatiently, Chin hui flicked his hand at it, dismissing it as he replied sharply. Samille stood beside her master, eyes lowered modestly. The Crab darted frequent glances at her and a queer sense of dread was born deep within her. Of what interest could she possibly be to this man—or more worrisome yet—to the master he served? With a final spate of words, Chin hui retrieved the herbal packet, turned on his heel and left without another glance at either of them.

Old Yen-shu sagged abruptly and leaned heavily against the counter. Hurriedly, Samille fetched the stool and helped him sit. With a quick glance at his drawn features, she ducked through the doorway and into the small partitioned kitchen, deftly loading tea and sugar onto a tray. Yen-shu had not moved. Silently, she poured the tea and placed a cup before him, then withdrew unobtrusively. Sorting quickly through the herbs and roots beneath the counter, she neatly lay out those necessary for Mrs. Pong's stomach remedy, then fetched a mortar and pestle from a shelf behind her and set to work methodically. Whatever had shaken the old man so badly, he would tell her in his own time or he would not tell her at all.

A steady stream of customers came and went all morning. Side by side they worked together. At noon Yen-shu sent her to market for Sakai, to the harbor to check on the arrival of a junk, and to deliver Mrs. Pong's remedy. When she returned to the shop, the druggist left her in charge while he made the rounds of his special deliveries. At length the long day drew to a close.

Yen-shu had not returned. Samille shut up the store, leaving the accounts for her master's quick eyes, and retired to the rear of the shop. She had bargained well in the market today—with a shake of the head and counting on her fingers, she'd managed for years. Stall-owners knew her to be Yen-shu's assistant and treated her well for the most part. This afternoon she'd obtained a fresh piece of pork. With bamboo shoots, water chestnuts, and bok choy, she would add a peanut sauce to the meat and serve with rice when Yen-shu returned.

As she worked, Samille heard him enter the shop. By the time he finished his accounts and shuffled slowly into the living quarters, the meal was prepared. Silently, Samille served the old man, and then made up a tray to take to Sakai. She found the elderly woman sleeping lightly and debated waking her. As she hesitated, Sakai opened her eyes. Setting down the tray, Samille propped her up and coaxed her to eat. When Sakai would take no more and her eyes drooped wearily, she made her comfortable once more and took away the tray.

Yen-shu turned a blind face to the warmth of the charcoal brazier as she served herself quietly from the remains of the dishes. He had, she noticed, eaten little and was deep in meditation. She ate quickly, gathering the remnants of the meal and slipping away to scour the dishes.

Her tasks completed, she retired to the storeroom, worry gnawing at her. Too restless to settle down, she began to stretch, carefully moving through a sequence of exercises learned as a child and other ones she'd watched the older dancers run through daily. With her stretches accomplished, she moved to the wall. Crates meticulously stacked waist-high created a make-shift bar. As a child, this had been her retreat from the memories that plagued her and from the strangeness of her new life. She moved through the positions mechanically.

From her days at Mme. Roussin's, she knew it was much too late for her to ever hope to dance with a company, as years of valuable training and experience had been lost and could never be regained. Yet, blessed with an acute visual memory—perhaps enhanced by a desperate need to focus upon happy memories—Samille was able to recall sequences of steps seen during those hours in Mme. Roussin's studio. Thus, bits and pieces of practice sessions were encapsulated in her mind, as well as fragments of the few ballets she had attended with her parents.

To escape to the hotel gardens or to some extravaganza hosted by the British coterie and to hear live music transported her to a world only music and dance could engender. Here, in the storeroom the music would play over and over in her mind and she would dance in her loose trousers and tunic, her slippers stiffened with fragments of scavenged wooden slats bound about with rags, the sounds muffled by the mats covering the hard-packed floor.

Tonight she would not be the dying swan, or a stylish sylph, but instead a member of the chorus dancing as the backdrop to some mysterious drama concerning her in some unknown manner to which she remained manifestly ignorant. Her candle flickered. She watched her shadow on the wall, taking on the persona of a living person, as if she and a separate part of herself danced together in a surreal pas de deux. As if she begged, pleaded, threatened, cajoled this shadowy dimension of herself to reveal some truth crying out for release. At last, exhausted, she flung herself upon her pallet. Only then did she notice Yen-shu.

He bowed his head gravely.

"Sparrow-dancer fill this night with beauty. You, Sparrow, have been good daughter to honorable parents." Tears started to her eyes, and she waited expectantly for what was to come.

"Chin hui say to me Wei-chu wish you to serve in his household. He say, Sparrow, you must come soon. I cannot disobey when Wei-chu speaks."

Her every sinew and bone seemed to writhe in pain as fear settled heavily over her. She could not find voice to reply.

"You very smart young woman, Sparrow. You know Wei-chu powerful man. Sakai—sick old woman. I cannot help you now. Wei-chu sees everything. What if he saw me go with you to mission?"

The bent, frail figure before her clearly did not expect an answer, but his eyes glinted and he shuffled closer to her, his voice a thready whisper. The very walls, it seemed, leaned closer to hear.

"But, if one day Sparrow not here and Yen-shu look for her in Chinatown, in bazaar, at harbor, then he must tell Wei-chu girl lost."

For a long moment piercing black eyes met alert green ones. Then, keeping her voice equally low, Samille spoke.

"Honorable Yen-shu and Sakai have given Sparrow a good life in Singapore. One night, Old Father, she will remember you and she will dance for you when there is a moon and the pear tree blossoms." Tears streaked her face. Yen-shu's tiny figure bowed deeply.

When he was gone, Samille clenched her fists against her forehead and fought down panic, trying to think. She must plan carefully and soon, but not too soon. Yen-shu had told her as plainly as he could if anything appeared remiss, he and Sakai would suffer for it. She must appear to have accepted her fate and continue on for as long as possible as if nothing untoward had occurred. Whatever her fate might be at the hands of Wei-chu, she could not accept the possibility it would be anything as simple as serving in his household. Chin hui's lascivious, inimical looks suggested such a life did not bear closer speculation, and Yen-shu's very reluctance to obey his powerful cousin bore this out.

But, where to go and how? Wei-chu's tong had eyes and ears in every part of Singapore from the harbor to city hall. In despair she tried to think of a way to escape and at last settled unhappily upon the idea of slipping out one night and into the mission. Surely, the reverend and sisters would watch over her until she could leave. Dissatisfied, but unable to come up with a more appealing plan, she drifted into a fitful sleep.

For the next week she forced herself to go about her appointed routine—marketing, running errands for Yen-shu, and working in the shop. At every jangle of the bell her nerves clenched into a single cordon of fear until her eyes registered someone other than Chin hui entered. Then she breathed freely once again. Bleary-eyed with fatigue, she moved like a puppet through the long hours of each day, feeling of no more substance than a shadow in the *dalang's* play.

This morning, Mrs. Sivachaipong stood deep in consultation with Yen-shu. Her husband had three daughters now and no sons. She entreated the druggist to provide her with the means of conceiving the desired male child. Samille forced herself to concentrate as Yen-shu reeled off a list of ingredients. This recipe was one she had not heard before and it was some time before the final blend of elements was reached. Old Yen-shu fussily weighed each ingredient, making minute adjustments and speaking short incantations over each addition.

At last he pronounced it ready and gave Mrs. Sivachaipong detailed instructions on brewing the tea for consumption. Her round, solemn face lit up with hope and she backed out of the shop with many bows and blessings for her benefactor. Straightening up, Yen-shu caught Samille's gaze.

"You doubt me, Sparrow?" He gave a dry chuckle. "I give her great hope and remove all responsibility from Mrs. Sivachaipong. Now if she bears no son, it is fault of gods and bad medicine!" Samille brought her palms together and bowed humbly.

"Master most wise and honorable man."

He bowed again, his thin mouth quivering with amusement. Samille could not stop the grin splitting her face from ear to ear. For the first time in a week, some of the tension left her and she relaxed. Yen-shu picked up a tray he'd prepared earlier in the day.

"I see to Sakai now. Ring bell if you need me, Sparrow."

Abruptly, Samille stopped smiling as the old man disappeared into the back of the shop. She could go into the storeroom at this moment, bundle up her few belongings, and slip away. No one would pay the slightest attention, and if they did, it would appear as if she were delivering another package for the druggist.

Indecisive, she checked an impulse to call out to Yenshu. Go, she told herself fiercely, go now! She pushed herself away from the counter, reached the curtained doorway. Behind her the shop bell jangled merrily as the door thrust open. She froze. If it were Chin hui? Slowly she released the curtain, turning squarely about to face the customer. A pair of azure eyes, alight with a lazy humor, met her startled gaze.

"Just the person I was hoping to see, Miss Samille Beauvoir Langley."

Chapter 3

"It's considered polite, Miss Langley, to respond in kind when a gentleman greets a lady. However, perhaps you will find this of interest. Permit me." Benjamin withdrew a slip of paper from his jacket.

Samille tore her gaze from his and glanced unwillingly at the paper, the blood draining from her face. She grasped the counter for support, the worn wood biting into her palms. The words written there seared themselves into her thoughts.

Prof. Samuel H. Langley unable to travel. Stop. Requests you return his daughter with all Godspeed. Stop. Authorizes Mercantile Bank to cover all expenses. Stop. Letter to follow. Signed Jane Langley Gooden.

Shock, swiftly followed by anger, blinded her. How could he do this? She could not find her voice. Years! The years spent in exile, hidden, so as not to betray her gentle, scholarly father. In one fell swoop, undone! Inarticulate in her fury, she raised green eyes sparking with rage to Benjamin. One thought, one hope flashed across her face. She could still disappear. Benjamin would appear mistaken. A hand thrust out suddenly, closed about her wrist like an iron fetter.

"How terribly impolite, Miss Langley, to think of departing without first taking your leave of a guest! Before you go, here's another item you may find equally riveting."

He unfolded the newspaper he carried. Apprehensively, she followed his pointing finger.

CHILD RETURNS FROM THE DEAD! The headline proclaimed. Scanning the paragraphs beneath, she read: *Samille Beauvoir Langley, long believed drowned with her mother in a tragic incident eight years ago, has been discovered alive and living in Singapore.... no memory of the events that claimed her mother, Francoise Beauvoir, wife of Samuel Hughes Langley, then a lecturer in American history at the Sorbonne in Paris....*

Professor Langley is reportedly overjoyed... teaches American history at the University of California, currently in ill health....

...taken in by a Chinese druggist and his wife, the child was rendered mute by the tragic consequences of her young life. A recent fright during a riot in the Indian quarter stirred her memory, and she wrote out her name and story for our reporter. The incident in which her mother lost her life was the infamous Malay mutiny aboard the barque Devon on September 12, 1888....

How long she might have stood there, rooted to the floor, she never knew. The shop bell rang, jerking her into the present with an immediacy surely even Benjamin must have felt as Chin hui advanced into the store. Benjamin dropped her arm and shifted slightly to face the newcomer. Samille watched her hand reach out to ring the counter bell. Its echoes resounded in the silence like the tolling of the great brass temple bells—clanging deep within her until the reverberations set her heart to pounding with a painful, shattering throb.

As Yen-shu entered, he bowed to Benjamin and Chin hui. The Crab spoke harshly to the elderly druggist, pointing his chin at Samille as he ended. Yen-shu turned to Benjamin.

"How may I assist you today, Mr. Greaves?"

After a rapid summing up of Chin hui, Benjamin picked up the telegram and tapped the paper.

"Astounding news, Mr. Wu. This young lady appears to be the daughter of an American citizen. I have here a telegram from her family, authorizing me to see to her immediate return home to the United States." He passed the telegram to Yen-shu along with the *Straits' Times*. "As you may read for yourself, Mr. Wu, her remarkable story has been given full coverage in today's *Times*."

Yen-shu's face quivered with a quickly hidden tremor of relief.

"Her family most fortunate. You will wait, Mr. Greaves, while Sparrow gathers her things?" A hint of entreaty colored his voice. Chin hui snapped a question. Yen-shu turned a querulous face to him, pointing to the newspaper and replying at length. Chin hui's eyes narrowed, he bowed abruptly, and hastily retreated. Yen-shu grasped Samille's arm.

"Hurry, Sparrow. Go now. Quickly, before the Crab returns!"

"Who is this man?" Benjamin demanded fiercely. "What does he want with this child?"

Yen-shu tugged at her. Samille shook herself and ran for the curtained doorway. In the storeroom she bundled her spare set of clothing together and grabbed her coolie hat. Short of the necklace she wore, she possessed nothing else. On impulse, she darted upstairs to where Sakai lay sleeping. Briefly, she knelt by the old woman and caressed her cheek with the back of her hand, leaned closer, and brushed her lips lightly across the soft, wrinkled cheek as the frail Malay woman stirred sleepily.

Downstairs again, she faced Yen-shu. Bowing low as tears started, Samille met the old man's eyes and gulped.

Yen-shu returned her bow.

"Remember your promise, Sparrow—when the pear tree blossoms and the moon is full."

The shop bell jangled. Two Chinese schoolboys entered shyly. Samille started around the counter, but Yen-shu checked her with a glance. Benjamin joined her as she slipped through the curtained back of the shop. A narrow door in the druggist's private quarters gave onto an alley. Samille led the way, Benjamin at her heels.

Crisscrossing the alleys, she brought them by a circuitous route within sight of Yen-shu's storefront. Whatever happened, she could not leave the old man to be harmed. Benjamin said nothing, settling to wait beside her. Samille sneaked a peek at his grave profile. Close as she was, she could sense the coiled readiness in him as he surveyed the street before them. He looked around after a moment, flashing her a thumbs' up sign.

For perhaps twenty minutes they watched the usual straggle of customers come and go, but with no sign of Chin hui. Benjamin touched her arm. She nodded and cautiously they made their way through the back streets to the European quarter of the city. Perversely, at this moment when she was safer than when she'd been creeping through the back alleyways, Samille hung back. This world had not been hers for a long time. What would happen to her? Where would she find a place for herself?

Benjamin took her by the arm and guided her through the noonday bustle to the imposing facade of the building which housed the *Straits' Times*. Inside, he whisked her past the curious stares of receptionists and reporters and advanced upon an opened door, knocking perfunctorily as he ushered her before him.

"What is it this time, Meecham?" A bellow erupted from a large, bewhiskered man who stood at the window, a sheaf of papers clutched in one hand and a cigar viciously occupying his teeth. "Well?" He looked up. "Oh, Benjamin, my lad. Why didn't you speak up, boy? Close the door, won't you?" He added irritably, "and sit the poor lass down." Striding over to a massive mahogany desk, the man tossed the papers he held onto an already precarious pile. Unperturbed, Benjamin shut the door and seated Samille before the desk.

"Miss Langley, I'd like you to meet my uncle, Nathaniel Hawkins, the *Times'* editor-in-chief."

Samille acknowledged the introduction with a wary nod, thinking as she did so she would never be able to slip out of this place unnoticed, but perhaps later it could be managed. Only one door led into this room, and Benjamin stood between her and it.

"Still won't speak, eh lass? Don't blame you, myself. This young whelp probably scared you out of your wits." He threw a pointed glance at his nephew, who lifted a brow in response but otherwise appeared untroubled. The burly editor stubbed out his cigar and grinned suddenly, the grin transforming his bristly character, his eyes snapping with frank curiosity.

"Always was my favorite and more's the pity, he knows it. Don't let it go to your head, lad.

"Now, Miss Langley, I'm sure you're wondering what's happening here and what's going to happen next.

"As you know, your father—" Nathaniel Hawkins' sharp glance caught the convulsive, white-knuckled grip on her bundled belongings, "your father is in poor health. We were told he's recuperating from a broken leg suffered this past spring. We've been authorized to assist you by your aunt, who," he paused and peered at a paper on his desk, bushy gray brows twisting with his momentary concentration, "lives with your father and cares for him since his accident.

"Professor Langley has arranged for credit at the Mercantile Bank to see to your needs and your fare home.

However," direct blue eyes met her own, "this won't be necessary. The *Times* will pick up the tab, Miss Langley. Your story, you see, is immensely appealing. We would very much like to hear it in your own words, and, of course, to cover your reunion with your father in America...." His voice trailed off hopefully.

Samille continued to meet his gaze squarely, lips firmly pressed together.

"Very well, lass, I won't press you." Unexpectedly, he continued, "but mark my words well, Miss Langley. Benjamin here is a man you can trust. You'll stay with the sisters at the American Episcopal Methodist Mission until the *Hesperia Joy* embarks. The sisters will see to it you are properly outfitted. Benjamin will look after you and make arrangements for you to travel home with an American family. Do you understand?"

She inclined her head fractionally.

"Good. He'll not let anyone hurt you, child. Remember that. Yes, yes, what is it?" He raised his voice in vexation as a knock sounded at his door.

A beaky nose with a pair of round glasses perched on it thrust into the office as the door opened a crack. Another inch and the rest of the face appeared. Mild gray eyes took in Samille in her coolie clothes, Benjamin suddenly at her side, and Nathaniel rising like a bull behind his desk.

"Meecham, Chief. Gilbert G's outside," a quick jerk of his thumb in the direction of the outer office punctuated this announcement, "demanding to know why the *Times* didn't give more coverage to the *Savage Club's* performance of MacBeth last night." A thin pair of shoulders shrugged and the corners of his eyes turned up mischievously.

Nathaniel Hawkins let out a huge, theatrical sigh.

"Good grief, Meecham! Why didn't you fob the pompous twit off on someone else? What do I pay you for, eh?" Muttering to himself, cigar once more crammed in the corner of his mouth, he came around his desk. "Bothering me will all this piffle and foolishness! Mnh...." He glared at his assistant. The miscreant Meecham dropped a wink at Benjamin and Samille as he followed his chief out.

Benjamin touched her shoulder.

"Come along, Miss Langley." As she stood obediently, he paused, commanding her eyes with his own. The midday sun struck golden glints from his hair as he tilted his head slightly to look at her.

"Uncle Nate's right, Sparrow. You can trust me." He spoke matter-of-factly. "Better yet, you can trust the word of Nathaniel Hawkins." His eyes narrowed as he studied her thoughtfully. "You're all shut up in there alone with your thoughts, Sparrow. Nothing stirring except those watchful green eyes.

"But, I can feel, my girl," he squeezed her elbow gently on the words, "the way your thoughts are twisting and turning, seeking escape. I don't know how or why," his idle, speculative tone hardened, "but don't try it.

"Can't you see, Sparrow, your safety lies in knowledge? The English-speaking world now knows you live. The whole world knows you are to be reunited with your father. And I'm here to see, young lady, t no one interferes with you between now and the time you board ship for home."

Almost she could believe him—this easy-going American with his cool, disinterested eyes and an inner edge of toughness and self-confidence. That he meant well, she did not doubt. But, a long-dead mystery revived and a dangerous game once more set into play? And he just one man against a tong! One man here and her father so far away! She was, she felt certain, somehow a pawn in the play—moreover, an unwilling pawn blinded by ignorance of her true role. How could he make empty promises to keep her safe? To know what disaster might strike her father before ever she could reach him? Samille pulled her arm from his grasp and stalked with stiff self-control to the door.

Downstairs, Benjamin hailed a rickshaw to carry them to the mission. Unaccustomed to such luxury, Samille sat quietly and gazed upon the city which she would soon leave behind. Due to the far-sighted vision of Sir Thomas Stamford Raffles, Singapore had emerged from languishing obscurity as the malaria-infested home of Malay pirates to become the bustling modern city it was in her day. Raffles had been a lieutenant governor of nearby Java in the early 1800s. Wanting to establish an economic and military toehold for Britain in the predominantly Dutch East Indies, he took advantage of the interminable successional squabbles among the local Malay rulers. In 1819 he established a trading post at Singapore for the British East India Company.

On the face of it, the British had officially disapproved of Raffles' action, but by 1821 Singapore was the most prosperous company port between India and China. Raffles' influence extended far beyond the founding of the port. Singapore, unlike other company ports, was duty-free. Immigration was encouraged and before long the settlement's original Malay population was outnumbered by Chinese and Indian laborers.

The admirable Raffles outlawed behaviors prevalent elsewhere in the Indies like cockfighting, gambling, and slavery. He oversaw the growth of the city, declaring the best lands public to limit land speculation, leveling hills, and laying out streets. Religious freedom was the rule in the polyglot city; free schools were established for Chinese, and later, Malay boys. The redoubtable Raffles even successfully rid the island first of rats, then of centipedes, by offering a bounty for each one.

More modern improvements had come to Singapore after Sir Raffles' death in 1826. Gas mains had been laid for the principal streets nearly forty years earlier in the 1860s. Not long after, petroleum oil began to be used, so now even native shops and residences could be lit by gas or oil.

But, she thought as they drew near the Mission, Sir Raffles would be shocked at the general condition of the city in her own time. Drugs and worse excesses of the flesh and soul catered to the sailors of six continents whose teeming presence thronged the streets of Singapore. Gangs of Chinese tongs grew more and more open in their lawlessness. Such things had become a fact of life. Samille shuddered. She was frightened at losing the anonymity the city had provided, keeping herself and her father free for so long, but she would not otherwise be sad to leave Singapore. It was a city of lions again—roaring with all the wild insatiableness of a beast gone mad.

Yet, the city's dangers were gilded with an exotic beauty. The British, for all their efforts, could not completely tame the foreign flavor of Singapore. Orchids spilled everywhere. The fragile beauty of a temple graced the gardens they now passed. This Singapore would always be a part of her. She sighed as the city streets slipped by her.

Benjamin, beside her, watching her drink in the city, watching the play of emotions cross her face in an unguarded moment, saw the shutters slip down, and felt her silent, resilient control firmly in place once again. How could such a child, he wondered, have become so centered in herself, so remote and self-sufficient?

"But not such a child, Benjamin," his uncle paused as he speared a slice of roast chicken from a serving dish, "or had ye not noticed she's a young woman now? And going to shock a few young men when she gets back to the States with those great bejeweled eyes and the grace of a doe."

"Really, Uncle Nate," Benjamin threw a reproving glance at him, "don't go all poetical on me. I just hope you know what you're doing this time." Worry heightened his usually calm features.

Nathanial Hawkins laid down his knife and fork and faced his nephew squarely.

"Listen, my boy, whatever drew her mama to her death, this Sparrow, er, Miss Langley, was but a child. From what you've told me, her mother didn't know what was behind the threats to her family. The child doesn't know either." He held up a hand as Benjamin attempted to interrupt.

"I know, I know," Nathanial said testily, "we know she doesn't know, but they don't, whoever *they* may be. Don't you see, it's a gamble any way we play it. This way, perhaps the unseen, unknown enemy will be drawn into the open. Until they show themselves, we've nothing to go on."

Benjamin was silent, staring into his glass of wine moodily. At length he downed the remainder in a gulp. Nathanial recognized the set of his nephew's chin and braced himself for whatever argument Benjamin was about to marshal.

"Uncle Nate," he began, and then shamefacedly grinned as he took in his uncle's wary expression. "I keep seeing her in my dreams—violated, cast asea, choosing certain death in an attempt to save her child's life. What a woman she must have been!"

Startled by his words, Nathanial Hawkins frowned.

"Remember, Benjamin, my boy, the child did survive."

The younger man stirred, looked at his uncle from the depths of blue eyes frosted with a hard determination.

"I intend to keep her alive, Uncle." He continued. "I propose to resign my position here and accompany her back to America. I've a hunch she holds the key to the heart of this mystery—locked away behind those stubborn green eyes."

Nathanial shook his head sharply.

"You're not thinking, boy," he thundered. "Something you're usually pretty apt at, when you put your wits to work. No," he raised an admonitory hand, "I know I've always said I wanted to be around when something or someone got beneath that cool exterior of yours and riled you up, but," he pushed back his chair, "you may as well face the facts." He counted them off, "one, the girl doesn't appear to want our help, and, two, I'm sure her father isn't going to welcome you into his home as a bodyguard!

"And, three, you can't suddenly take up residence near her without someone noticing," he finished drily.

"Okay, okay!" Benjamin threw up his hands in surrender. "As I see it, we still have several options. First, you arrange through your infinite and convoluted connections for someone over there to keep an eye on father and daughter. Second, we run down any other leads we can find.

"Right now, I think the most fruitful lines of inquiry are here and in Paris. I know the trail is eight years' cold, Uncle, put something happened there to set Françoise—Mrs. Langley—secretly on her way to Singapore. Perhaps I can dig up a clue to point a definite finger at someone here." He ran a hand through his hair.

Nate pulled thoughtfully at his beard.

"Like Wei-chu Chuang, you mean? It's worth a gamble, Benjamin. When do you propose to leave?"

Benjamin looked up in surprise, pushing back his chair and rising.

"Why, when Samille's safely on her way, Uncle, of course. I want to see her before she goes." His eyebrows quirked, and this time the blue eyes sparkled and his grin was genuine. "I don't want the child to go away angry with me."

His uncle rose slowly from the table and stared in amazement at the retreating back of his youngest nephew. The boy never ceased to surprise him—how he would care about the opinion of a child! Halfway to the door, he bit off his silent amusement.

Not such a child, after all.

Samille discovered in the following days she was a *cause célebrè* at the mission. The sisters fussed over her, soliciting items from their female parishioners when she steadfastly refused to use the money Nathaniel Hawkins gave her, giving it instead to the mission. Benjamin had been right—a great deal of interest and sympathy was evident in the overwhelming donations of apparel pouring into the mission. Samille selected three skirts—once the hems were let out, they were nearly long enough for her. Shirtwaists, washed and mended, were added to her trunk. Undergarments, stockings, nightgowns, and a pair of ladies boots completed her wardrobe. Sister Deborah Carole, the matron who looked after her, remarked with cheerful acceptance that Samille's presence at the mission was a blessing. Many of the mission's orphan charges would have new clothing thanks to the curiosity about the girl come back to life. A heavy cloak, a hat, and a handbag were also contributed by Mrs. Sarah Weams.

Mr. Jasper Weams was an accountant for one of the older Singapore banks. When he became afflicted with malaria, the bank had offered him early retirement. He and his wife had eagerly accepted. In return for their chaperonage on the voyage home, Samille was expected to help in the care of Mr. Weams.

Dressing for her first meeting with Mrs. Weams, Samille clumsily pulled on the Western clothing. Cinching up the slightly wide waist of her skirt, she caught sight of herself in a mirror—skirt too short, wrists hidden in the too-long sleeves of her blouse—and burst into tears to her embarrassment and the surprise of Sister Deborah Carole.

"There, there, child," the older woman murmured, producing a handkerchief from one of her voluminous pockets and pressing it into her charge's hand, "I'm sure your father will provide you with pretty dresses and ribbons. But," she added firmly in a tone that spoke volumes of no nonsense, "we mustn't be ungrateful for what the good Lord has provided."

Samille dried her eyes. How could she explain she'd seen not her own ungainly, certainly unfashionable figure in the mirror, but her mother's? Mama, who always took her breath away with her delicate gowns in subtle pastels, or her immaculate, lace-trimmed shirtwaists and finely tailored skirts. Tiny, sparkling, beautiful! For herself, so tall, gangly, small-busted, such clothing would be entirely wasted. Already she missed the freedom of movement and comfort, the easy familiarity of her tunics and trousers, although she knew better than to say this to Sister Deborah Carole. She had, however, packed them carefully in the bottom of her trunk. Her necklace, as always, hung securely about her neck, its thin gold wire hidden by the high, starched collar of her blouse.

Mrs. Weams arrived a few minutes shy of noon. Dressed soberly, she looked Samille over approvingly, and perched on the edge of the seat of a chair. The older woman, Samille thought, was like a shore bird—thin, long neck, long limbs, her neck twisting nervously as she darted a glance continually between Sister Deborah Carole and Samille. As if she might take fright at the slightest gesture and wing away.

"What a lucky young lady you are, to be sure. As I said to Mr. Weams, most fortunate to escape this heathen city." Her voice squeaked tremulously. Clearly, she felt herself to be equally fortunate.

"Mr. Weams is not at all well, not at all...." She had a disconcerting habit of popping her eyes wide open, her voice trailing off even as her thoughts did. "It will be a blessing to have help. Not a good sailor, not at all...." she finished up with a great deal of grimacing and a deprecating shrug.

With a sinking feeling, Samille deciphered this last to refer to Mrs. Weams herself and possibly to the unseen

Mr. Weams as well. At least it would leave little time to brood alone on the voyage. And, she thought later, after luncheon, Mrs. Weams had not seemed put off by the fact her charge had not uttered a word during the entire interview. They would board ship in three days.

The days passed quickly with Sister Deborah Carole's watchful, encouraging eye always upon her. Early on her last evening in Singapore, Samille sat quietly in the mission chapel. She could not marshal words into the proper prayer structures of her childhood, but instead strove to clear her mind of all troublesome thoughts. How would the father of her memories greet her—the living reminder of his wife's death? How would her aunt, whom she could not remember, receive her? What would life be like in California? Her earliest memories were of Paris. She could not recall San Francisco, the city of her birth.

Gradually, the swirling tangle of her mind slowed. A sense of peace and comfort crept over her. She rose and bowed before the altar. Turning, she started. Benjamin sat relaxed and easy in the last pew. He neither spoke nor moved, but followed her with those watchful blue eyes as she advanced down the aisle towards him.

When she would have passed him without pause, Benjamin rose unhurriedly and fell into step beside her, matching her pace for pace the length of the small mission courtyard before taking her arm and tilting her chin up so she had to stop and face him. His touch, like a sudden chill, sent tiny shivers along her spine.

"Don't bristle so, Sparrow. Here," he drew her down upon a bench. "Speak, Sparrow. Tell me why you're still angry with me." His moustache quivered as he regarded her steadily. "No one is in sight. You won't be overheard."

Mute and accusing, she stared at him until, unexpectedly, all her anger left her to be replaced by an overwhelming sense of bewilderment and fear.

"My mother woke me in the middle of the night, Mr. Greaves. We stole from my father's house like thieves before dawn. Mama met a man—Kwang-ju, she called him. I could not see him very well in the darkness, but he said Father would die if we did not come with him. To Singapore! Mama later reassured me my father would be safe as soon as we went to Singapore and saw a man there. This man wanted something he thought Mama had, but once he saw she didn't have it, we would be free to come home to my father.

"Don't you see, Benjamin," in her need to make him understand, she clutched at his arm, his Christian name slipping out unawares, "Father was a hostage. Once Mama—and I—died, then he was safe. Whatever Kwang-ju's master wanted, the matter would have died with us. Father didn't know anything, or he would have been brought along with us.

"And now—" she choked, anger returning in her frustration. She shook his arm. "Now he's in danger again. All because you meddled in something that doesn't concern you!" In disgust she turned away from him, rigid, gripping her arms tightly as if she could force away the hot tears glistening on her lashes.

Benjamin's arms came around her. She struggled, but he pulled her against him as the tears splashed over. He held her until he felt the stiffness of her body relax, her fingers burrowing in her pocket for her handkerchief. After she wiped her face, sighing raggedly, he regarded her somberly, the blue eyes deepening in the twilight.

"I'm sorry, Sparrow," his voice was gentle, as if he feared her fragile composure might crack at the slightest rough sound, but he spoke firmly, too. "Think on this, if you will. The mystery lured your mother to her death," a muscle tightened in his neck, "and it didn't die with her, nor with you. Your father was safe as long as you were thought dead, but to what kind of life were you condemned? To live as a shopkeeper's helper in Singapore? Or as a concubine to someone else?

"Don't you think you deserve a chance for a happy life? Don't you think your father deserves to have his only child home again? Don't you want to see your mother's killers brought to justice?" He let her go, then grasped her hand in his as if to telegraph his electric sense of outrage and determination through her.

"There's a chance, Sparrow, in eight years' time, this secret is no longer of importance to our mystery man. Perhaps he's dead himself. No," he met her skeptical glance, "I don't think it's wise to assume he's dead. Whatever drew this person to threaten your mother may just precipitate new actions now the world knows you survived.

"And in those actions, reveal his identity and his motive. Remember, Sparrow, you'll be there to help keep your father safe. San Francisco is not like this wounded old tiger of a city. You'll both be surrounded by family and friends. Friends here as well, Sparrow, if you'll trust us."

"I want to go home, Benjamin!" she cried softly. "Truly!" She was astonished at how fiercely, suddenly true she meant what she said. "But not at the expense of my father's life. Nothing will bring Mama back again. How can I—can you—think to put him at risk?"

Benjamin was quiet for a moment, his hands stilled, his breath let out in a curious little whistle under his breath.

"I don't think, Sparrow, Professor Langley's life is at stake." He spoke slowly, carefully choosing his words. "After all, you were a child when you left Paris. Now, you've appeared on the scene again, but traumatized, apparently mute. I think it's likely we'll succeed in flushing these people out into the open. They'll want to find out what you know, what your father might know once you are reunited."

Her face set, Samille considered his words. Her own mind, she conceded, had been clouded for so long by the horror wrought on the terrible night her mother died. What Benjamin said had a logic to it she could not deny, but.... What?

"You may be right. He's not been harmed in all these years. And I haven't a clue as to what's behind this—what anyone thought Mama might have. Oh, Benjamin!" She stopped abruptly. Beside her, he felt her small shrinking gesture of embarrassment.

"It's okay, Sparrow." His voice was unexpectedly rough, "Benjamin T. Greaves, Benjamin to my friends."

She looked up swiftly, not at all shyly, the ghost of a grin passing so quickly he might have imagined the quick look of amusement she threw him.

"Right," he said, oddly disconcerted, standing and tucking her hand under his arm. "Come, Sparrow. Let's get you back to Sister Deborah Carole before she sends out the troops."

Seventeen going on twenty-five, the irrelevant thought crossed his mind, and suddenly he had a great desire to shout with laughter.

Morning dawned in the midst of a steady downpour. Sister Deborah Carole's broad features momentarily creased as she fastened Samille's small trunk, tut-tutting as Samille came away from the window.

"You'll be soaked through, child, before ever you reach the Roads. Oh look, there's Mr. Greaves. He's hired a covered chair. How thoughtful!"

Downstairs Samille ducked her head at his greeting. He handed her into the chair, efficiently stowing her trunk at her feet before turning to the sister.

"Thank you, Sister, for your kindness and your help. My uncle will wish to see you are more properly thanked as soon as possible." With a lightning grin and a tip of his hat, he settled himself beside Samille. The rickshaw driver picked up the shafts of the chair and started off. Benjamin grimaced.

"Sorry, Sparrow, but I can't get used to a human being used like a donkey."

"He'll make enough money, Benjamin, to provide his family with decent housing and regular meals. His children won't have to beg or live in a shack on the canals." She kept her voice low.

"I'll bear in mind your words, Sparrow. Meanwhile, I understand you've met Mrs. Weams. We're to meet her and her husband at the *Hesperia Joy*. You'll be steaming to the Philippines, then to Yokohama, Japan, before crossing the Pacific to San Francisco." Benjamin raised his voice over the cacophony of the streets.

Their driver slowed and forced his way with increasing difficulty through the crowds. Claustrophobic, Samille longed for the days when she could have slipped through this mass of confusion and swarming humanity with ease in her coolie hat and Chinese costume. Suddenly, she gasped. Her fingers dug into her companion's arm.

"Benjamin!" she hissed, stabbing a finger to their right. "Chin hui!"

"What?" Startled, he looked where she pointed and saw a milling crowd of vendors and customers thronging the streets. "Who?"

"The man in Yen-shu's shop. Look, there!"

This time there was no mistaking the man who had confronted him in the druggist's storefront. Chin hui jerked his head. To the right and left of him, men moved from his side and started towards them.

Samille shot a frantic look about the streets.

"Benjamin! There!" From their left, two more men were making a determined progress towards them. She knew others would follow. They were scarcely making any headway now. Benjamin's hand closed reassuringly about her own. He leaned forward and addressed their driver. The man twisted about, shrugged eloquently at the tightly packed throng before him.

Chin hui stood unmoving, watching as his henchmen closed in on their goal.

Pop! Pop! Pop! Suddenly, the street before them was alive with smoke and noise. Firecrackers! People scattered wildly as another string danced in the air. Their driver bolted through a gap, the crowd surging together behind them.

"We've done it!" Benjamin grinned at her. "He'll be a long time trying to get through the crowds back there, Sparrow."

Samille looked back, blinked, craned her neck for a long moment. On the edge of the crowd, standing on sacks of rice, Penang saluted her with two fingers, watching their rickshaw out of sight. She became aware Benjamin was asking her a question.

"Why do you suppose this fellow is determined to keep you here, Sparrow? What did you do, sell him a poor potion?" Beneath the light tone, a flint-edged curiosity glinted. Samille met those cool blue eyes directly. Today they gleamed like water pooling in a deep lagoon. A slight flush bloomed on her pale cheeks.

"It isn't what you think, Benjamin. Oh, I suppose it's possible Wei-chu, Chin hui's master, may have wanted me as a concubine. More likely I would have been a scullery maid or put on the streets. No, I think my escape will cause Chin hui to lose face with Wei-chu, and worse, for Wei-chu to lose face because someone so insignificant has outwitted him."

"A female at that, and one aided by a Westerner," Benjamin added with quick insight. His eyes deepened, like a blue flame flaring before the night. "We've made an enemy, Sparrow, but I don't see how we could have avoided it." A breeze lifted the fine hair away from his face, cheekbones sharp and firm before her. "I'll not breathe easily, my dear, until you're safe with Professor Langley."

What answer could she make? Even San Francisco would not be far enough away with a man like Wei-chu for an enemy. But surely, he would not be bothered with such a one as herself once she was gone from Singapore. They rode in silence to the Roads.

Benjamin delivered her to Mrs. Weams. Mr. Weams was much like his wife, but with all his nervous energy depleted by his illness. He sat apathetically in his chair and waited patiently to be carried aboard the *Hesperia Joy*. Mrs. Weams made up for her husband, flitting anxiously from the baggage to the purser to her husband. Benjamin stood beside Samille until two seamen carried Mr. Weams aboard, Mrs. Weams fluttering beside them. He accompanied her on ship and to her quarters. She would share a cabin with Mrs. Weams, whose husband would share quarters with a single gentleman traveling to Manilla.

"His medicine," Mrs. Weams quavered, peering uncertainly about. "The bed...." she waved a hand awkwardly, "rest?"

Samille lifted a brow at Benjamin, who covered a smile, stroking his mustache. As Mrs. Weams popped out of the cabin once again, he turned to her with mock formality.

"I won't keep you, Miss Langley. Bon voyage." He took her hand in his, looked at it as if not sure why it was there, then patted it absently. When he spoke, his voice was deep and roughened about the edges.

"Remember, Sparrow, I'm your friend. If you ever...."

Abruptly he dropped her hand as a fresh-faced, red-haired purser stopped, a gleam lighting his eyes as he took in the girl before him.

"Miss Langley, isn't it? I thought so," as Samille nodded woodenly. "Would you see Mr. Weams gets this?" He handed her a small case. "A slight mix-up with the baggage. So sorry," he finished smoothly.

Samille bit her lip. Her throat tight, her mind whirling, she sought for words to express her gratitude, her friendship. How could good-bye have come so quickly? Benjamin, Penang, Yen-shu and Sakai—she could count her friends on the fingers of one hand, and now she was leaving them all behind. Mrs. Weams loomed up beside her.

"Mr. Weams... discomfort...." Samille thrust the case at her, drew a deep breath, turned—to find Benjamin gone.

He'd not even waited. Sparrow. A child. Sighing, half-angry, half-saddened, Samille followed her new companion slowly into the cabin. It was going to be a long, demanding voyage. She had only time to wonder what he might have meant. If she ever needed a friend... if she ever found herself in Singapore... if she ever....

Chapter 4

San Francisco was hot. Not a breath of air stirred bay side. Tired, sticky with perspiration in her long-sleeved blouse and long skirts, apprehension further darkened Samille's mood as she stood woodenly by Mr. Weams' chair. His wife, true to form, darted like a bee on a string away from her husband and back again.

"Oh dear, Miss Langley! Will they... soon... do you think... how?" She sputtered and buzzed. Samille tuned her out, much as old Mr. Weams did, she suspected, and scanned the busy dock. Who would come for her? The aunt she'd never met? Surely not her father. A lump lodged in her throat. To be so close. Without a single incident from the time they'd boarded the boat three weeks ago until now. Her nerves were strained to the breaking point. She could not accept the possibility she might be free of fear.

"But, Papa, you never said she was going to be beautiful!"

Startled, Samille turned about at the accusatory tone coming from immediately beside her. A child—a girl—she guessed about ten or twelve years old, tugged at the sleeve of a slightly rotund gentleman with merry brown eyes. He took off his hat and made a graceful bow.

"Miss Samille Langley? Allow me to present myself. Michael C. O'Grady. Your father is a dear friend and colleague of mine. He's entrusted you to me—to us—" he said and his eyes twinkled as he corrected himself, "as your final escort home."

"How do you do, Mr. O'Grady?"

It seemed her body remembered and thought for her, for without thinking to do so, Samille curtsied with an elegance bespeaking her travel-weary appearance and put out her hand.

"It's most kind of you."

Mr. O'Grady beamed at her, patting her hand gently, his bald pate gleaming with sweat, dark brown porkchop sideburns quivering.

"My dear, if you could but see the change in Samuel, in your father, you would know it brings me nothing but joy to see you safely home."

Samille nodded stiffly. Scarcely an adequate response, she thought, but fear and apprehension together choked her until she thought she couldn't breathe.

"Oh dear, oh dear, oh dear!" Mrs. Weams, looming up suddenly beside her, pressed an ice into her hand. "So hot... so hot! And you, good sir, you are come to escort our charge to her father?"

Samille blinked and stared in open-mouthed astonishment at her shipboard companion. It was the most complete, sustained utterance she'd yet heard from Mrs. Weams. The lady turned to her.

"We must be on our way, Miss Langley. Many thanks for your kind assistance—most, most helpful to Mr. Weams and me. The Lord bless you, child."

She had, Samille noticed, garnered two stalwart porters, one of whom stood behind Mr. Weams' chair and one by their cases.

"Thank you, Mrs. Weams. I was most grateful for your company." Surprisingly, it was true, too. Mrs. Weams hadn't pried, hadn't tried to exact confidences, hadn't offered advice or sermons. She hadn't even mentioned the obvious: her charge could speak again. In short, she had kept Samille just busy enough to make the passage tolerable.

With a brisk nod for Mr. O'Grady and Samille, the indomitable lady pointed her umbrella and led her small procession to a waiting carriage.

Samille became aware of an intent stare and looked down to find an unblinking set of brown eyes meeting her own determinedly. A sharpish tug was administered by the young girl to her father's hand.

"Beautiful, kind, and graceful, Father," she reported in a meaningful tone.

O'Grady rolled his eyes in mock despair and with a flourish of his hat, presented his daughter.

"Forgive my manners, Miss Langley. My daughter, Eleanor Jane O'Grady."

Save for the twinkle in her large brown eyes, Eleanor bore no resemblance to her father. Tall for her age, she was all sharp angles with slim wrists outgrowing the sleeves of her dress. Strawberry-blonde curls sprang about her head, escaping the careful blue ribbon vainly attempting to contain them. Instead of curtseying as Samille had done, Eleanor put out her hand in a forthright manner.

"Pleased to make your acquaintance, Miss Langley. My friends call me Lennie. Father's right, you know. Uncle Samuel is all in a dither about you not being dead and coming home and everything.

"He's walking around, thumping his way back and forth across the garden. Aunt Jane's beside herself for fear he'll fall. I don't expect he will, though," Lennie considered as she paused for breath, "'cause he doesn't go very fast."

Mr. O'Grady raised an amused brow at Samille.

"We have our entire cab ride in which to engage Miss Langley in conversation, Lennie. Shall we find a porter to take up her trunk," he glanced questioningly at the single small trunk left beside Samille, "and make haste so Samuel can stop thumping about the garden?"

Lennie grinned saucily at her father and Samille, stuck her fingers in her mouth and whistled shrilly. Samille spoke without thinking.

"I once heard a sailor hail a rickshaw just like that. Do you think you could teach me, Lennie?"

The young girl beamed, and it was then Samille saw her resemblance to Michael O'Grady.

Solicitously settled in the hansom cab, Samille took in her surroundings with a blurred sense of awe. The streets twisted away from San Francisco Bay and wandered up and down the hills of the burgeoning city. Their cab halted periodically for the trolley lines which crisscrossed the wide, unpaved streets. Sprawling, busy working-class neighborhoods gradually gave way to more prosperous streets, full of shops and well-tended houses. This city was her home, she thought with a growing sense of nervousness. Her father's home. Once her mother's home.

It was far different from the lush, overwhelming beauty of Southern Asia, and equally distant from the ancient, civilized worldliness of Paris and its environs. The air, now they were leaving the bay behind, was reviving. Samille drank it in greedily, feeling a sense of wonder and welcome and relief with every breath she took, with every block they advanced, with every spinning turn of the cab's wheels bringing her closer to her destination.

At length she looked away from the streets and met Mr. O'Grady's quiet, thoughtful gaze. Lennie, opposite Samille, was absorbed in a book. After all, it was not so difficult to begin.

"Tell me about my father, Mr. O'Grady," she asked simply, turning upon him two fathomless, remote pools of green in which some deeper waves of emotion flickered against the light, revealing only her need to know.

Her father's friend gently shifted his daughter, slipping his arm about her, then spoke softly—whether because of the child beside him or fear of stirring the pain which he recalled to life once more, Samille was never after certain.

"Samuel and I have been friends, my dear, since our undergraduate days at Harvard. We were two Westerners drawn together for survival at first, and then later because we suited so admirably as friends. When our studies ended and we went our separate ways, we maintained contact and rejoiced when eventually we became colleagues at the university. By which time, I'd married my Marta, Eleanor's mother.

"Your father was making a name for himself with his scholarship on the foreign policy of Thomas Jefferson. He was invited to lecture at the Sorbonne in the fall of 1876. A month after his arrival, we received a glowing letter. My serious, charming friend had met a beautiful young Parisienne, whose parents were transplanted San Franciscans, like he himself. Françoise was also witty, sparkling, and intelligent with a remarkable degree of self-possession, according to your father. He had fallen head over heels in love with her.

"He was older, by a good ten years, and dull by comparison, or so he told us. What hope had he with such a woman? Marta and your Aunt Jane, however, were quick to reply: he was afforded a fine sense of humor, looks, grace, kindness, and charm. And, they told him, he must trust his feelings, for they knew him to be a most excellent judge of character.

"So fortified, he began to court your mother in earnest, writing to us at length of each new discovery—of how her mind leaped to new ideas, to the humor in a situation, to the joy of small pleasures. We were not surprised when their engagement was settled less than a year later. By then, Samuel had been offered and accepted a formal lectureship at the Sorbonne. Jane and Marta and I traveled to Paris for the wedding. It was a small service, with Françoise's father, your grandfather, recently deceased, and her mother in poor health. We rejoiced in our friend's happiness, for his bride was all he had said. A more honest, open friend I have never had."

Michael O'Grady paused, cleared his throat, and looked away for a long moment before turning his attention back to Samille, who sat before him, emotions collected and reposed, all energy held in abeyance, the city passing unnoticed around her.

"In the years which followed, your parents were two of the happiest individuals you could ever hope to see. We visited them occasionally; they came here infrequently. However, Françoise insisted on having their child—you, my dear—here in San Francisco, to be, as she put it, surrounded by family. Your grandmère came with them. She died before they returned to Paris when you were still a babe in arms.

"Nothing disturbed the serenity, the overwhelming contentment of their marriage. Your father was filled with a profound gratitude because his life was so rich. It brimmed over in his work, to his friends. Imagine, then, what it must have been like to awaken one morning and find his wife and child gone as completely and utterly as if they had never been. With no word, no explanation."

Samille's eyes blurred. She could not bear to think of it, and yet, she had asked him to tell her.

"Samuel was beside himself—he cabled us and we went to him immediately. For weeks he hounded the authorities in France. Every call, every unidentified female body, every hospital and orphanage in the area filled his waking hours. Then, out the blue, so unexpectedly t it was the last straw crushed in his grasp, came the unfathomable news—Françoise Beauvoir Langley and her child had been murdered during the mutiny of a Malay crew on a steamer bound for Singapore. Their bodies had not been recovered. A fellow shipmate and survivor, a Mr. McNamara, reported he witnessed the death of your mother and that you had been lost overboard.

"Your father suffered a complete collapse, Samille. We—your Aunt Jane and my Marta and I—arranged to close up the apartment in Paris and brought Samuel home to San Francisco, where he had been offered a teaching position at the university. Months passed before he would do more than eat a little of what was set before him, sleep, stare out the window, or walk at all hours about the city and the shore.

"Then, at the beginning of the following fall term, he appeared one morning in class and proceeded to give as brilliant an opening lecture as he had ever done in the past. From that moment on, he threw himself into his teaching and research.

"He never spoke again," O'Grady's voice faltered, "of the glowing, golden years behind him. But he has never stopped grieving either, my dear, for the daughter who never came home, not in all these long years since."

"But you should see him now, Miss Langley!" Lennie, silent and unnoticed until then, chimed in. "He's so full of laughter and fussing over the house and food and flowers. But," she paused, her brows drawing together in perplexity, "he seems a bit nervous, too. Isn't it odd?" Her gaze cleared and she looked directly at Samille.

"He's your father, but even if he weren't, one couldn't help but adore him. He always tells the best stories...." She halted abruptly as her father squeezed her shoulders in warning.

Seeing nothing, the streets and hills oblivious before her, Samille half-whispered to herself.

"Yes, the most marvelous, wondrous stories. Once I was his little girl...." and her face closed, all the grief, the pain, the feelings playing about her features moments before now locked tightly inside once again.

The hansom cab rattled down a planked street with rows of smart wooden houses. Rioting with color and curlicues and furbelows, tower rooms, and porches, their vitality and vulgarity overwhelmed Samille. She was obscurely reassured when her companion spoke to their driver and they slowed, halting before a house on Divisadero Street which stood as a marvel of simplicity and restraint among its ornate neighbors. Tall and narrow, a white gingerbread frieze relieved a gray clapboard front. A series of large windows jutted out, one above the other, from the main rooms on each floor. This was, surely, much more in keeping with what she remembered of her parents.

Samille's hands tightened and she tried to steady the sudden, rapid beating of her heart as Mr. O'Grady helped her from the cab, aware of Lennie chattering happily behind her, the door before her opening, and a tall, spare-boned woman with russet waves softening a severe brow stepping forward. She knew those high cheekbones, the height and lean frame for her own. This, then, must be her aunt, Jane Langley Gooden.

"Samille?!" Hands extended, Jane hurried forward, gray eyes alight and a slight flush rosy on her cheeks. She hesitated awkwardly before her newfound niece. Samille stepped back a pace, dipping a cool little curtsey in deference.

"How do you do, Aunt Jane?" she inquired stiffly, aware of a stubborn, frozen core of ice within herself, one which would not allow her to embrace this woman, aware, too, of her aunt's quickly-masked disappointment. She forced herself to meet her aunt's gaze, then turned away with relief to Michael O'Grady.

"Thank you so much for your time, Mr. O'Grady. It was a most comfortable journey. I look forward to seeing you again, Lennie."

She sensed, rather than saw the shrug her father's friend gave as she turned back to her aunt.

"I should like to see my father now, if it is convenient for him."

Picking up her skirts, she advanced before her aunt into the cool, dim hall where a Chinese houseboy stepped forward to take the trunk deposited there by their hansom cab driver.

"Leave it, please." Her curt tone brooked no argument. The young man rolled his eyes questioningly at Aunt Jane, and then bobbed his head and retreated silently down the hallway. Her lips uncompromisingly set, Samille faced her aunt.

"I have labored all my life, Aunt Jane, and prefer to see to my own needs insofar as this does not disrupt your life, or my father's, of course.

"May I see him now?"

Disconcerted by the cool self-possession of her niece, Jane Gooden raised an eyebrow briefly.

"Certainly, my dear. Come this way."

She moved across the hall, opening a set of double doors and gesturing for Samille to precede her into the room. Books filled the walls to capacity, sparing only the fine, bowed windows and the austere, simple fireplace gracing one wall. Two leather Queen Anne chairs flanked the hearth where even at this hour a small fire flared and popped. Vaguely, Samille took in the large desk before the window, the scent of old leather, cracked bindings, and faint trace of a sweet tobacco as her Aunt Jane withdrew and closed the doors to her brother's study firmly behind her.

All of her attention was riveted upon the man who sat in one of the leather armchairs, his left leg propped up before him, cushioned and elevated on a stool.

Tall, slightly stoop-shouldered, his dark hair was graying untidily, though touches of white graced the temples, highlighting the wounded, harsh set of brooding gray eyes. Some spark of hope and instant recognition lit them briefly, far in their depths. Gravely, he attempted to rise with the aid of a cane lying next to his chair.

Gaunt, with deep furrows ringing his cheeks, Samille saw clearly how grief and advancing years and something else—something colder and more insidious—had stealthily eroded away the health and vigor of the man she remembered.

"Please don't stand upon my account, Father."

She curtsied with a natural, effortless grace, never taking her eyes from his face, and so caught the sharp spasm of pain violently contorting his features. She followed the flick of his gaze to the portrait hanging above the fireplace mantel.

Her mother's eyes met her own. Half-smiling, a pale blue ribbon wound through the thick black plait drawn over one shoulder to lie glittering against the graceful arch of a white throat. Those eyes betrayed an eagerness and joy indulgently mirrored in the face above hers. Older, but with the same slightly exotic hint of Asian blood, her grandmère looked not at the world, but at the daughter seated before her who would bear her only grandchild—another daughter.

Abruptly, Samille tore her eyes from those twin pairs of soft green eyes and sat down carefully, like an obedient child, on the stool before her father's chair.

"Françoise was sixteen, then," her father indicated the painting. "Your grandmère gave the portrait to me as a wedding present."

Her father's voice held none of the pain and anguish his appearance had led her to expect. With surprise, she noted his voice was strong and firm, a half-timbre deeper than her memories. Unexpectedly, he smiled at her and light stirred, rippled in the depths of those dark eyes.

"Let me look at you, child. To have you back again, whole and safe and sound!"

He paused, pouring a glass of sherry for himself with a shaky hand, whether from age or infirmity or excitement, she could not guess, handed another to her, and seemed unconcerned about her lack of response. He raised his glass, not to her, but to those two dark heads in the portrait above them—those heads so much like her own such that she sat before him like an echo, a living extension of the portrait.

"To the women of the House of Chui!" Her father's eyes met her own. "I knew she would have somehow saved you, Samille, and one day you would return to me."

He toasted her. Her mouth opened, her head tilted, the sherry trickled down her throat, an unfamiliar, slightly sweet taste on her tongue with the unmistakable bite of alcohol beneath. Staring at her father as if mesmerized, Samille found her thoughts swirling, her head whirling.

She closed her eyes against the light, against the sight of her father, against the sudden flood of memories which threatened her precarious calm. Gently, Samuel removed the small glass from her fingers and chafed them. She opened her eyes. Still she could not speak.

"I hired a detective, Samille, every year for five years, to search for you. Each time they began in Singapore and came away empty-handed, although once or twice I was led to believe they had found you—closer scrutiny proved otherwise. I became convinced, then, either you had truly perished, or, more likely, you were alive somewhere within the sprawling city of Singapore, and in your own time you would be restored to your home."

Every year for five years he had searched for her. Samille's eyes smarted and it seemed to her those two pairs of emerald eyes misted with tears even as hers did. She covered her father's hand with hers and lay her cheek upon it, crying silently. Her father stroked her head, murmuring incoherent, comforting sounds. Within her, something gave way with every tear sliding across their entwined hands, something she dimly recognized as a deep, unacknowledged fear that her father had never come for her because he did not care, shame because she had not deserved to be found, and anger, too, because he had not come.

How long they sat there, she did not know, aware only of a kind of peace slowly filling her as her tears ceased. At last she lifted her head. The sunlight had slid farther across the books and slanted palely across the rich burgundy of the carpets. Her father, she noted with a catch in her throat, seemed to have shrunk in his chair, looking older, frailer as the light left the room. This interview had tired him, taxed him, as if his strength had surrounded her, borne her child's grief, filled her with a sense of peace. Now she summoned a tremulous smile.

"Yes, Father, I've come home in my own time, and I've every intention of staying.

"May I ring for my aunt? I think I'd like to wash and rest now."

Unexpectedly, prodigiously, she yawned, finding the prospect of a moment's rest enormously appealing. Her father chuckled, patted her hand.

"But, of course you may, my dear child." He rang a silver-chased bell at his side. "If you prefer, Jane will have a tray sent to your room later."

"Oh no, Father." She spoke quickly. "I'd much rather join you for dinner, if you don't mind."

The doors opened. Her Aunt Jane stepped into the room.

"Mind?" Vividly, pain etched her father's features and his voice was gruff as he finished, "how can you think it of us, child? We dine at seven. Jane will wake you."

On impulse, she stooped and shyly brushed a kiss across his forehead.

Samille floated up through layers of sleep and disorienting, dream-fragmented images. Soundless laughing puppets had loomed like shadows over her bed. Gold had glittered, dazzling her. Some flicker of movement, green and menacing, had come and gone in a split second. She rolled over on the bed, sitting up hazily as an echoing sound collected into a knock. Someone was at her door.

"Yes?"

The door opened. Aunt Jane stepped in, bringing a breath of fresh air into the room to dispel the last vapors of the dream web tangling her attempts to awaken.

"You've time to bathe, Samille, if you haven't already done so. Soon Lee has put fresh towels in the bath. Come down when you've finished." She turned to go as matter-of-factly as she'd come.

"Thank you, Aunt Jane," Samille called belatedly.

Thirty minutes later, Samille rebraided her hair, pulled on a fresh shirtwaist and skirt, retrieving the necessary belt, hesitated, then went to her trunk and dug out her slippers. It had been such a relief to shed the ill-fitting boots she'd been given in Singapore. She could not bring herself to don them yet again tonight. Before she could change her mind, she slipped quietly from her room.

Seated at her father's right with Jane Langley Gooden across from her, Samille noted the Oriental screens and the ferns arranged in a corner, the Ming-dynasty style vases gracing the ornate fireplace mantel. Rich carpets cushioned her feet. When Soon Lee served the first course, the familiar hot and sour soup barely raised a brow. Her father sampled his soup, and complimented Soon Lee.

"Please tell Ho Lee he has excelled as always."

A small smile briefly turned up the corners of Soon Lee's mouth. Professor Langley turned his attention to his daughter.

"You'll find we dine well, Samille. Ho Lee is an artist with his native cuisine, but has also very cleverly mastered many other styles of cookery from San Francisco originals to Italian and some French dishes."

He put down his soup spoon abruptly, stretched his hand hesitantly toward her, and picked up his spoon again.

"I'm sorry, my dear, to be babbling on about cookery as if you were a comfortable hausfrau, but you... you seem thin, child." He stopped, looked helplessly at his sister, and started to rise. Samille reached out and clasped his hand.

"Please, Father, don't distress yourself. I've been a fortunate child." She paused, gently squeezing his hand as her father settled in his chair.

"I'm sorry, Samille." Her father apologized, giving her the ghost of a smile. Soon Lee cleared the soup course, following it with steaming bowls of rice, followed by a savory shrimp and vegetable dish which he set before them. Samille unrolled the ivory chopsticks, took them up and casually positioned them, thinking quickly. Then she looked from her father to her aunt.

"I'm sorry, too, Father. You've lost a child and regained a grown daughter. No," she insisted, as he started to protest, "please, Father. That child is gone forever. I... I think she died on the day I watched Mother drown. You mustn't forever guard your tongue for fear of hurting me.

"The past is behind us." Her voice softened, faltered as she struggled to find the words to put them all at their ease. "I don't know how I actually came to Singapore. I suppose it was the shock of Mother's death, but I can't remember much of the days which followed. I'm not certain how long I wandered the streets and canals, but, but," here she paused, rubbed her forehead as if to smooth away an ache. Her aunt glanced anxiously at her father.

"No, please, Aunt Jane, I want to tell you. I think, Father, it was not very long. At any rate, one morning a tiny Malay woman woke me. I'd gone to sleep in her doorway. In the doorway of her husband's shop. Her name was Sakai, his name was Yen-shu.

"They took me in, Father, giving me shelter and food. I helped them in the shop. My mas—Old Yen-shu," she hastily corrected herself, "was a Chinese druggist. They had no children, you see," she spoke to her aunt, "and they became fond of me, and I of them.

"I expect they told you, Father, I could not speak when they found me." When had she decided she would not share her burden of fear and terror with him? "But Yen-shu and Sakai treated me kindly, and I never wanted for food or shelter.

"That's all, really. I worked in their shop and lived with them until the day I was caught in the middle of a street riot on my way home from the Roads, the harbor," she explained at her aunt's quizzical expression. "Malay and Hindu religious societies were fighting amongst themselves. The sudden fright brought back the memory of my past. Mr. Greaves, luckily, was nearby and came to my rescue when he heard me cry out.

"Because I had cried out in English, Mr. Greaves became curious and was able to ferret out the story of the mutiny from the *Straits' Times* archives and then contact you."

She toyed with a piece of shrimp and met her father's eyes.

"I don't know why Mother and I were on board the boat, Father, except someone threatened your life if she did not go to meet a man in Singapore. She told me as soon as we saw this man, we would be able to return to Paris."

Professor Langley sat silently for several interminable moments, and then he sighed. Tired gray eyes searched her face.

"I must confess, dear child, I had entertained the faintest of hopes you might know something, in spite of your tender age at the time, to shed some light upon your mother's motives for leaving as she did.

"However," his gray eyes deepened with emotion and intensity, "let me tell you, Samille. When I realized my love and trust were intact, I began to recover from the shock of losing you both. Françoise loved me. I know that absolutely. I know, too, why ever she left, she had a compelling reason for her actions. And if you say she meant to come back, it is only what I have always known. If she had not been prevented, she—and you—would have come back to me."

Aunt Jane stirred. Samille saw the gray eyes, so like her father's, fill with tears. She sniffed.

"It's only what we all said and felt, Samuel. All of us—Michael and Marta and Alfred and myself—who also loved her, and you, too, Samille."

"Thank you, Aunt Jane." Samille flushed a little with shame as she recalled her earlier behavior toward her aunt. "I'm so glad you believed in her, Father, but I am home again. All I want now is for us to pick up our lives and go on."

"You see, Samuel," Jane smiled shakily at her brother, "your daughter has the strength and commonsense of Françoise. I think she's right, you know. We must put the past behind us now." She spoke encouragingly, almost with an entreaty.

Professor Langley surveyed his sister and his daughter, a faint humor brightening his features.

"You needn't fuss so, either of you. I can see you're both determined to let the past lie. I don't dispute the logic or the wisdom of what you say.

"Eat child," he urged Samille. "Let me savor the small ordinariness of coaxing my daughter to eat her peas and rutabagas."

Samille's nose wrinkled in automatic distaste, and then her eyes widened with astonishment and chagrin as memory came flooding back.

Samuel's laughter rang out richly.

"'Rutabagas are fit only for pigs and little boys,' eh, my dear?"

Samille flushed, caught her aunt's bewildered eye and grinned in spite of herself. Her father turned to his sister.

"Only four or five at the time, she was, Jane, but quite opinionated, and, if I recall correctly," he paused and glanced at his daughter with loving amusement, "the remark, along with a generous spoonful of the detested vegetable, was directed at Jean-Pierre Robard, who'd pulled her pigtails just before supper."

Soon Lee padded in with a tray of dessert ices, his soft footfalls covered by the sounds of laughter.

Chapter 5

Dressing slowly, Samille made her way cautiously downstairs, careful not to wake her father or her aunt, and let herself out by the side door to the gardens. On Saturdays the usual traffic and commotion of the street was lacking and in its place a tranquility presided over the morning, a tranquility rarely to be found in Singapore. Breakfast, she'd discovered over the past month, would be leisurely, *chacun á son gout*, her father having fallen into the habit of taking his breakfasts in bed since his accident, along with the morning paper and any personal correspondence to which he cared to attend.

Distractedly, she drew in the dew-spangled morning air and settled on a bench in full sun. Here, Soon Lee, under his father's painstaking direction, had lovingly, methodically landscaped the backyard into a series of gardens. To one side, tidy and luxuriant, grew vegetables and herbs. Samille recognized peppers, peas, onions, and lettuces. Other plants sprouted—stalks of some root crops—while sprawling tomato plants bearing hard green fruits were staked next to the high wooden fence surrounding the back lot of the property. Further along the fence, es-

89

paliered trees had lost their blossoms and green nuggets of fruit were just now appearing.

A stone path, casually meandering, separated the vegetables from rioting purple hibiscus, pink and red azaleas, white camellias, and masses of showy pink, white, and red roses. Ferns calmed the spirit in shadowed corners, while irises, mosses, and other plants unknown to her carpeted the ground beneath decorous shade trees. Vibrant and joyous, the garden's splendor reminded her of Singapore's tropical effusiveness, and for once this thought did not dismay her. Narrow strawed beds followed the circuitous winding of the path through this profusion of scent and color to the rear, where potter's and storage sheds flanked a gated tradesman's entrance onto an unpaved alley.

Despite the tranquil setting in which she sat, Samille was aware of her fingers twisting a leaf absentmindedly, and her gaze unfocused on the beauty before her. She sighed and deliberately stilled her restless movements, her hands clasped solidly in her lap, her thoughts drifting over the recent weeks since her arrival in San Francisco.

Quiet as the dawn stealing in across the carpet, across the foot of her bed, she woke each morning and contemplated her room with a guilty pleasure. Delicate yellow and blue violets entwined in regular columns across the papered walls, while woodwork, mantel, curtains, and coverlet were all of white. A golden pine bed and chest of drawers, a dainty ladies' writing desk, a white rattan rocker, and a window seat with a shelf beneath it furnished the room, which was nearly the size of Yen-shu's entire shop and living quarters. A landscape—a haunting vision of Yosemite by Lionel Adams—graced the wall above the mantel. Overlooking the back gardens, this had been her mother's room before her grandparents had decided to live in Paris.

The house had never been sold and had passed to Françoise on the death of her parents, and hence to her husband after her death. In plan, it was very simple. A central hallway divided each floor with two rooms on either side. Of the three other bedrooms on the second floor, her aunt occupied the other rear room across the hall from her own, with her father's bedroom at the front and separated from Aunt Jane's room by a commodious bath. The spare guest room also fronted the house and was occasionally used when Lennie visited overnight. At the rear of the hall a narrow stair led up to the unused third story—a nursery stretching the length of the house on her side, with rooms for a nanny or governess and live-in maid opposite—and down to the back hall and kitchen.

On the first floor, a wide entry separated her father's study from the large, comfortable parlor at the front of the house. A second, smaller bath was situated between the study and Aunt Jane's morning room behind it, while the dining room completed the square—opening from the parlor and having a door onto the narrow hall which led to the kitchen addition. This was a single story which housed both the kitchen and the Chinaman's room, occupied by Ho Lee since the death of his wife three years earlier. Soon Lee, it transpired, still lived in Chinatown, but frequently came up the hill to help his father. An attic and a cellar provided storage.

Before her arrival, she learned the household had run on a fairly flexible schedule, revolving around certain fixed points. Her father lectured three mornings a week. On those days he rose about eight o'clock and repaired to the downstairs bath. Aunt Jane usually woke shortly thereafter and made her way to the upstairs bath. Her father would breakfast lightly and leave by nine-thirty to catch the Central and Sutter streetcar down to the foot of Broadway Street on the harbor and hence to his ferry across the bay to Oakland. Owing to his injury, he now took a hansom cab to and from the ferry.

Depending upon his appointments and whether his students or his research sidetracked him, Professor Langley would either return directly to the house on Divisadero Street after his lecture or remain at his office until such time as he was free. It had not been uncommon, Samille understood, for several of her father's colleagues and students to cross the bay back to North Beach with him and continue an argument or discussion over supper at Luchetti's or one of the other little restaurants crowding thickly in the neighborhood.

Now, however, her father had taken an extended leave of absence from the university, spending all of his time with his daughter. Along with Aunt Jane and occasionally Michael O'Grady and Lennie, they'd toured the University of California, taken tea at the fabulous red-brick Palace Hotel, ridden a cable car, picnicked at the inn on the side of Mt. Tamalpais after taking the steam engine to the top of the mountain, and dined at several French and Italian restaurants. With her father abstaining, she'd even bicycled with her aunt through German neighborhoods and Golden Gate Park.

Jane Langley Gooden, for her part, had also taken several mornings with Samille in tow to make the rounds of the small shops lining nearby Fillmore Street, where she purchased such ready-made articles of clothing as possible, and ordered other shirtwaists and fine woolen skirts fitted to her niece's tall, supple figure. Over Samille's futile protestations, several dresses were also ordered.

Half the population of San Francisco, particularly the residents whose homes filled Russian Hill, seemed to be acquainted with her aunt. Her late husband, Alfred W. Gooden, had been a local writer greatly admired for his wit and good-nature. Along with Marta O'Grady, Lennie's mother, he had perished in a conflagration which had broken out in the aftershock of an earthquake several years previously. With his intelligent, handsome wife, Alfred and Jane Gooden had from the outset fitted well into the bohemian, artistic community of Russian Hill. Her aunt, Samille discovered, rented her cottage there to a writer and his wife for a pittance. Eventually, with urban expansion, the Western Addition where her brother lived and the built-up areas of Nob Hill, Pacific Heights, and Presidio had been claimed by the upper middle class and upper class. They had hired a carriage one day and driven along Van Ness, where the elaborate, ostentatious mansions of the Silver Barons and other wealthy citizens stood.

For the most part, Samille found herself readily accepted as the Professor's resurrected daughter with barely a raised brow. Far from the gilded, prescribed social rituals of British Singapore. Samille found her father's and her aunt's friends met frequently in groups whose interests spanned a wide range of literary, political, and educational topics. At the moment, Jane Gooden was heavily involved in the promotion of public kindergartens for all of San Francisco's children, female suffragism, and Mexican religious folk art. These seemed a bewildering mélange of activities, yet revealed an oddly appealing enthusiasm on the part of her aunt, tempered by the famous Langley practicality and foresight. Jane, however, had also curtailed her daily activities severely since Samille's precipitous return to the household.

Therein lay the rub, Samille admitted. While San Francisco presented an ever-changing montage of activities and delights, the role of tourist was wearing thin. Her days were constantly structured around new activities. She had no time for reflection, no time to think of what the future might hold. Well-aware of the sacrifices being made for her, she had tried hard to be gay and cheerful and uncomplaining. Yet she felt increasingly uncomfortable at keeping her father and Aunt Jane from their regular pursuits.

The toll was telling in her restless nights and when she woke far too early in the morning. Now, the truth jolted her in its clarity. Boredom, plain and simple, assailed her.

She missed the daily business of Yen-shu's shop—her master's quick patter, the constant flow of customers, the myriad necessary trips to market, to the Roads, to the bazaar.

What could she find to do here? In spite of her hasty words to her aunt, her assistance was not needed in the running of the household. Between Aunt Jane and Ho Lee, the household functioned smoothly. Her feet tapped a staccato rhythm as her thoughts tangled, led nowhere. Samille sighed. As enjoyable as it was to have her father's and the city's libraries available to her, she could only spend so many hours reading. She knew herself too well. She needed some pattern of activity to her days—something satisfying and challenging.

At last she sighed again, stirred as a warm, stray breeze teased tendrils from her braid. Somehow, without hurting his feelings, she must find a way to tell her father this. Or, perhaps it would be better to approach Aunt Jane first. The unguarded intensity she occasionally surprised in her father's face worried her.

Idly sweeping her glance across the garden, Samille checked, for even as she watched, the latch lifted on the gate to the alleyway and the gate swung open. A heavyset youngish Chinese man stepped onto the path, swinging his pole with its bundles clear of the gate as he fastened it behind him. Advancing toward the kitchen entrance, he caught sight of Samille, rising suddenly from her seat. Bobbing his head in a quick, deferential gesture, the curious dark eyes, hooded and sly, took in her heightened color, the fingers clutching the touch of lace at her throat. He stopped.

"Ah Sing Lee, Missy. I come to bring the laundry for honorable uncle." A slight shrug set his bundles to dancing.

Samille recovered her composure, stepped ahead of him onto the path.

"Yes, Mr. Lee. I'm sure Ho Lee will be expecting you."

He followed her silently. A few steps from the kitchen Soon Lee appeared at the back door. His eyes widened, his gaze briefly flicking from Samille to Ah Sing and back again.

"Mistress Gooden asks if you will join her for breakfast, Missy?"

"Yes, thank you, Soon Lee. This gentleman," she gestured self-consciously, "has come with the laundry."

Making her way to the side entrance to the house, which entered the back hallway, Samille stopped to pluck a rose and cast a covert glance behind her. Soon Lee and Ah Sing stood as she left them, staring after her. As she moved on, Soon Lee took a step back into the kitchen and gestured sharply for his kinsman to enter.

Inside the hall bath, Samille noted her too-pale features and trembling hands with dismay. Her last few weeks had been free of fear and distress. She'd thought she was beyond reading something sinister into every new face. She pinched some color into her cheeks and went to breakfast.

"Good morning, Samille."

Her aunt passed her a basket of hot sourdough rolls.

"Thank you, Aunt Jane."

Samille busied herself with honey and butter and pouring out her morning tea. Jane read the morning's *Examiner* in her usual undemanding silence. At length Samille stole a glance at her and resolutely put down her cup.

"Aunt Jane?"

"Yes?"

"Shouldn't Father be getting back to his classroom and his studies?"

Her aunt's gaze swept up in surprise. So much for subtlety, Samille thought ruefully.

"Why do you ask, dear?"

Her niece hesitated, fidgeting with her napkin and eying Jane uncertainly.

"Aunt Jane, please don't think I'm not sincerely grateful for your time and patience in helping me adjust," she met her aunt's eyes, "but it seems to me we would all get on much better if we allowed our lives to return to their normal patterns.

"Father tries to hide it, but I can tell when he's bored and, frankly, longing to be back at the university."

She finished all in a rush and waited. Jane Langley Gooden folded her newspaper slowly and considered her niece with a look of quiet amusement tinged with respect.

"You're absolutely right, my dear Samille. We can't go on treating you like a guest in our home, though," the look she gave the younger woman was warm with affection, "don't think we haven't enjoyed every minute of these past few weeks with you."

She paused, picked up her coffee cup and turned away to fill it. Samille saw her wipe at a surreptitious tear, and then her aunt faced her and spoke with a resolute steadiness.

"I'm afraid, Samille, unlike your father, I gave you up for dead years ago. There seemed no way you could have survived when Françoise was killed."

Her throat tightened and she swallowed quickly before her rueful gray eyes met Samille's.

"Samuel never lost faith in your return. But, now, I think he's very much afraid if he lets you out of his sight, he'll come home someday to find you gone again."

Samille's involuntary protest died unspoken. The past was always with them. She saw bitterly how it would refuse to die until somehow, some way it could be laid to rest. And that circumstance, she feared, would come only with an explanation for the inexplicable flight of her mother from Paris nearly nine years earlier. She raised troubled eyes to her aunt.

"Perhaps, Aunt Jane, if you resumed your own activities, Father would be reassured?"

Her aunt's eyes narrowed, and then her lips pursed and she shook her head.

"We'll have to let him find his own way, I'm afraid. As for myself, I hardly feel comfortable leaving you to your own devices."

Jane picked up her coffee cup and viewed her niece searchingly over its brim.

"You seem to forget, child, this family now consists of three people. Perhaps when you feel settled and secure, Samuel will be reassured.

"So, dear, what do you want to do with your life? Heaven knows," she spoke with a burst of savagery, "you were certainly denied the normal childhood most children would've had. Would you like to marry, child? Or, find your own interests, pursue a career?"

At Samille's look of distress, her aunt rose and bent her towering form to quickly embrace her niece.

"You don't have to decide this minute. Think about it—try anything that strikes your fancy, my dear. You can be sure your father and I will support you in any way we may."

"Why do I have to learn to dance, Father? I'm going to college and learn to be a scientist. I won't have time to dance."

Brows knitted ferociously, Lennie glared at Michael, her face twitching to contain the humor echoing in her father's indulgent eyes.

"You need to know how to dance, Eleanor, because as soon as this confounded limp is gone, I'm going to kick up my heels. I'll need a dance partner," Professor Langley said. His gray eyes gleamed in the rich flare of light from the candles on the table.

"No fair, Uncle!" Lennie shot a baleful glance at him, and then perked up, pointing her fork triumphantly at

Samille. "But you'll have Samille, and," she added for good measure, "Aunt Jane *and*," she grinned wickedly, "the Widow Healy for partners. You won't need me after all!"

Samuel threw his god-daughter a look of mock reproach and concentrated on his spaghetti before replying.

"Younger men than I will claim Samille and Jane, and" he paused, grimacing exaggeratedly and stretching a pleading hand toward Lennie, "you, my dear, are supposed to keep me from the dire clutches of the Widow Healy!"

He rolled his eyes dramatically. Michael chuckled. Lennie cast a beseeching glance at Jane, who simply shook her head helplessly laughing. Admitting defeat, Lennie took her godfather's hand.

"Oh, all right, Uncle Samuel, you win. But I want you to know you play dirty," she finished doggedly.

Samille touched the young girl's arm lightly.

"Do you truly not know how to dance, Lennie?"

A decisive shake of the head, sending blonde curls bouncing, answered her. Michael O'Grady, face carefully grave, looked from his daughter to Samille.

"Three tutors, my dear, and—."

"And I still have two left feet," Lennie interrupted her father glumly.

"Then I'd like to try and teach you, Lennie, if you're willing."

Samille turned an earnest glance upon her father. "We could practice in the nursery, Father, and move the gramophone there. If you don't mind? I don't think the noise would be a problem up there."

Samuel looked startled, followed by a pleased smile.

"I think it's a wonderful idea, Samille."

She turned eagerly to Lennie.

"We could practice in the afternoons, Lennie, when we're home from school."

Her father started.

"'When we're home from school'?" he repeated.

Samille caught her aunt's eye, who smiled warmly at her.

"Yes, Father. I want to go to college and be—" here she stopped, laughing, reaching out a hand to tug gently at one of Lennie's blonde curls. "Well, I'm not sure what I want to be just yet, Father, but I'd certainly like to be better educated."

From beside her, Jane let out her breath in a sigh of relief. Her father's friend, beaming with approval, nodded his head vigorously. Samuel's astonishment gave way to interest. He lifted his glass of wine.

"There's more than one way to get around your father, isn't there, my dear?"

Green eyes, glinting with affection and amusement, met his own. Samille did not reply, lifting her glass to clink with the others. It had dawned on her, as Lennie had spoken, how school would give her a purpose and structure in which to seek the pattern of her future. More immediately, it was a means of getting her father back to his work, to his life—and keep her relatively close at the same time.

A mist swirled fitfully in the gardens below her room as Samille watched. Michael had taken his daughter home shortly after dinner, Lennie promising solemnly to help Samille with her studies in return for dancing lessons. Her father had spoken to her then of preliminary tests to ascertain her skills and described the college application process to her. Now, her father's and her aunt's conversation welled up the stairs with the light, their voices rich with contentment. Samille sat, knees drawn up, on her window seat, thinking sleepily.

Amazingly enough, the idea of attending university excited her, and the decision to teach Lennie was equally satisfying. The child, she'd observed, had a natural rough grace; confidence and practice could strengthen and polish her innate ability. Samille turned her head away from the light of her bedroom to the mist-enshrouded night beyond her window. Perhaps school would give her a sense of confidence and belonging to this world as well. Maybe friends of her own. A friend.

The mist before her shifted, altered, coalesced. A fair-haired, strong-featured face, tanned and smooth, took shape. Blue eyes smiled encouragingly at her, and a mobile mouth grinned beneath a trim mustache.

"Benjamin!"

Samille blinked, palms outstretched against the window screen. The image shattered as the mist eddied in a pocket of wind. Unaccountably annoyed with herself, she reached out to pull the window down, but halted abruptly. Down below, there in the gardens and the mist, a pinprick of light blinked back at her. Samille rubbed her eyes and peered intently into the mist. It was gone. If, she jeered to herself, it had ever been there.

She was tired. Time to get into bed. This was hardly the time to let an over-active imagination conjure up secret prowlers or erstwhile friends. She shut the window impatiently, flicking the curtains into place, went to her bed and switched on the light. The ormolu clock on her bedside table showed ten o'clock. Not even the dead of night. Too early for morbid imaginings. Samille stood thoughtfully, then quickly, decisively, went to the little writing desk and pulled out a sheet of paper.

Writing for several minutes, she read and reread her letter, crossing out phrases and whole sentences. Muttering to herself, she crumpled the paper and reached for a fresh sheet. This time she sat in silence for several minutes before putting pen to paper. Then she wrote steadily, stopping at length to scan her words and sign her name. Addressing an envelope, she folded her letter and tucked it inside. Tomorrow, if she did not lose her nerve, she would mail it. A small, hopeful glow warmed her as she tried to calculate how long it might take her letter to reach Singapore and for a reply to come back. Picking up her robe, she padded along the hall to the bath.

Outside, the mist spiraled and coiled like some primordial, sentient being settling about the night, its one red eye unblinking.

Chapter 6

The cold sleep. The eternal weight of the centuries abating breath, time. The green dragon's slitted eyes were closed, its scales quiescent. Samille watched, afraid to breathe, aware of the terrible fragility of its sleep, knowing the slightest sound, the slightest breath would be echoed in the rippling, tensile stretch of scales and the doomed, great head would rise, the gleaming red eyes open, and the mouth spout the first engulfing flames of death. "Don't breathe, don't breathe..., don't breathe!"

Desperately, the warning sounded over and over again in her mind, her lungs bursting with the need to dispel the indrawn air. She could feel the ragged remnants of self-control slipping, hear the soft whisper of breath escaping. A slow rattle reached her ears, like the sliding of scale-clad muscles over stone. *The dragon!*

"Ah-h-h!"

Samille fought for light and air, flinging the enveloping shroud from her. Her flailing hands struck something smooth and hard. Her eyes flew open.

With the top sheet knotted and twisted about her torso, she lay scrunched up at the head of her bed, under a pillow, her knuckles banged against the headboard.

Samille rolled over on her side and lay gasping as panic subsided and her eyes focused on the little ormolu clock at her bedside. Barely half-past seven o'clock in the morning. She pushed herself up precipitously. Not just any morning, either, but Tuesday, the fourth of July 1899. Tonight was the Fireman's Charity Ball which she was attending with the dozen or so current students of the Beauvoir School of Dance.

Samille grabbed her robe and padded downstairs. Her father was not due to return for several days yet, having traveled to Sacramento to attend a conference on *Thomas Jefferson: Statesman and Scholar*. She and Aunt Jane, in the meantime, could be as comfortable as two cats in the pantry in his absence.

"'Morning, dear."

Aunt Jane yawned, looking as sleepy as she herself felt, Samille noted. What a dream, she thought! Nightmare, more likely. And likely as not, brought on because she'd worked too hard these past weeks. Between her studies, dance classes, and getting her father ready for his trip, not to mention helping with Aunt Jane's banners for the fourth of July suffragettes' rally, it was no wonder she'd suffered a nightmare.

"Here, Samille, have a biscuit," her aunt pushed the basket toward her. "You eat like a sp—bird, child."

Samille, absently stirring cream into her tea, put down her spoon hastily. Aunt Jane had almost said sparrow. It reminded Samille unpleasantly how it was nearly a month ago when she'd found a sparrow, three mornings in a row, dead, broken wings dangling, in the basket of her bicycle. The first day, shocked and sickened, she'd stood frozen on the doorstep, holding herself in on a painful, indrawn gasp. Trembling and shaken, her mind had conjured before her a quivering bundle of rags—a long ago Sparrow huddled in Yen-shu's doorway.

Professor Langley and Jane, coming out together, had seen the ghastly sight and hastened to call Soon Lee. Unaware of that other Sparrow, they could not make the same connection as she had done, but put the incident down to the depredations of the great yellow tomcat known to roam the neighborhood. The cat, moreover, was seen in the yard two days later when the third dead sparrow was discovered. Soon Lee gave chase noisily and vigorously, and the fourth morning, when Samille opened the door with a sinking feeling in the pit of her stomach, the basket had been empty. She had not quite rid herself yet, however, of the same moment of dreadful anticipation upon leaving the house on Divisadero Street each day.

Red highlights glinted among russet waves as Aunt Jane reached out quickly to touch the younger woman's hand.

"You aren't worried about tonight, are you, dear? I'm sure the children will perform beautifully." She paused, looked at the hollows under her niece's eyes, and continued. "Why don't you skip your studies this afternoon and rest, Samille? You look too pale, my dear."

Samille shook her head automatically, and then relented as she took in the strained forbearance on her aunt's face. She picked at her napkin.

"I'm sorry, Aunt Jane. Truly, I don't mean to distress you." She gave a deprecating grin. "Who'd ever have thought Lennie's success would've had all those mamas lining up at the door? All those awkward sons and less than eager daughters?"

Jane laughed softly.

"It was your success as a teacher they sought, Samille. Though, heaven knows, I thought it certain that Durwent Appleby would defeat even your infinite patience!"

They laughed together, remembering the butter-haired boy, too large for his age who'd come twice as long as any of his peers and persisted in spite of their teasing to become quite presentable on the dance floor. But, Samille remarked unhappily, the little worry lines did not fade altogether from her aunt's countenance.

"If it will set your mind at ease, Aunt Jane, I'll stay home this afternoon and indulge myself with some entirely frivolous reading," and, she amended mentally, go to the library tomorrow afternoon to make up the lost time.

"Thank you, darling. There..." her aunt paused, uncharacteristically at a loss for words, "there isn't anything on your mind, is there, dear? Something... someone... troubling you?"

Samille looked up swiftly, shocked for one tiny moment as if her aunt had read her thoughts, before comprehension dawned, and she wrinkled her nose.

"If you mean am I having second thoughts concerning the almost courtship of Jason Randolph McGuire, the answer is still no." She spoke firmly, but her eyes now held a shadow of amusement.

"Oh dear! I don't mean to annoy you, Samille," her aunt flushed a rosy red as she sometimes did when she suddenly found herself feeling as though she were the younger and her niece the elder. "But then," she persisted, laughingly protesting, "they've all been perfectly charming, presentable young men.

"I swan, child," Aunt Jane maintained severely, half-laughing and half-serious, Samille guessed shrewdly, "you're either setting your standards impossibly high, or, you've already lost your heart to someone and you aren't telling."

Exasperated, Jane shrugged as Samille sat unperturbed, meeting her aunt's gaze and calmly popping the last bite of her biscuit into her mouth.

"I won't press the matter, dear, but I can't help feeling as though you're holding out on your father and me when you sit there looking like the cat who's been at the catch of the day!"

Samille eyed her aunt crossly.

"Don't be ridiculous! You know all of my friends!" She fairly snapped the words out, stopped, and held her hand to her mouth as if to catch back her words. "Oh my, I am sorry, Aunt Jane. But I can't encourage a fellow to hold out hope when I don't feel anything more than friendship for him.

"I've had to work so hard to make up the lost time with my school work, and now, there's so much to do! I can't possibly consider marriage seriously before I've earned my degree. And besides, I've got you and Father and Lennie and Michael to love, Aunt Jane. There's nothing left to spare."

Nor would there ever be, she told herself silently, fiercely. These were the people who loved her, who she could trust not to abandon her.

Her aunt took in the bowed head, the eyes perilously close to tears, and gently patted the fingers clutching the napkin so tightly.

"I won't badger you, Samille. You'll make an admirable architect, you know. But," she added softly, "don't ever underrate yourself, my dear. You're a woman now, and you've a heart as wide and free as the good earth you walk upon.

"Now," the older woman changed the subject determinedly, "I can't wait for your father to see the design you finished for Professor Maybeck. I find it exciting, but I'm not quite sure why. It's so simple on the face of it."

Samille took her up eagerly, as Jane must have known she would.

"Do you, Aunt Jane? I think the design works because I've finally managed to channel the sense of freedom and movement I feel in dance into structured spaces—the cathedral ceilings and the expanse of glass in the living room open up the house and let it flow into its environment."

Her aunt considered her words.

"You may have something there. I think I see what you mean, and the use of native materials—the natural redwood outside lends to the tie between environment and enclosed space." Jane sighed. "That's just the kind of house my Alfred would have enjoyed."

Samille glanced covertly at her aunt's face. Regret was written there, mingled with love and a kind of acceptance, too—the same elements present in her father's face whenever he spoke of Françoise. Jane stirred from her contemplation.

"Well, I must get these banners distributed by mid-morning." She rose, bent briefly to press her cheek to Samille's. "Michael will meet us here at seven o'clock this evening. Oh, and I've arranged for a late lunch to be delivered, since Ho Lee and Soon Lee have the day off."

True to her word, Samille stayed home and fielded several frantic telephone calls from over-anxious students or their mothers. Her lessons for Lennie had grown by word of mouth to include a dozen or more students three afternoons a week. Lennie now accompanied Samille on an old upright piano which Professor Langley had purchased for Samille on her eighteenth birthday—nearly three years ago now. How like him, she thought affectionately, to have raised no objections, realizing the joy she took from teaching and from maintaining a certain degree of independence. The money she earned went toward books and tuition at the University of California at Berkeley. She'd never even considered another school.

Her dance students, upon graduation, were chaperoned to one of the many annual charity balls. This term the dance was a masked ball given by the San Francisco Fire Department to raise money for fire victims. She'd choreographed a short piece for four of the youngest girls, who would open the ball escorted by four of the most dapper members of the Fire Department. They would be followed by the rest of her students, and then the dancing would begin in earnest. Ranging in age from a precocious set of four-year-old twins to several thirteen and fourteen-year-olds, the children would be allowed to remain until the first interval, during which they would have an early supper, afterward being chaperoned home. The thought crossed her mind that she might return home then as well.

Restlessly, she wandered upstairs. Maybe she could release some of the physical and emotional tension she felt by dancing. Yet, once in her nursery-studio, no music stirred within her. Since her arrival at the house on Divisadero Street, she'd shut away all thought of the dancing which had been her private retreat from pain and fear and loneliness in Singapore. Except to illustrate steps for her students, she had not danced once for her own pleasure. And yet, how she wanted.... The thought trailed away uncompleted. She sat down dispiritedly at the piano and idly plunked a key. Silence. She struck another key and then another one. How odd! They had last used the piano on Friday afternoon for the final dance practice. She saw to it that the piano was kept perfectly tuned as a necessary business expense. Puzzled, Samille lifted the top lid and peered inside. To her amazement, each wire had been neatly clipped. She whirled about, but the room was empty. Lowering the lid once again, she went slowly down to the first floor.

The house was still, as if listening with her. She moved from room to room, reassuring herself the kitchen, side, and front doors were all secure. She and her aunt had been in and out of the house all weekend and on Monday, what with their various engagements. So too had Ho Lee and Soon Lee. Anyone could have slipped in and out again unseen, particularly on Monday afternoon. She had been in classes, Aunt Jane had been attending meetings, and Ho Lee regularly went to market then. Frowning, she recalled it had been raining in the morning and a fog had rolled in late and persisted until early evening.

Who could have done such a malicious thing? And why? There'd been no disgruntled students—at least none who would have been driven to this point of revenge. She debated whether to try and reach her aunt by telephone at her club's headquarters, then thought better of it. This was something that could wait until later. The damage was already done.

Curled up in her favorite leather armchair in her father's study with the latest issue of the *Lark*, a small literary monthly featuring local writers and artists, Samille started violently at a loud rapping at the front door. Glancing at the watch pinned to her shirtwaist, she saw with surprise it was nigh on one o'clock. Hastily, she stepped into the hall and nearly collided with someone.

"Soon Lee!"

Her voice not quite steady, Samille gave a weak laugh and eyed Ho Lee's young son.

"You startled me!"

"Most sorry, Missy Sam."

Unperturbed, Soon Lee moved past her to open the front door. A burly, bald Chinese man balanced a tray, his pedicart visible on the street.

"Order for Mistress Gooden?" he inquired, moving forward as if to step into the entryway. Soon Lee turned to Samille, inadvertently blocking the big man's way. Almost stumbling, the man righted his tray with an effort and shot a rapid look at the younger man.

"Mistress order meal, yes?" At Samille's nod, Soon Lee patted agitatedly at his pockets. "Petty cash in kitchen, Missy Sam. You fetch?"

"Of course, Soon Lee. Just a moment, please."

Hurrying into the kitchen, Samille tipped down the petty cash jar only to find it empty of funds. Oh dear, it was probably her father's turn to fill it before he'd left for Sacramento, she decided. She'd have to dash upstairs and retrieve her purse, but better tell Soon Lee.

Rushing back to the front hall, a shrill exchange of Chinese met her ears—Soon Lee's voice high and sharp, and a deeper, guttural response. As they came into her line of vision, she saw Soon Lee pressing some bills at the man. He glanced at Soon Lee, caught sight of her standing motionless beyond the houseboy, and stuffed the money into his pocket with one hand as he shoved the tray at Soon Lee. As he did so, his wide sleeves rode up slightly. Samille stared. Some flicker of coiled green slid into sight before the man abruptly straightened, jerked his head sharply at Soon Lee, and lumbered toward the street.

Soon Lee turned with the tray, his face impassive as Samille stepped aside to let him pass on his way to the dining room.

"Forgive carelessness, Missy Sam. I find money in pocket."

He padded on into the dining room. Shivering, Samille caught sight of her face in the mirror which graced the wall above a small console table in the entry hall. Her cheeks were pale, but otherwise the crashing thump, thumping of her heart was invisible and she was thankful.

"What a heavenly smell!"

Samille whirled about as her aunt strode briskly into the hall, rakishly tossing her reticule on the table beside Samille.

"Just let me wash my hands, and I'll join you for lunch, Samille. I'm utterly famished."

Her aunt disappeared into the hall lavatory. Samille leaned weakly against the table, and shook her head impatiently. What a namby-pamby baby she was! They had been safe and undisturbed ever since her return nearly three years' ago. It was ridiculous for her to see monsters in every shadow, or to read sinister happenings into sheer coincidences. It wouldn't do at all for her to go on in this vein. She moved toward the dining room, wrapped in her thoughts.

She couldn't afford to get distracted by anything at this point in her studies. Professor Maybeck, a renowned architect with innovative ideas for the adaptation of oriental designs to American settings and materials, was exacting in the high standards he demanded of his students. Facing this, she hadn't needed the example of Julia Morgan, the first female to study with him, to tell her the pressure would be even greater because she was female. Everyone in the university community knew of Julia, and out of curiosity, she had attended one of Professor Maybeck's lectures to see what had attracted the other woman. The familiar elements of his designs, transposed to the modern American world, had resonated some deep chord within her, awakening a hunger to explore this world in depth. Her studies, along with her dance classes, filled part of an aching need her secret ballet practice had once assuaged.

Professor Maybeck had agreed to take her on as a student after she'd made up her deficiencies. She couldn't afford to let her concentration slack now when the meat of her coursework was finally underway. Her glimpse of the tattoo on the deliveryman's arm could have been anything—a snake, a sea monster—anything. And what if it had been a dragon? Surely it was just a coincidence. It occurred to her that it was probably some local tong emblem.

With three-quarters of all Chinese immigrants to America settled in California, Samille hadn't been at all surprised to find several notorious tongs existed in San Francisco, controlling an assortment of illegitimate waterfront vices like the slave girl traffic and prostitution cribs, opium and gambling dens, and labor racketeering just as similar organizations had done in Singapore. Here, however, they did not yet rule the city itself. From the newspapers she'd gleaned the information that the tongs were thought to have grown out of the ranks of the Taiping rebels who'd fled China beginning in 1851. Today their members fought openly in the streets of Chinatown and the waterfront, often armed with knives, cleavers, and guns which they concealed in the voluminous sleeves of the oriental dress most Chinese still wore.

Their activities contributed greatly to the anti-Chinese sentiments of local San Franciscans, much to the chagrin of the *Chinese Six*, the heads of the combined family associations whose members had emigrated from the same district of their homeland. Certain family associations often dominated one business. She'd found, for example, many members of the Lee family were cooks, with several having their own restaurants. The Hang Far Low restaurant on Grant Street, where she'd celebrated her recent twentieth birthday, was owned by Ho Lee's elder brother. But, she reminded herself impatiently, the tongs didn't reach here, beyond Chinatown, and this wasn't the waterfront, but a comfortable, upscale neighborhood.

She attacked her lunch with renewed zeal. Aunt Jane, preoccupied with a letter she'd received in the afternoon's post, had not noticed her niece's drawn-out silence, but she would certainly notice if her lunch went untouched. A cool breeze blew in through the dining room windows. Samille rubbed her temple gingerly. Perhaps if she took her reading outside to the garden, she'd rid herself of the headache threatening her peace all morning. Suiting action to the thought, she stood. Jane glanced up absent-mindedly.

"I'm going to sit in the garden and read for a while, Aunt Jane."

Jane took in the sunshine and the cool, wandering breeze, and sighed longingly.

"What a heavenly idea! I wish I could join you, but I need to think about this letter and what it means to our own activities."

Seeing Samille's blank expression, she laughed and rattled the sheet of paper she held.

"Our sisters in New York are suggesting a national suffragettes' conference to be held in Albany this fall. We'll have to think about the advantages of such a meeting and whether we'll want to send a local or state delegation. It means a flurry of telephone calls and long committee meetings, I'm afraid!"

Samille left her aunt to the details, retrieved her magazine and a rug, and made her way to a small, willow-shaded spot of lawn next to the fence. For once, Bruce Porter's witty story barely held her attention. She felt her head nodding again, gave it up, and settled herself more comfortably. A ten-minute nap might work wonders for her head.

Her head jerked up, her eyes abruptly open. One minute, ten, an hour might have passed. What had startled her into sudden wakefulness? The garden was like an oasis of quietude in the midst of the holiday. Not a bird sang. Only the normal daytime sounds were evident. She caught at the thought. Not a bird sang? Then, it came to her—the odd note—the small repetitive sound that hadn't been there when she settled down with her rug and her reading material. The creaking hinges. The back gate, opened, swinging gently to and fro in the intermittent breeze. Had Soon Lee come through the garden as she dozed? Odd. He was usually careful about latching the gate, especially since the unwelcome antics of the yellow tom.

Her fingers tightened convulsively on the flimsy bamboo paper of the issue of the *Lark* which she held. Someone stood silent, listening, concealed somewhere in the garden. All the alertness born of her years in Singapore came back to her. She could feel the tension, the awful crowding excitement, the thickening of her throat. Nonsense, she told herself savagely.

"Ee-ee-ei...." The screened back door slammed with a protesting squeak as Soon Lee emerged, whistling tunelessly, a basket in one hand and shears in the other. Samille popped up like a jack-in-the-box and made a business of shaking out her rug and folding it as Soon Lee stopped whistling and proceeded down the garden path toward her.

"Missy Sam, Mistress Gooden say you come in now. I take rug, okay?" He reached for the rug. "Missy okay? Too much sun?"

Samille glanced sharply at the thin, hooded features of Soon Lee. Clearly, she'd been sitting well in the shade. Just as clearly, something of the absurd relief she'd felt at his opportune appearance must have communicated itself to him. Casually, she handed the rug to him.

"I expect so, Soon Lee. Thank you."

She turned as if to leave, adding over her shoulder, offhandedly as she raised her voice a fraction, "You might check the back gate, Soon Lee. I think maybe the tomcat's gotten in again."

Dark eyes gleamed at her.

"Yes, Missy Sam. I fix."

Samille forced herself to walk away leisurely. Was that the gate she heard now, creaking sharply? Her steps faltered, but she determinedly kept walking without looking back until she was inside the house. Then, peering out the window, she saw basket, rug, and shears abandoned on the path. Soon Lee was nowhere to be seen. A moment passed, and then he came in swiftly from the alley and secured the gate behind him. Samille, hidden in the shadows of the dining room, knew he could not see her, but stepped back involuntarily, her thoughts buzzing.

Soon Lee had been given the day off, she was certain. Yet, he'd come back early, appearing twice today—once in the hallway and once now—both times when she'd been alone. Friend or foe? She bit her lip. Had he vandalized the piano? But how could he possibly bear a grudge against her or her father or aunt? If only there was someone in whom she could confide these gnawing fears. Some friend. But though she moved in a loose circle of fellow students, she kept her distance—a distance she found herself unable, unwilling? to bridge. Her fingers found the thin gold chain and pulled the jade talisman from beneath her bodice. *Oh Mother*, she cried silently, desperately, tears starting to her eyes. Is this how Françoise must have felt with only a child at her side?

Sternly, she blinked back a precipitate rush of tears. If Soon Lee had any sinister motives toward her or anyone else in their home, there'd been ample opportunities for him to act. She often worked alone in the house or at the library, riding her bicycle to and from the ferry each day. She moved reluctantly out of the shadows. After her exams were over, after this project for Professor Maybeck was completed, she'd slow down and work less. Aunt Jane was right. She definitely needed a rest.

Still, she caught herself, later, after she'd bathed, listening for a moment on the threshold of the bathroom before she scooted quickly down the hall to her bedroom. Mocking her cowardice, Samille lovingly drew from the closet the dress with which her father had surprised her at breakfast before he'd left for Sacramento.

A creamy Belgian lace bib rose to a high collar, gracing a heavy silk blouse of the same lustrous color. Lace edged the cuffs of the long sleeves, while the skirt draped full and luscious over petticoats. A broad satin bow nipped in the slender waist. High-topped, buttoned boots peeked from beneath the skirts, and a lace fan dangled by its ribbon from her wrist.

Samille pirouetted before the cheval glass she'd salvaged from the attic, delighting in the sweep of the skirts. Then, she held the sequined, feathery ivory mask to her face, considering her appearance. The thick black cloud of hair, loosely knotted at the crown, gleamed about the pale, composed features. A hint of color graced her cheekbones and the green eyes shone as if to hint at some tantalizing, secret expectation. The swell of her breasts stirred the lace as one shapely hand captured a perfume bottle. Thoughtfully, serenely, she touched the crystal stopper to the visible pulse in her throat, to her wrists, to the nape of her neck. The slow curving of her lips dreamily mocked her, as if, she thought ruefully, this masked woman was set to entice some handsome partner to her side, when nothing could be further from the truth. She'd heard the names given her by young men she'd scarcely noticed—Samille the Scholar, the Diligent, and, less charitably—the Remote, the Marble Princess. Returning the perfume bottle to her dressing table, Samille picked up her fancy reticule, her shawl, and her ivory mask. It was time.

Nate and Charlie, the four-year-old twins, presented their partners with a flourish amid thunderous applause and laughter. Lennie, flushed and laughing, joined Samille with the young fireman in black tie and tails who'd partnered her. His dark eyes danced behind his mask.

"A delight to partner such an accomplished dancer, Miss Langley!" He gallantly swept Lennie a bow, and addressed Samille. "May I have the privilege of leading out her teacher for the first waltz?"

Lennie, blonde curls tamed for once, gave her friend a tug.

"Oh do, Samille! Mr. Beaumont is a wonderful dancer. Go on!" she urged.

Samille tucked her hand into the crook of the dark-haired young man's arm and allowed him to lead her to the floor. It was the last time she saw her charges until the first interval, when she gathered them together, saw them all provided with punch, and solemnly toasted their graduation. Beaming parents swept their respective offspring off to their suppers and then to home. Several new ladies, husbands in tow, approached her about lessons for their children. Samille demurred politely, suggesting they call to make an appointment to visit her studio with their child.

Tonight she did not want to talk business or to think of her studies. Tonight she wanted to dance. Perhaps it was the mask, but tonight the Sparrow was spreading her wings again and no one would be the wiser. A tall, elegant woman in black lace and satin dress, russet tendrils curling about the edges of her mask, bent toward her as Samille stood on the sidelines after another breathless series of partners and looked about her vaguely for her program.

"Enjoying your evening, my dear?"

"Oh yes, Aunt Jane! Wonderful!"

"I'm glad, Samille. I thought the children were marvelous. Michael's escorting Lennie home. He'll return shortly. Come find one of us if you tire." Then she was gone as a portly gentleman pulled her onto the dance floor once more.

After the next set, Samille became separated from her most recent dance partner in the milling crowd and found herself alone in a side gallery of the ballroom, isolated from the main room by towering potted palms and banks of white azaleas and camellias. Tapestried seats were pushed against the wall where several sets of tall French doors stood open to the drifting night breezes. The scent of flowers was heady. Samille sat on the edge of a chair, snapped out her fan, and tapped her toes to the music reaching every part of the ballroom.

All evening an undercurrent of excitement had run through her—as if her mind sensed some portentous moment in the offing. She felt her senses heightened, alive in every molecule, her skin electric, her rational mind remote and watching from a far distance. The music, the dancing, the whirl of colors of the women's dresses, the fantastic masks, and above all, the fragrant banks of flowers, took her back to those stolen moments in the gardens of the *Hotel L'Esperance* in Singapore.

She could not contain the emotion, the music, the energy funneling through her. And who was there to see, after all? She had made a promise once. The moon was full—or would be—and, somewhere, a pear tree would be in blossom. Her arms entwined and she rose in one lithe, swift movement, as if a spring released within her, her body responding to the rhythms of its own making. Softly, softly, as if magic sparked from her fingertips and guided her heart, she danced alone and celebrated love—for Yen-shu and Sakai, for her mother, her father, and Aunt Jane. And if there was some other nameless, formless yearning behind her steps, she would not admit it. Let the reality of her hopes and fruitless longing lie beyond rational thought, in the realm of moonlight and wishes.

At last the music ended and she sat breathless, eyes closed, and let the light, loose state of enchantment engulf her as it always did when movement flowed as liquid as the sparkling champagne she'd drunk earlier in the evening. Now, if she opened her eyes, the perfect partner would appear before her.

"Mademoiselle, s'il vous plait?"

Her eyes flew open.

A lithe, muscular figure bowed gracefully before her. She put her hand, trembling, into his. Strong fingers closed about hers, and she rose into his embrace, little shocks spreading from her hand to her stomach to her breathing as azure eyes regarded her unwaveringly from behind the black mask that swept fine, sun-blessed blond hair back from a high forehead. The masked face bore a mouth marked by laughter and care and concern.

Soft laughter bubbled out of her throat, and the formal grasp about her waist tightened, pulling her closer, the blue eyes snapping as she whirled about—the black halo of her hair threatening to cascade about her shoulders. A rich, deep chuckle escaped him and was lost in the moment.

Chapter 7

Snap! Exasperated, Samille stared at the third pencil tip she'd broken in a row. The intimate silences of the library, so familiar and commonplace, offered no comfort, no surcease from her tempestuous mood.

"Hey Princess, care to dance?"

Samille raised furious green eyes. Jason Randolph stepped back hastily, holding up his hands in mock self-defense.

"Whoa, Princess! Don't look daggers at me! You danced divinely with me last night. Will you join us for an ice cream?"

Samille flushed and dropped her pencil.

"Sorry, Jason. Some other time, okay?"

He grinned, gave her a thumbs-up, and moved off to rejoin a group near the door. Samille waved as they left, noting sourly how Carilla DeMondeley didn't seem at all sorry at her refusal. Carilla could have Jason Randolph and his father's burgeoning china business for all she, Samille, cared. Angrily, she gathered up her books and papers. Why kid herself? She could no more concentrate on the paper she was supposed to be writing than she could forget last night. Forget the witching hour when the clock struck midnight and she'd unmasked, turning about to find Michael and Aunt Jane beside her and her black-masked dance partner nowhere to be seen.

Books and supplies cached in the satchel she used to carry her school work, she strode outside to stare with bewilderment at the empty rack where she'd left her bicycle. Not again! She stamped her foot in frustration. She frequently rode her bicycle to the university, taking it across on the ferry with her to and from school to avoid the crowded streetcars and get some exercise as well. Several times in the last few months, however, she'd come out from class or the library—as now—to find her bicycle missing. A few days later it would suddenly appear again, exactly where she'd originally parked it. None of her friends owned up to the mischief. Now, she set off on foot, irritated and uneasy, for the ferry. She could only hope the jokester was one of her friends and would return her bike yet again in a few days' time. And if, a small voice whispered, the miscreant was not one of her friends? Her nerves could not take much more. Why did *they*—whoever *they* might be—not confront her directly? Why all the petty, frightening mischief?

Still disturbed on the trip back across the bay, Samille gazed at the city without noticing the scampering goat herds on Telegraph Hill or the colorful feluccas—Italian fishing boats—with lateen sails skimming to berth at Fisherman's Wharf. As the ferry docked at the huge Ferry Building, she impatiently worked her way through the crowds to the plaza, the building simply an obstacle to be negotiated. Begun two years before her arrival in San Francisco, the massive edifice was not yet finished and boasted a central clock tower inspired by the Cathedral of Seville. Most days she never failed to pause in the rush of commuter crowds to and from the ferries and streetcars, to admire its continuing construction. This afternoon, the shoppers and excursionists were merely a nuisance to be endured until she could catch her car up Russian Hill. Here it came—no, this car was the smaller line to Dolores Street.

On impulse, Samille caught up her skirts and ran, oblivious to the surprised, amused glances cast in her direction as she swung herself agilely aboard the moving streetcar. Her mood was yet too foul to inflict it on the household at Divisadero Street. The short run from downtown, along the quiet boulevard of Dolores Street with its central island of palm-studded grass, might sooth her frazzled nerves. She hopped off quickly at her stop.

Before crossing the street to her destination, she drank in the Mission of San Francisco de Asis, or the Mission Dolores, nearly hidden by the huge, double-towered modern church erected adjacent to it. The little church had drawn her from the first moment she'd set eyes upon it. With its whitewashed adobe walls and arched central portal, it lifted a single cross from the peak of its rawhide-lashed, redwood timbered roof, covered with red clay tiles. A low abode wall led around the building. Covered now with a mantle of purple bougainvillea, the wall hid a maze of tumbling tombstones and monuments and an equally riotous garden.

Entering the cool, dim interior of the mission church, Samille hesitated for a moment to allow her eyes to adjust to the lighting. The eighteenth-century Mexican carved altars, hand-whittled wooden statues of saints, and the richly painted ceiling scenes—done in the softly fading organic colors of the Native Americans, were familiar and comforting. But now, in her haste, she dismissed them and trod unerringly to the back of the church, where a door opened to the cemetery.

Here, along paths chased by violas and blue hydrangeas, she sometimes wandered, looking at the tombstone inscriptions in French, Italian, Spanish, and all the other mother tongues of those who'd come to San Francisco. Here lay children long dead in cholera epidemics, victims of fire and drowning, suicides, and those who'd died violently at the hands of frontier vigilantes. Yet, here too stood a statue of Fra Junipero Serra and the tomb of Don Luis Antonio Arguellos, an early governor of California. Pacing past yew and poplars, oxalis, and a fountain, she came at last to the great toyon tree with its hanging baskets of fuchsias. Here, a marble bench was placed beneath the spreading branches of the ancient tree. Samille sat her satchel on the ground next to the bench and stared at the garden without seeing.

A great knot of confusion and pain swelled with each beat of her heart. Try as she might, she could not doubt it had been Benjamin who swept her into his arms last night at the Fireman's Charity Ball. Her Benjamin! The man who'd named himself her friend, then hadn't written her, or contacted her in any fashion in nearly three long years. Here, in his arms. And, his touch! Palm to palm sealed in as ardent a caress as any medieval lover might have longed for—and yet, he had disappeared again as surely as if she'd dreamed it all.

Her head ached from going over and over it all. Perhaps she had dreamed the whole vivid encounter. She was losing her mind, and doubly so at what the mere thought—if it had only been a dream—of what those eyes and lazy mouth, those hands could do to her. How could he just waltz back into her life and awaken this cauldron of emotion—set to boiling all those feelings she'd kept so tightly under rein all this time? How dared he! She could not bear it. Numbly, she dropped her head into her hands.

A feeling of lethargy stole over her. The tension began to drain from her shoulders. Warmth, infinitely gentle and persistent, spread. Angels might have stood behind her and massaged away the burden she carried. She leaned her head back against that strong, reassuring pressure. Suddenly, she twisted about, standing so abruptly she might have fallen if a long arm hadn't caught her by the wrist to steady her. She snatched her hand away as if the touch stung.

"You!"

All the force of her anguish and anger snapped behind the single word in vehement accusation.

Benjamin's mustache twitched and blue eyes deepened like clouds passing over the sun, his lips turning down in mock reproach.

"Don't be angry with me again, Sparrow—not when we parted the best of friends." He let his words hang, and she blushed furiously, recalling last night and—. And the touch of his hands just a moment ago—known and accepted on some level before her conscious mind was aware of his presence.

Ruefully, he stepped around the bench as she stood fighting for self-control and the words to marshal her indignation against him.

"I can explain, Sparrow. Truly. Truce?" He lifted a cajoling hand toward her. "Samille, please!"

The light bantering tone dropped at the first furious tears escaping from those luminous green eyes. At his soft, urgent entreaty she saw the dancing devils in those eyes stilled, the mobile features twist with concern and something deeper, more assured, with none of the raging bewilderment battling within her. It wasn't fair! She turned away from him, wiping at the frantic, hot tears with the back of her hand. Behind her, a slight stir reached her, then a handkerchief was pressed into her hand. He did not speak, nor did he touch her, but retreated as she fought for control. At last she swung about to face him. Benjamin sat, composed and grave, on the bench she'd abandoned.

"You said you were my friend, Benjamin." Her face crumpled, and she blinked rapidly. "Then you sent me on my way and forgot me. In all this time you never wrote to ask how I was, n-never sent a single word of how you were.

"Never," she repeated, looking at the handkerchief as if it had suddenly spoken to her, her voice faltering, lowering. She gave a great heave of breath and raised her tear-stained face to him. "It was cruel of you not to answer my letter, Benjamin." She cringed now to remember the oh-so-casual missive in which she had told him rather primly she was fine, thanking him, and closing by asking if he was well and did he plan to come to San Francisco any time in the near future? She swallowed hard. "Better if you had simply sent it back unopened."

Benjamin raked his fingers distractedly through his hair and stood up, as if he could not speak and sit still in the face of her discomposure.

"Can you understand, Sparrow, when I tell you I thought it best not to answer, that you should be left to seek your friends among the children of Professor Langley's friends?" He gave a pale imitation of his impudent grin, "and it seems I was right. It took me nearly the whole evening to catch you alone, Miss Langley."

When she did not smile in response, he sighed, seated himself again, and searched her face.

"In truth, Sparrow. I'd nearly forgotten the young girl-child."

Samille winced as the brutal force of his confession struck her. Benjamin gave an odd, quick glance at her as he continued rapidly.

"I knew she—that you, Samille—were safe and happy in San Francisco. You see," he reached out suddenly, capturing her hands, the fine hair fanning forward with the movement. He met her eyes squarely, his own blue eyes sober, full of humility and—surely?—a touch of chagrin.

"I chased a phantom, Samille—one crying out for vengeance for a dead woman's soul—and found myself consumed by the chase, by that woman—by Françoise."

Her hands jerked involuntarily and Benjamin's grasp tightened.

"And then one day, Samille, as I spoke with an elderly Frenchwoman, I saw your mother's face clearly—and it struck me all of a sudden how her face was—well, it came to me that you lived and what I did, I did for you."

"And so you traveled all the way to San Francisco to confess you had fallen in love with my mother, who is no longer alive, and now you want to be my friend?" For the life of her, she could not keep the bitter, jeering sarcasm from her words, masking her pain. She had been nothing to him, a duty, perhaps because he had rescued her from a riot in the bloody back streets of Singapore? She hadn't needed his rescuing. She and Yen-shu had already worked out a means for her to leave Singapore!

Benjamin flinched and dropped her hands.

"Believe what you will, Sparrow. There is more, but now, I think, is not the time for it. Shall I take you home?" At her wary look, he continued wearily, "I think it's time I met your family. There are things which must be told."

Jane Langley Gooden sat at her leisure in the parlor, guiltily looking up as Samille and Benjamin entered the room. She was, Samille, noted, reading the latest London fashion magazines.

"Aunt Jane, I'd like you to meet—"

"Benjamin T. Greaves, Mrs. Gooden," he finished for her. "An old friend of Samille's from—"

And was in turn interrupted by Jane, who ended smoothly, "Singapore." She rose and extended a firm hand, eying him with candid interest. "Delighted to meet you at last, Mr. Greaves. May I say you danced divinely with my niece last night?"

She cast a droll look at Samille's swift intake of breath and chuckled softly at Benjamin's arched brow.

"Come sit beside me on the sofa, Mr. Greaves, so we may become better acquainted. Samille, dear, ring for Soon Lee and ask him if he will serve soup and sand-wiches in the dining room in half an hour."

Samille did as she was bid, settling herself in a corner chair and gazing unseeing out the window. The drift of her aunt's and Benjamin's conversation eddied about her. She could not bear to look at him as reality hit her. How long had she measured every man she'd met against Benjamin? Against his humor, his strength, the neatly trimmed moustache, the slightly rough edge to him as if he moved well in the worlds of both city and country. How had she hidden even from herself the knowledge of her love for him? Perhaps because of the other hurt eating into her. The fear that Benjamin, too, had abandoned her?

She bit her lip. This was one humiliation she would spare herself. He would never know about those foolish, youthful daydreams. The way she'd imagined him striding up the walk one day, come to claim her, throwing his arms around her, and declaring his love. Nor the way those dreams had slowly died, strangled in her shame and misery when he never wrote, never answered the pathetic missive she'd sent soon after her arrival in San Francisco. Well, she had her father and her work now. Those were the only certainties in her life. To hope for more was only to invite pain in once more. She'd learned her lesson well—a trusting heart led only to a broken heart.

Her gaze sharpened to attention. A tall, gray-haired gentleman descended from a cab and advanced slowly upon the house. His limp was noticeable, now, when he was visibly tired. Samille slipped from the parlor, flung wide the door, and hurried down the walk to meet her father.

"Father! How lovely! We weren't expecting you until tomorrow." She slipped an arm about his waist. "Here, let me help you with your things. Ah, there you are, Soon Lee. Here's Father's case."

Soon Lee hefted the older man's valise with ease, flashed him a smile, and followed as Samille walked her father into the house.

"All right, all right, Samille. Don't fuss so, darling." Snapping gray eyes met her sheepish glance, then her father brushed a kiss across her cheek. "I'm happy to be home, my dear, and yes, the journey was tiring. But, I feel all the better for seeing you."

They halted in the parlor door, Samille, in spite of herself, tensing as Benjamin rose and faced her father. Gently, she disengaged her arm.

"Benjamin, I'd like to introduce my father, Professor Langley.

"Father, this is Benjamin Greaves. Benjamin is—."

"I know who he is, Samille. I'm not mentally feeble." Her father's fierce visage raked the younger man. Her breath came out in a slow, inaudible hiss as the Professor advanced and held out his hand to the younger man. "You're the man who restored my Samille to me." Her father's voice caught. "I've often wondered about you, Mr. Greaves. There's much I would like to ask you."

He glared at his sister and Samille, who'd moved to sit next to Jane, as if he were certain protest would come from their quarter. Benjamin grasped his hand in a firm handshake.

"It's an honor to meet you, Professor Langley. I'm more than willing to answer your questions if I can."

Jane cleared her throat as Soon Lee appeared briefly in the parlor doorway.

"Samuel, Soon Lee has set out soup and sandwiches in the dining room. When Michael rang up to say he'd spoken with you this morning and you might be returning this afternoon, I thought you'd welcome a light supper."

Her aunt met Samille's quick gaze. "There wasn't time to tell you, my dear, when you came in."

The front doorbell rang. Soon Lee could be heard opening the door.

"I see Michael's punctual as well." Jane stood. "Shall we adjourn to our meal? I took the liberty of inviting Mr. Greaves to join us."

Without waiting for a reply, she took her brother by the arm, greeted Michael serenely and steered him toward the dining room as she casually introduced Benjamin. He, in turn, offered his arm to Samille.

"Will you do me the honor, Miss Langley?" His blue eyes held none of the smoldering fire that had warmed her so treacherously the night before, but a puzzled, wary look, as though what he saw now he could not understand. She brushed past him into the hall.

They ate in silence for several minutes after Benjamin had told of tracing the story of the Malay mutiny in the *Straits' Times* morgue. Samille saw nothing, looking inward, willing herself not to relive again those moments when rice knives had flashed red in the sun.

"I've another story to tell now, Professor, as much as I would prefer not to do so. You might say I've a confession to make."

Samille's mouth went dry. A quick, hopeless glance showed the attention of her father, Aunt Jane, and Michael O'Grady riveted upon Benjamin. His next words took her completely by surprise.

"Since Samille's return to America, she and this household have been under constant surveillance."

"What?!" Three heads swiveled to confront Samille, who sat dumbfounded, staring open-mouthed at Benjamin. Absently, he stroked his mustache.

"I think, young man, you'd better explain yourself."

Samille's heart sank to see the rapid aging of her father's features once again as strain and worry rushed back. Benjamin's cool glance swept them all, Aunt Jane wary and tense beside her brother, Michael quiet and watchful, and herself—with her heart in her throat, watching her father.

"My uncle, Nathanial Hawkins, and I—despite your misgivings, Samille—felt a great deal of responsibility for making your story public. You know," his words may have been addressed to the room at large, but his eyes commanded Samille's attention, " we did so deliberately, hoping to provoke some reaction on the part of the unknown person or persons who'd precipitated Françoise Langley's inexplicable flight to Singapore.

"But, having drawn attention to our lamb, we could scarcely send her to slaughter. Someone was set to watch over her, to keep her and her family safe."

Michael stirred at this and asked drily, "So you have been here for three years, Mr. Greaves, protecting this household?"

Samille spoke without conscious thought, but with conviction. She hadn't lived all those years in Singapore without knowing how some things could be accomplished.

"No, not Benjamin. Soon Lee."

Her aunt set down her cup of coffee, nodded. She met her brother's drawn face.

"Think, Samuel, how unobtrusive he is. Always helping Ho Lee, working in the garden or the kitchen when Samille is home."

"Always with work of his own to do elsewhere when she's gone," Samuel concluded heavily. "How were you able to arrange this, Mr. Greaves? I take it he reported directly to you and your uncle? You are here now because of something he reported?"

Benjamin nodded curtly.

"Uncle Nate is well-acquainted with a respected restaurant owner in Singapore—Min Lee. Min Lee happens to be Ho Lee's elder cousin. He recommended Soon Lee on the strength of his devotion to family and to his studies. Soon Lee is," Benjamin's wry grimace checked his words, "a master of the martial arts. I've since learned he's highly intelligent, observant, and thoroughly cautious as well.

"He communicated directly with Min Lee, who then passed Soon Lee's messages on to my uncle. Uncle Nate has long been a patron of the *Emperor's Lotus*, Min Lee's flagship establishment, and a personal friend of Min Lee."

"Why, may I ask, was all this cloak and dagger secrecy necessary in your dealings, Mr. Greaves?"

Michael put the question forward curiously, speculatively, to the younger man. Benjamin caught him up with a sharp glance.

"It was obvious some powerful connection to Françoise's death must have been centered in Singapore. We thought it best to be prudent in a city where the British veneer of law and order is spread thinly."

Michael persisted politely.

"You did not, then, suspect some particular figure as this Singapore connection?"

"You're too quick by far, Mr. O'Grady," Benjamin tipped his head in deference. "Yes, we did suspect someone, but had no real proof of their involvement."

"And your job, since you were not present to receive Soon Lee's reports, was to find such proof?" Professor Langley interjected. At Benjamin's nod, he added, "you used the past tense just a moment ago, Mr. Greaves. Have you then found the proof you for which you were searching?"

Benjamin's eyes widened slightly. Clearly, Samille's father and his friend were not two academics with their heads lost in their academic studies.

"Exactly, Professor. I saw Samille safely aboard ship bound for home, and then I traveled to Paris to see if I could discover the connection from there."

Samille noted with a pang the sudden stillness of her father's features, the way he blindly lay down his spoon, the slight flutter of anxiety across both her aunt's and Michael's expressions.

"I managed, Professor Langley, to track down the present whereabouts of Madame and Monsieur Eloyse and Manard Verhautier, your housekeeping couple. They retired as pensioners to St. Briere, a village just south of Paris. Madame Verhautier was still spry and remembered you well."

Samuel leaned back in his chair, his eyes closed.

"I'm sorry, sir," Benjamin addressed his host quietly, "if this distresses you. Perhaps I should wait...."

"No!" The single syllable exploded harshly from the professor's mouth. He opened gray eyes deepened with the pain of remembrance. "Pray continue, Mr. Greaves. No other time will ever ease the impact of what you must say." He opened his eyes and his glance pinned Benjamin in his seat. Samille had seen unprepared students quail under that same look. Benjamin waited.

"It seems to me, however, young man, you took it upon yourself to involve yourself in our affairs far above the calling of your professional duty." The brooding gaze shifted imperceptibly to Samille and back again to Benjamin.

"We—my uncle and I—hoped to solve the mystery behind your wife's death, Professor Langley, for only then could the real murderer be brought to justice.

"It also seemed a monstrous sort of crime to deprive a young girl of her childhood and a loving family. For all of this, then, I hunted the Verhautiers." Benjamin paused as though to collect the elements of his tale. So still were the occupants of the dining room Samille swore long afterward that a redbird perched upon the windowsill and peered inside the room.

"Monsieur Verhautier was an ill man, it appeared, for some time prior to your wife's and daughter's disappearance, Professor. He and Madame were saving even then to retire to the country. Two years after they retired, the old man died, leaving a sealed letter with the direction it should be given to anyone who came asking about the death of Madame Langley."

He reached inside his jacket to pull a folded square of paper from his pocket and offered it to Samuel, who took it with a hand which shook. Benjamin addressed the rest of his audience as Samuel read the letter to himself.

"Briefly, it states Monsieur was paid by a *chinois* to be given access to the house for the purpose of speaking with Madame Langley. Having taken the money, Monsieur Verhautier was afraid to speak up later when his mistress and the *petite piaf* disappeared, afraid he would be arrested and go to prison.

"Then, after...after it was discovered that the Madame and her child had both perished and the Professor returned to America, the old man saw this same *chinois* one day on the streets of Paris and followed him to a curio shop on the Left Bank." Benjamin turned to Samille, "the *chinois* was the man you've identified as Kwang-ju. The name of the shop was Quon-Li's Curio House. Monsieur had the *curé* write it all down, along with the address of the curio shop.

"I found the shop still exists and is owned by a wealthy Chinese. From a fellow journalist, I learned it was managed at the time of Françoise's disappearance by a nefarious man known as the Crab, who later disappeared from Paris in connection with the murder of a shop clerk whose body had been recovered from the Seine."

Samille shivered involuntarily as the cold, clear memory of Chin hui's vicious features came to her, then felt, beneath the tabletop, the slight pressure and warmth of Benjamin's fingers closing over hers. For a moment she relaxed, taking comfort from the warmth off his touch, then she caught herself and jerked her hand away. Benjamin's mustache twitched. A pulse pounded in his throat and the azure eyes were awash with a momentary gleam. She looked away from him to her father's bent head. Benjamin took up his tale again.

"This man, Professor, was already known to us as a powerful thug in the pay of Wei chu Chuang—a wealthy Chinese merchant in Singapore, who is, moreover, a cousin to Yen-shu, Samille's friend and master. Wei chu, through Chin hui, had attempted to take our Sparrow from Yen-shu's shop shortly before I contacted you. He also attempted to prevent her from leaving Singapore.

"It was not hard to discover the same Wei-chu so respected in Singapore owned a curio shop in Paris—one associated there with the opium traffic and a great many other criminal activities. Wei-chu, then, represented the link we'd sought.

"Curiously enough, it appears my friend had been approached many years ago by another man concerning this same shop. He even recalled the name—a Monsieur McNamara."

Samille's head jerked around. She spoke as if some suffocating weight bore down upon her.

"Who died with Mama," she whispered.

"No," Benjamin corrected her, "his body was discovered on the coast. Apparently he made it that far before he died of his injuries. I think perhaps he was the reason you made it safely to shore."

Professor Langley raised great bruised eyes to Samille, his voice cracked and old.

"You are the Sparrow, my dear?"

Jane started violently and exclaimed.

"Samille!"

"Yes, Father. Yen-shu's name for me was the Sparrow, since I could tell him no other." She went on, almost to herself, "I'd forgotten *Ms.* Verhautier used to call me *le piaf.*"

Samuel gripped the edges of the table before him.

"Then you are here, Mr. Greaves, after all this time has passed because this man, this Wei-chu, is once more seeking my daughter?"

"Yes. Two years ago Soon Lee reported the presence of someone watching this residence. No one made any attempt at that time to enter the house, or to approach Samille. However, six months ago, a series of seemingly unrelated incidents began which alarmed Soon Lee. He cabled for further instructions and assistance."

"The sparrows, of course." Professor Langley looked at his daughter. "You knew, didn't you? Why didn't you say?" The older man answered his own question. "To spare us, obviously. What else?"

"Most recently, the reappearance of the watchers, an aggressive delivery man who tried to enter the house, and someone hiding in the garden."

"My disappearing bicycle," Samille added reluctantly, "and the cutting of the piano strings in the dance studio."

As four pairs of questioning eyes focused on her, Samille hastened to explain. When she finished, her father thumped his fist on the table.

"What could this man possibly want from my family? First my wife," he choked in his anger, "and now my daughter! Tell me, how in heaven do we make an end to this when we remain ignorant of his motives?" In frustration he turned from his old friend to his sister and Benjamin. "Why can't we go to this man and ask him what he wants?" His face blanched and drained, he seemed shrunken and vulnerable. His hands quivered as he spoke.

Samille could bear no more. She went quickly to her father and knelt before him, chafing his hands with her own. Fighting tears and a hard, deep knot of grief and anger, she forced herself to speak calmly.

"Please, Father. Whatever his secrets, I don't believe Wei-chu is the kind of man with whom one can reason and explain. If he is moving into the open once again, maybe we'll be able to end this nightmare once and for all. But, you must promise me, Father, you won't do anything rash. I promise, in turn, to be careful, not to travel alone, to come straight home after classes."

Professor Langley stood, pulling Samille to him for a fierce, brief hug. The barest gleam of humor lightened his features.

"I notice you did not offer to give up your studies, my dear child." He smoothed back a stray wisp of hair from her forehead. "You are the most precious reason I have for living. I won't do anything to jeopardize your safety or mine." His hard eyes sought Benjamin's.

"I take it, young man, you'll be staying in San Francisco for the time being?"

"Yes."

"Good. We seem to be heading for a crisis of some sort. An extra pair of eyes and ears won't go amiss. Stay close to my daughter, if you will, Mr. Greaves. I trust you with her life.

"Now, I would like to go to my room. Will you come up with me, Michael? I've one or two papers in my valise which you're sure to find of interest."

Seated once more in the parlor, Jane surveyed Benjamin and Samille bleakly as Michael O'Grady rejoined them.

"Samuel's lying down. I think he'll sleep."

"Thank heavens!" Jane held Samille's hand in hers. "It's like a nightmare, isn't it? We seem frustrated by our ignorance." She took a deep breath. "I think, you know, whatever the source of this man Chuang's actions, his motive must lie in the past. Farther back, even, than Françoise." Her eyes glinted suddenly. "Come into Samuel's study for a moment, won't you?"

Samille, guessing her aunt's intent, led the way across the hall and threw open the door to the study. She was drawn, as always, to the portrait of her mother and her grandmother. Eying the picture thoughtfully, she turned about. Michael, Jane, and Benjamin stared at her.

Michael was the first to speak.

"The resemblance is quite striking, isn't it?"

"Ye-es," Benjamin agreed slowly. "But you meant something more particular, didn't you, Mrs. Gooden?"

Jane Gooden met his gaze candidly.

"Yes. There's just the hint of some exotic strain in their blood. As if somewhere, some ancestor was Asian by birth."

"*'the women of the House of Chui'*"

Excitedly, Samille fingered the golden wire of her necklace.

"That's what Father called us, my first day home. What did he mean, Aunt Jane?"

"Not what you're thinking, Samille. He often teased Françoise, when she was being stubborn about something, about being part of the women of the house of Chui."

Crestfallen, Samille shrugged.

"I suppose if it were something so obvious, you and Father would have thought of it years ago. What are you suggesting, Aunt Jane?"

Her aunt pursed her lips and waved her hand at the room in which they stood.

"This house belonged to your mother's parents, Samille. They lived here with Françoise until your mother was about twelve years' old, then moved to Paris where your grandfather had business interests. As far as I know, your grandmother never returned to this house until shortly before her death. All of her belongings are here, however. Stored in the attic. Perhaps somewhere among her things we will find a clue to her background."

"Or," Michael O'Grady interposed thoughtfully, steepling his fingers and resting his chin on them, "it may be the answer to our riddle lies in your grandfather's business dealings in Paris. Exactly what was his business, Jane? If I ever knew, I've forgotten."

A swift frown creased Jane's brow.

"Mr. Beauvoir was a jeweler and did quite well for himself. His work caught the eye of the Silver Barons and other wealthy San Franciscans. So successful was his business, he took his wife and child and went off to study in Paris. His work was equally well received there. He opened a small, very exclusive establishment and never returned to San Francisco. But, he'd been retired for several years before he passed away."

Benjamin stirred for the first time.

"Best, I think, not to overlook any possible connection, don't you agree?" At their nods of assent, he continued, "I propose to begin with a search of your grandmother's effects tomorrow, Samille. The rest of the household can go about their normal business as usual. You could explain my interest as a visiting scholar, holed up with Professor Langley to do some research." He cocked a dubious eye at Samille, who turned remote green eyes upon him.

"We'll put it about you're moonstruck over the professor's daughter, as well, Mr. Greaves," Aunt Jane might have read his thoughts, "to explain your attachment to her."

If the slightest hint of amusement tinged her voice, it was studiously overlooked by those concerned parties.

"Yes," Michael chimed in helpfully, "you can arrange a picnic in a nice public place like Golden Gate Park—you'll be surrounded by people. You could also go sailing in the bay. Whichever, of course, you prefer," he hastened to add as Samille's color rose. "And we can pitch in, naturally, with the boxes in the attic."

"Oh yes, indeed," Jane agreed. "You've no idea how much is stored away, Mr. Greaves."

Michael O'Grady got to his feet.

"I must be getting home to Eleanor." He kissed Samille's cheek. "Lennie will be waiting up for me, the little minx. Mrs. Donohue tries her best, but the child doesn't like to go to bed without saying good-night to her papa." He nodded briskly in the direction of Samuel's bedroom above them. "Try not to worry so much about your father, my dear. He's stronger than he looks, though I'd see he sleeps late in the morning."

"An excellent suggestion, Michael. I'll speak to Ho Lee about it at once." Aunt Jane stood as Michael turned to Benjamin.

"I don't know how you're situated for lodgings, Mr. Greaves, but I've a room in my home I've let to students in the past. You're most welcome should you wish to make use of it." He drew a card from his case. "Here's my address."

"Another excellent suggestion, Professor O'Grady. I've cousins who live in San Francisco, but I'd rather not disturb them with my comings and goings."

Michael shook hands with Benjamin, made his goodbye to Samille, and followed Jane out of the study.

Benjamin sighed softly. Samille, standing before the mantel, hugged her arms to her, stifling a sudden shiver that engulfed her. Utterly weary, she closed her eyes as if to blot out the evening's revelations, frustrations, her father's fear, and the face swimming so enticingly before her.

A feather-light touch tilted her chin up. Startled, she opened her eyes. Close up, Benjamin's face mirrored her own bone-aching tiredness.

"I think your father's right, Sparrow. A crisis is brewing. It's why I came back to San Francisco now to help—or part of the reason—" his blue eyes flashed with some unreadable quicksilver emotion. "If you will allow me to help you, Samille?"

She twisted her chin free. Why not? She had herself well in hand. She returned his gaze. Justice, he'd said earlier.

"I want an end to this, Benjamin. An end to the threat, to the fear, to my father's pain. To get on with my life—my work. I have no choice but to allow you."

"I see." Plainly, he saw all too clearly. "Until tomorrow, then, Miss Samille Beauvoir Langley." The blue eyes flared, but whether they mocked himself or her, she could not tell.

Jane, pausing on the landing at the top of the stairs to the second floor, heard the closing of the front door, and watched in surprise as her niece flew from the study, faltering as she reached the door, both palms against it, her head bowed between them, her shoulders heaving with the force of silent, pent-in sobs.

Chapter 8

Slithering out of the corner of her eye, the green dragon un-folded two great, age-encrusted wings to the sun and with a silent, heavy majesty flew high against the sky. As if she rode upon its massive, scaled back, Samille could see far below, in the dizzying depths of the earth, a thin golden river snaking across the green valley. The dragon lurched suddenly. She went spinning, spiraling down....

"Ouch!"

Samille's head snapped back and her eyes popped open.

"What? Oh dear, Lennie! I'm terribly sorry!"

Leaning over, she retrieved the heavy tome that had fallen from her tottering pile of books, striking the girl on the top of the head. Ruefully, Lennie rubbed her head.

"Honestly, Sam, why don't you take a break?"

Samille surveyed the litter of papers and half-opened textbooks scattered across the desktop before her and shrugged bleakly. Pushing back her chair, she threw up her hands in despair.

"There aren't enough hours in the day. Look at this! I'm not nearly finished as it is." She waved a hand at the stacks of paper, dislodging one as she did so. "Oh, for pity's sake!"

Frustrated, Samille grabbed for it and in her haste sent several long rolls of drawing paper flying. Lennie dodged them, laughing, and a long, lean arm restored two of them as she gathered her papers.

"Listen to the young lady, Sparrow, she's wise beyond her tender years," Benjamin drawled, dropping Lennie an exaggerated wink. She giggled and stood up, casting a beleaguered eye at her friend.

"Sam's working too hard, Benjamin. She fell asleep over her plans again and nearly knocked me silly with one of those great fat books she's using to weight them down.

"She sits up half the night poring over her grandparents' papers and the other half reading for old Professor Maybeck's classes, then she's up by dawn tinkering with this latest project." Lennie took a deep breath. "What are we going to do with her, Benjamin?"

Samille groaned mentally. The young girl and the news reporter had taken to each other like goldfish to a lily pond, Samille reflected as Benjamin eyed the stacks of papers and the scattered piles of books ringing Lennie and shoved precariously on every available surface in the study.

"Why, I'm going to kidnap her for the rest of the afternoon and take her rubbernecking in Golden Gate Park. After we've seen the sights, we're going to settle down in the sun and picnic on cold roasted chicken, cheese, and sourdough bread. We'll finish with a bottle of California wine and fresh strawberries from the valley. What say you, Miss Langley?"

He swept his cocky straw boater across his heart and grinned winningly at her, rolling mischievous blue eyes at Lennie as he did so.

"Thank you, Benjamin," she replied stiltedly. "It's very kind of you to offer." She came around the desk, gave Lennie a quick, affectionate hug. "Promise me you'll have Aunt Jane give you lunch soon, Lennie, and you won't spend all afternoon cooped up indoors."

"Oh do go on, Sam. Don't worry about me." She gave Samille a playful push. "Run along and enjoy yourselves!"

"We will, my sweet, we will. After all," Benjamin reminded Samille, "you're my excuse for being here, don't you recall?"

Jerking her head around sharply, Samille noted with surprise while his tone was light, his eyes were oddly grave, his expression contemplative. She caught her breath quickly and held her tongue.

The Regina lily blossomed across the quiet expanse of water in the sunken pool like a silken mirage, exquisite, larger than life. The calm green surface of the pool mocked him, Benjamin thought as they stood looking at the impossible flower, like the fathomless depths of Samille's eyes as he stole a glance at her.

Their lunch had been a sedate affair—Benjamin at first exerting himself in a running, amusing monologue on the day, the art museum, the recently constructed bandshell, and the horde of sightseers thronging the paths. Samille had tried hard to match his carefree tone, but eventually Benjamin's patter slowed and she could not summon the energy to carry on by herself. Now they meandered aimlessly among the obligatory sights of the park with nothing to say to one another. Yet, neither turned their steps away, back to Divisadero Street.

Samille paced silently beside Benjamin. In the nearly six weeks which had followed his abrupt reappearance in her life, she had seen him almost daily. Sometimes he went off on mysterious errands, but mostly, true to his word, he worked diligently, futilely, on the ever-diminishing boxes of her grandparents' effects.

Sometimes they labored together—bittersweet occasions when she was reminded over and over he was here only because of some noble sense of duty—and she represented an obligation to be discharged. She would torment herself with imagining he was anxious to return to Singapore, where someone fair and blonde and dimpled—and in such moments, these nameless young women all looked like Carilla DeMondeley—awaited him.

At these times she would grit her teeth and work doggedly beside him. Every little joke, every casual moment's forgetfulness, when she allowed herself to enjoy his easy companionship, came back to stab at her until she felt as fragmented and fragile as a sparrow's egg shattered on the garden walk.

Slowly they strolled along the paths of Golden Gate Park. At length Benjamin broke the silence that lay between them.

"I'm going away, Samille."

She halted in mid-stride, gaping at him, stumbling as the force of his words struck so pat upon her thoughts. She shook off his instinctive move to aid her and turned glittering, cold eyes on him—eyes as hard and chilling as malachite chips.

"It seems futile to continue, Sparrow. We've found no clues in your grandparents' things. No one has approached you or your father. There seems to be nothing more I can accomplish here. Unless," he cast an oblique look at her stony features, "you can think of some other reason why I should stay?"

Tell him! The thought fairly shrieked inside of her. *Tell him you love him!* She took a deep breath.

"Benjamin!"

"Yes?" The single word exploded like a hawk pouncing on a rabbit. She faltered before the fierceness of his gaze. If he wanted so desperately to leave, then let him.

"I...I think it's probably a wise decision. There's no reason for you to waste your time here any longer. I've Father and Jane and Michael to look after me, and there's the close of the semester to deal with as well," her words tumbled out. "I've really no time to keep stumbling about on this wild goose chase," she ended lamely.

Beside her, Benjamin echoed her nod, his voice wooden as he replied.

"I'll see you home, then, Sparrow, and tell your father. I've an old friend to look up in Singapore and I don't want to wait too long."

Into Samille's mind flashed a vision of an imaginary blonde—all smiles now. It seemed her guess had hit the mark. She flashed a falsely brilliant smile at him.

"Then we'd best be on our way, Benjamin. Shall we go?"

All things considered, her father took the news of Benjamin's imminent departure well. Professor Langley had doubled Soon Lee's salary as houseboy and watch dog, and now he seemed considerably relieved that Benjamin's departure signaled an end to the danger. The tension which had driven haggard lines into his face lessened. Occasionally, he stopped again for lunch or supper with colleagues and students. Samille spared a moment to be glad for him, but threw her energy into her studies with a grim determination.

The plans for her semester project had been completed. She'd discovered the perfect site for what was, in her mind, *her* house, and had risked tailoring her ideas to a small clearing which swept against the hillside two-thirds of the way to the top of Telegraph Hill. Trees and boulders tumbled near the edge of the clearing which had escaped the dynamiting so common on the hill. The site appeared to her as an untouched, natural refuge high above the growing city and the bay. Sometimes in early afternoon, after her morning lectures and lunch, she'd go there and sketch, finding release and refuge from her thoughts and emotions, if only momentarily. It did not matter to her that the land had been sold recently. Clearing had begun, but halted abruptly. No one bothered her on her visits, and the peace and quiet was all that mattered.

She had the queer sensation of a spring winding deeper and deeper into her, one twisting flesh and soul into one taut coil threatening to release at any moment, shattering mind and body forever. If only Benjamin's ship would steam out of harbor! Once he was well and truly gone, perhaps then this pain and frantic fear could be fought to control. Aunt Jane seemed to share her feelings, for dark rings mocked her once lively eyes, and she hadn't resumed her usual activities in spite of her brother's evident relaxation of his guard. Lennie, as determinedly cheerful as always, shadowed her older friend as unobtrusively as did Aunt Jane, the young girl frequently spending the night at the house on Divisadero Street. Samille felt ashamed, as now, that she could not hide her own fears and bring them some measure of peace.

Only Michael O'Grady seemed untouched by the miasma of emotions gripping his friends and his daughter. He insisted they be his guests for dinner on Benjamin's last night in San Francisco and took them all to Luigi's small trattoria on Russian Hill. A mingled sense of freedom and sadness pervaded their conversation as they sat at a terrace table and enjoyed a carafe of the house wine, steaming plates of pasta and *frutti di mare*, the seafood fresh from San Francisco Bay the same afternoon, and long loaves of fresh bread.

Across the terrace, another couple was being seated. The woman, fairly young and slender with a ready grin, seemed slightly familiar to Samille. Her companion was a considerably older gentleman, heavy-set with neatly trimmed gray hair and hooded eyes. Catching Jane Gooden's eye, the woman waved enthusiastically.

"Excuse me, Samuel, but I must speak with Isabella and James Forelli. Isabella's succeeded in getting pledges to fund a new kindergarten. She's part of the Public Kindergarten Society—the one Phoebe Hearst has thrown her support behind. Isabella's set to open a new kindergarten on the waterfront. I must offer my congratulations."

Samuel nodded pleasantly to the couple, distracted by the sight of Lennie surreptitiously eying the pastry cart, and crooked a finger at their waiter. As Lennie gleefully took her time over her selection, he turned to Michael with a fresh attack upon his colleague's interpretation of President Jefferson's motivation for funding the Lewis and Clark expedition. Samille toyed with her coffee cup. Michael deliberately baited her father, she realized, just to have the pleasure of arguing with him. Her head ached. She rubbed a temple cautiously and touched her father's sleeve.

"I'm going to get a breath of fresh air away from the tables, Father. The cigar smoke...." She shrugged, indicating the thick swirls from a neighboring table. Worry momentarily overshadowed the professor's features as she walked away, but his face lightened with relief as Benjamin followed the retreating figure of his daughter.

Leaning her elbows on the terrace wall in a quiet, secluded corner, Samille breathed the sweet night air deeply. Straining a little to see, she picked out the dark blot of space on Telegraph Hill that was her inspiration for her architectural project. At the crunch of gravel behind her, she jumped, startled immediately into the present, into wariness at the silhouette of Benjamin as he joined her.

"I thought I could walk away, Sparrow, without looking back, but I can't." Benjamin's strained voice came through the darkness to her as he leaned against the terrace wall, pointing toward Telegraph Hill. "Whatever dream you're hiding in, Samille, build it well. As sturdy as the fence you've built around yourself and as long-lasting."

His quiet, bitter words cut into her as deftly and deadly as a rice knife.

"I came to San Francisco to find that young girl, so beautiful and courageous, the one who lived a life of spartan comforts and filled with dangers, but who risked life and limb to dance in a moonlit garden. A girl who loved loyally and ferociously." She couldn't see his face, but could feel his eyes boring into her. "I came here to see what kind of woman she's become, and I found a shell of that girl. Someone so centered in her comforts, in her fear of pain, she's afraid to live at all. I can't help you, Sparrow. Only you can free yourself from your gilded cage."

A shrill, mirthless burst of low laughter escaped her.

"Of all the pompous...! How noble, how righteous of you to judge *me*, Mr. Greaves!" Her words spurted viciously out in a desire to strike at him. "I didn't ask for your help, either in Singapore or here. I'm sorry you no longer find it convenient or profitable to linger in San

Francisco to pay off some quixotic debt you think you owe to me—or to my mother!"

His shoulders tightened. She knew her words had struck a nerve and was glad. But as quickly as the urge to wound him had flared, it died. "Oh, just go away, Benjamin. Go back to Singapore where you belong—to your friend—whoever she is. You've done more than enough to solve a puzzle with no pieces." She stepped away from the terrace wall, and like an echo of another time, two strong, familiar hands turned her about. The moonlight shifted across Benjamin's features, his eyes startlingly brilliant in the ebb and flow of light.

"*She*? You're mistaken, but I'll go, Sparrow. I've things to do that won't wait. I can feel time slipping away even as we speak." His words held an urgent note of worry, a note that deepened her sense of shame and grief. She stared at him in misery. Was he so glad, then, to leave her? Unwilled, her hand went out and brushed his cheek just where his mustache ended in a fleeting good-bye caress.

"Then go, Benjamin," she whispered. "I wish you the best of luck, and if you ever...." Her voice faltered. Valiantly, she smiled uncertainly at him. "Take care of yourself, please, and give my love to Yen-shu and Sakai and Penang, if you should ever come across them."

She turned then and fairly ran back to the lights, to her father, to the safety of her own life. How could it matter if he were right, when the key to her cage was her undoing—the love of a man who would never touch her life again?

One day edged nervously into two, and then into one week, until a month passed since Benjamin Greaves had left San Francisco. Nearly mid-August now, Samille mused as she stole a glance at her father's profile. He stood deep in thought at her side as they rode the ferry home together. She'd been dead wrong about the effect of Benjamin's departure on her, on them all. They were edgy still, prone to nervous starts. Desultorily, she and Lennie had decided not to reopen the dance studio until autumn, completing instead the exhausting task of sorting and repacking her grandparents effects.

List after list of inventoried pieces came to light, a testimony to her Grandfather Beauvoir's prodigious output. Meticulously drawn sketches of his best work, accompanied by notes in her grandfather's hand, were also unearthed. None of these, to their increasing frustration, had been commissioned by mysterious or not-so-mysterious Chinamen. The task, however, fascinated Samille, as the evidence of her grandfather's work revealed a master artisan and craftsman—one who had taken great pleasure and pride in his designs. She set his sketchbooks aside to peruse at her leisure. Vaguely, she thought she could remember her mother wearing some of his pieces.

Unconsciously, Samille hugged her father's arm to her. He glanced around at her touch, giving her an absent-minded smile. The patchy fog seemed to thicken, enclosing them in a world of their own, the ferry gliding soundlessly through the mist-enshrouded waters of the bay. She leaned her head against Professor Langley's shoulder. She'd meant to ask him if her mother had had any of her grandfather's pieces of jewelry. But, one afternoon, going in search of her father, she'd come quietly to the door of his study to find the same thought must have occurred to him, for he sat in his usual armchair with a box opened on his lap. Something in the way he reached into the case arrested her greeting unspoken. She watched in helpless silence as he dangled a pearlescent pink opal earring before him, his gentle smile twisting. Clasping the fragile earring to him, he shook with hard, rasping sobs. Samille backed away in panic and fled to her room. The sight of his grief, still so fresh and deep, shocked her.

Now, she squeezed her father's arm again as they disembarked at the ferry building.

"Father," she urged on impulse, "let's stop for dinner at Luna's—just the two of us. It'll be cozy there, out of this fog. You know Ricardo can always find us a table. I've a terrible craving for chicken tamales. What do you say?"

Professor Langley eyed his dark-haired daughter indulgently.

"Capital idea, my dear, but your aunt will worry if we're late," he chided her gently.

"We'll call from Luna's or send a messenger. Aunt Jane's not alone tonight, Father. Soon Lee's there and Michael's dropping Lennie by while he gives his lecture at the faculty club tonight. Please?"

Her father's rare grin flashed. He gave in with one final caveat.

"We'll call as soon as we get to Luna's. I'm sure Ricardo can arrange it if we ask."

Ricardo, the long-time maître d' at Luna's restaurant, twirled his luxurious white mustaches, his one good eye veritably snapping as he beckoned imperiously to a young server. With his patch and his gleaming red sash, he was a highlight of any visit to Luna's. His regulars were treated like royalty.

"Alejandro, show *el professor* to *el telefono*," he commanded. "Tell me, *Senorita* Langley, what will you have tonight?"

Requesting coffee for them, Samille resisted the impulse to order dinner for her father and herself. He hated her to fuss over him, and tonight she would wait. He came back almost immediately, however, clearly agitated and reached for his hat.

"No one answered, Samille. Jane might have changed her mind about dining in, but it's inconceivable Ho Lee would be gone when he expected us for dinner. We must go at once."

Professor Langley explained rapidly to Ricardo they would not, after all, be dining, and tipped him handsomely for his trouble. Samille was on her feet before her father had finished.

Once outside, they hurried toward the trolley stop, until Samille, in her nervous haste, dropped her satchel of books.

"Sorry to be so clumsy, Fa—" she halted mid-word as the swirling mist cleared briefly, straightened slowly, and clutched her father's arm with a shaking hand. "Keep walking, Father. Two men are behind us. Chinese. One, I think, our deliveryman." She turned a worried face to her father. "What are we going to do?"

"Can you run, Samille? Our stop should be just along here. There are bound to be other people about at this hour." Even as he spoke, Samille felt him stiffen, his pace check. Two Chinese in western garb stepped out of the fog drifting from an alley, half a block ahead of them, and turned as one in their direction. The professor took his daughter's arm and together they fled across the street. Samille threw a glance behind her.

"Two of them are following, Father." The men did not close in, however, and five minutes later, the scenario was repeated. Samille and her father were forced into a side street by the sudden appearance of two men in front of them.

Twenty minutes later, Professor Langley gripped Samille's arm tightly. Judging the distance of a trolley which could be heard slowly approaching their direction, and the measured, relentless footsteps behind them, he ordered.

"Now, Samille! Run!"

Together they sprinted for the trolley car as it emerged from a patch of mist and swung aboard just as it picked up speed. Samille landed first, dropped her satchel at her feet, and reached a helping hand to her father.

Paying their nickel fares, the professor grimly eyed his daughter as she anxiously scanned the fog-enshrouded street they were traversing.

"Never mind, dear. If I'm not mistaken, we'll be left alone now." At her puzzled look, he explained. "You noticed none of these men made an effort to approach us, Samille? Nor to harm us? It's all too common knowledge the kind of weapons which are frequently concealed about their persons. What was their mission, then?"

Samille considered her father's words.

"They hoped to force us in a certain direction, where others would be waiting to deal with us?"

Her father shook his head.

"I think you've got it backward, my child." He swung off the trolley with her as they made their connection for Divisadero Street, and then finished heavily as they boarded the second trolley. "They hoped to delay us, to keep us from returning home as expected."

Heart in her throat, Samille turned a sick face up the hill. They rode in silence and strode quickly toward home once they left the trolley. The house loomed menacingly before them as they approached, not a single light shining. Apprehensively, they reached the front entrance. The door creaked faintly in the breeze that had lifted the mist from their neighborhood.

"Steady, Samille."

Professor Langley cautiously pushed the door open wider, switching on the front hall light as he did so. Ho Lee lay sprawled on the stairs, his white queue darkened and sticky against his cheek. Samille dropped her satchel in horror and ran to the old man's side, where she quickly felt for a pulse.

"He's alive, Father!"

"Sh-h!"

A muffled thumping came from the back of the house. Samuel Langley picked up a stout umbrella with a steel shaft from a receptacle next to the hall console table, and started down the hallway. Samille catfooted along behind him. Gingerly, he poked at the door to the kitchen with the tip of the umbrella, pushed the door wide, and switched on the light.

Soon Lee's angry, frustrated eyes blinked in the sudden glare. He lay on the floor, gagged and trussed tightly to a ladder-backed chair. Samille seized a knife and cut his bonds, the professor freeing his mouth from the gag.

"My father?"

They helped him stand.

"Alive, Soon Lee, but unconscious. Where's my sister? Tell me what happened while I ring for the doctor."

He threw the words over his shoulder as he hurried back to the telephone in his study. Samille and Soon Lee covered Ho Lee's fragile, crumpled form with a throw hastily taken from the sitting room. The professor barked urgently into the telephone mouthpiece, stopped, grunted, and hung up.

"The doctor is on his way." He looked at his pocket watch. "And I imagine Michael will be here shortly; his lecture should have ended long before now. Soon Lee?"

The young man sat back on the stairs beside his father's form.

"Four men come through kitchen, Professor. I was in dining room, setting table for dinner. Mistress Gooden and Missy Eleanor were in parlor. Father call out to me. When I enter kitchen, one man holds honorable father, one has knife to his throat. Two men tie me up and gag me. They take my father with them to front of house.

"I hear my father cry out. Hear Missy Eleanor scream, Mistress Gooden's angry voice. Then silence. Then telephone ring, ring, ring. Maybe half-hour or more before you come." Soon Lee's shoulders sagged, and he bowed his head. "I fail you, Professor. I most unworthy son, most unworthy servant."

"Nonsense." Samuel briskly clasped the tense shoulder of Soon Lee. "Samille, see if there's any brandy in the study. Bring three—no, four—glasses. Dr. Adams will want one, too.

"There was nothing you could have done alone, Soon Lee. None of us expected an attack of this nature. Ah, thank you, my dear." His keen gaze took in the same look of defeat on his daughter's face. "Don't waste time blaming yourself, Samille."

The doorbell sounded. Samille wrenched the door open to admit the doctor, a stoop-shouldered, white-haired man with the saddest eyes she'd ever seen. Michael O'Grady trod hard on his heels.

"Oh, Michael!" Tears ran down her face. She could not squeeze speech past the awful tightness of her throat.

They sat grimly staring at the piece of white rice paper clutched in the professor's fist. Dr. Adams had bandaged Ho Lee's head wound and Soon Lee and Michael had carried him to his bed. The elderly man would wake up by morning, the doctor assured them, but with a walloping headache. After a critical examination of Soon Lee's wrists and a quick shot of brandy, Dr. Adams had taken his leave, asking no questions, but giving his old friend a shrewd appraisal, said he'd send the bill around in the morning.

Professor Langley, Samille, Michael O'Grady, and Soon Lee—at the professor's insistence—had retired then to the sitting room. According to Soon Lee, Jane and Lennie had been reading bits from the newspaper to one another here, waiting on the professor and Samille to return for dinner. There, the square of white paper sat ominously, centered on the mantelpiece. *Call police at peril of women's lives*, it read. *Do nothing. Instructions to follow.* As they contemplated the implications of the note, Soon Lee quietly left the room.

"Michael?"

The robust, cheerful Irish face, now gray and haggard, met his friend's query.

"I'll wait here, if I may, Samuel. I don't think I can bear to go home."

Soon Lee reappeared, bearing a tray with a steaming tureen of cioppino and a basket of bread, bowls, spoons, and napkins. This he deposited on a low table.

"You must eat, " he insisted. "Honorable father will be distressed if you do not."

Professor Langley nodded brusquely and handed around the bowls. "Thank you, Soon Lee. Please, will you join us?"

Samille's heart lifted. Her father could not have shown the young man any more clearly he did not blame him for the events which had transpired this evening. Soon Lee's dark eyes dropped.

"Thank you, most honorable professor, but I must sit with my father." Quietly, he left the room.

Michael made a pretense of eating, pushing his spoon around as if to give his nervous fingers something to do. Samille forced herself to concentrate only upon the next spoonful of soup, willing the sound of the mantel clock into oblivion.

Chapter 9

Vaguely wondering why she was so uncomfortable, Samille stretched and heard a groan. Sitting up, she saw Michael and her father sprawled in their chairs. She had fallen asleep on the sitting room settee. Early morning sunshine streamed through the lace panels framing the sitting room's windows. The aroma of coffee and biscuits reached her, followed by the rattle of crockery from the kitchen.

Michael O'Grady blinked bleary eyes and slowly pushed himself upright with one stiff arm. Samille watched the awful realization hit him. Wearily he rubbed a hand over his face. Her father spoke without moving, his voice deep and resonant in the morning stillness.

"We'll get them back, Michael." He rose and extended a hand to his friend. "Come along. We'll look in on Ho Lee, have some coffee, and see what's to be done."

Samille, in the upstairs bath, pulled her rumpled shirtwaist over her head, tangling her fingers in her haste in the fine golden strand of her necklace. Blindly, she tried to disengage her fingers, and then felt the necklace give way.

"Oh, no!"

With dismay, she retrieved the necklace where it had fallen, and then quickly splashed cold water on her face before donning a fresh shirtwaist and skirt. She made equally quick work of brushing her hair and plaiting it. Grabbing her necklace, she thrust it in the pocket of her skirt and hurried downstairs. After she joined her father and Michael, she'd examine the damage to the necklace given her so long ago by her mother.

Her rush down the stairs skidded to a halt. Mesmerized, she stared at the front door. A buff-colored oblong fell through the bronze mail slot and came to rest silently on the hall runner. Galvanized, she flew down the remaining steps and stooped to scoop up the envelope. It bore her father's name in Jane Gooden's small, careful script.

Professor Langley tore open the envelope, withdrew a single sheet of dirty paper, and read aloud:

My dear brother Samuel, darling Samille, and dear friend Michael,

By the time you hold this in your hand, Eleanor and I will be bound for Singapore on this grimy, ramshackle steamer. It belongs, of course, to Wei-chu Chuang. I have been instructed to give you the following information.

Eleanor and I are unharmed and shall remain in Singapore, until Samille returns to Wei-chu with the 'Green Dragon's treasure.' If she has not done so by November, Wei-chu will see that I am introduced to the drug opium. His minion assures me soon I will live only for the drug. Eleanor is to be sold into the white-slave traffic.

I have attempted in vain to discover more of this 'Green Dragon,' and have been told only that the secret has been passed from mother to daughter. We must be correct in assuming, then, that the origins of this puzzle lie with Samille's grandparents.

I am forbidden to write more. They are treating us as well as can be expected, and I fully expect they will continue to do so. Please keep your spirits high and do not lose hope. I know in my heart we will be reunited. All of our love,

Jane Langley Gooden and Eleanor

"'The Green Dragon's treasure," Samille repeated the phrase aloud as she paced back and forth before the dining room windows. "The green dragon... the sleeping dragon...'Beware the green dragon!'" she whispered, her eyes growing large. The pounding of her heart rang in her head as the vivid memory came flooding back to her. Stopping in her tracks, she became aware of her father's and Michael's puzzled, hopeful glances.

"In the *dalang's* play—evil forces were chasing the princess and the *dalang* warned about a green dragon sleeping." Samille sank into a chair and distractedly pulled at her plait. "There was more, but I can't remember."

"The *dalang*?"

"The word refers to a Malay shaman, Michael. My friend Penang used to take me to the *dalang's* hut for the shadow-play." Seeing their confused looks, Samille hastened to explain. "The shadow-play is done with puppets. The *dalang* manipulates the puppets, but the audience doesn't watch the puppets. Instead, one watches the puppets' shadows upon a wall. Not long before I left Singapore, Penang took me once again to the *dalang's* hut. She always seemed to feel the shadows were foretelling my future. The last time, evil figures were chasing a princess, who met up with two good figures, but she was still not out of danger because of the green dragon."

She lifted her eyes to Michael O'Grady's face, saw the hope drain from her father's friend as he buried his face in his hands.

"I'm sorry, Michael. I know it doesn't help us."

Michael raised his face suddenly from his hands, a gleam lighting his tired eyes.

"Samille, do you still have those sketchbooks of your grandfather's?" At her uncomprehending nod, he continued, "it seems to me he did some sketches for some brooches—or pendants—pieces with a distinctive, Oriental flair."

Her father scratched his chin thoughtfully.

"If you will get the sketchbooks for Michael, please, Samille, I will see if I can contact Banks and James—your grandparents' solicitors. I'm virtually certain the original founders—old Banks and James—have long since retired, but if they are still in San Francisco, it is possible they can be of help. They knew the Beauvoirs for a long time. Perhaps our tale will strike a chord of memory."

Samille rang for Soon Lee and told him of the letter. He helped her carry her grandfather's sketchbooks from the study, and then together she pored over them with

Michael O'Grady. Professor Langley poked his head into the room a half-hour later.

"We're in luck. Mr. James is out of town, but I've made arrangements for us to lunch with Mr. Banks at the Palace today."

"Here!" Michael exclaimed, lifting the book he held so they might all see. The sketched piece was indeed a brooch—the barest outline of a dragon, wings furled with diamond eyes and gold flames escaping the mouth. Beneath it was scrawled a scribbled notation.

Fine-winged brows nearly meeting in her fierce concentration, Samille frowned.

"I don't ever remember seeing such a pin. Father?"

"Are you quite certain?" Michael's voice, barely controlled, raked her with its raw emotion.

She shrugged helplessly. "Is it among Mother's jewelry?"

The professor shook his head decisively.

"I'm sorry, Michael. I'd not forget something so exotic, but I'll look again to be sure."

Shoulders slumping with defeat, Michael pushed the book away. Samille picked it up and peered closely at the sketch. It seemed tantalizingly familiar, although she'd never seen the brooch or its like before. Idly, she glanced at the sketch again and tilted the sketchbook into the light in order to examine the scribbled note better. She straightened abruptly.

"Father! Look at this!" She held up the sketch again. "It says here, *for Samille*. How could Grandfather Beauvoir have designed this for me when he died before ever I was born?"

Eyebrows arching in astonishment, Samuel pursed his lips and let out a long breath as he considered.

"I'd forgotten, my dear. Your mother and your grandmother chose your name. Samille was Françoise's own grandmother. *Père* Beauvoir must have made the brooch for his mother-in-law. She lived in this very house. It was only after her death that Françoise and her parents went to live in Paris."

Exasperatedly, Michael shoved back his chair and stood.

"That's all very well, Samuel, but it gets us nowhere further along, does it? Three deceased women, a daughter who knows nothing, and my own daughter—!" He stopped, looked aghast from one stricken face to the other. "Forgive me, I don't know what I'm saying. Perhaps I'll go home after all. I'll change and meet you at the Palace.

"But, Samuel, I feel you should be warned I've made up my mind to catch the first steamer to Asia. Once the authorities are alerted in Singapore, perhaps they'll be able to find my Eleanor and Jane."

Samuel regarded his friend steadily.

"I've already seen to it, Michael. A wire was sent to Nathanial Hawkins this morning, advising him of the situation and asking him to spare no expense, but to make use of his contacts, the local constabulary, the British government, and anyone else he can think of to discover their destination and whereabouts."

The professor's longtime friend paled, swallowed hard.

"Thank you, Samuel. I'll see you at noon."

"Yes, yes, yes. I see, I see." Old Mr. Banks, eighty-seven years old and as dry and thin as eucalyptus bark, nodded his head so fiercely Samille feared it would roll from his shoulders. "Let me think a moment, Professor Langley, let me think."

Samille and her father had met Michael O'Grady promptly at noon outside the Palace Hotel. Inside, they'd found Mr. Joshua Banks and his nephew, young Mr. Oliver Banks, sixtyish, already seated at a table. Joining them, Samuel succinctly recounted the events which had led to his telephone call to the offices of Banks and James this morning. Samille held her breath as the elderly lawyer considered their story, closing his eyes in concentration.

The senior Mr. Banks' eyes were closed so long, his bald pate with its ring of neatly-clipped white hair bowed over his clasped hands, she began to fear he'd fallen asleep, or worse. Michael cleared his throat. Samille was relieved to see her father's best friend had recovered some of his usual ruddy color, though his round face was un-smiling, and his worry and anxiety were ill-concealed. The old man jerked his head up.

"A beautiful woman she was. Wore those Chinese silks like royalty, she did. With gold combs in her great mass of black hair. Green eyes glowing like gemstones. No wonder he lost his head." He caught Samille's eye on him and snorted, pointing at her with a bony index finger.

"Rather like you, young lady. What'd you say your name is, eh?"

"Samille, Mr. Banks."

He snorted again.

"Why, Samille was her name, too!"

"Ahem," young Oliver Banks interjected, "they know, Uncle. Perhaps...."

Oliver Banks, Samille saw, would be a carbon-copy of his uncle in a few years' time. His hair was just thinning on top, and his eyes masked the slightest twinkle. His mild impatience was tempered by an obvious affection for the old man.

"What? Yes. Treasure, you say? Green dragon, what? No, I'm afraid I can't help you there."

Acutely disappointed, Samille exchanged miserable glances with her father and Michael. A long silence ensued, and then Samille prompted the elderly man musingly, encouragingly.

"You must have been only a very young man at the time, Mr. Banks, but you seem to remember my great-grandmother quite well."

His pale, blue-washed eyes fairly snapped with pleasure.

"I never forget a beautiful woman, m'dear young lady. My father was solicitor to your great-grandfather, Captain Andrew Hooper Winslow. Captain Winslow plied the Orient from San Francisco to Shanghai and back again—silks and spices and woods—a highly profitable trade. On his next-to-last run, he brought her back with him.

"She was the daughter of a Chinese woman, a member of some great merchant's house at Peking, and a French merchant. Her mother was disowned for marrying a foreigner, and her husband took her and their daughter—the first Samille—to Shanghai. It's where Captain Winslow met and married her."

The frail old man fell silent.

"And Captain Winslow brought her to San Francisco," Samille prompted him gently.

He nodded abruptly and drank thirstily from his glass of water.

"Aye, he did. Built her a fine house on Fillmore—er, no—"

"Divisadero Street, Uncle," Oliver Banks murmured.

"What's that you say? Divisadero Street? They know that. Live there now, Oliver. Really, your wits are getting soft, young man. Not too built up in those days, you know. Pretty house. Shame he didn't get to enjoy it."

Michael stirred restlessly.

"Why, what happened to the captain?"

"Why," Joshua Banks eyed Michael peevishly, "I was just getting to that part of the story. The old mandarin was on his death-bed and called his grand-daughter Samille home to receive her inheritance.

"The captain returned with her, of course. But he took sick—some heathen illness—and died on the voyage back. She came home with his body, a widow with a young babe of her own to raise. Did well for herself, too."

"And the inheritance?" Michael asked eagerly, leaning forward as if he could drag the information from the old man.

"Pah!" Surprisingly, Joshua Banks wheezed with indignation still. "Inheritance, my foot! Never heard of such a fool thing. But those Chinese, they're big on their ancestors, you know. No, no, no. No money. Nothing at all like that. Gave her a trinket, the old man did. A flat green stone, if I remember correctly, strung on a thin golden wire. Not even worth insuring. Sentimental value, I suppose."

Samille's hand crept to her neck, and then, remembering, she felt in her pocket, withdrew her necklace, and lay it on the table before the old lawyer. He poked at it with his finger, darting an abashed glance at his nephew. Oliver Banks reached into his coat and withdrew a case, taking from it a pair of spectacles which he handed to his uncle.

"Vain old cuss," he murmured as his uncle examined the necklace.

"Same piece, on my oath. Funny looking thing, isn't it?"

Joshua Banks wheezed again, and then shook with a coughing spasm. His strength, which had carried him through their luncheon and his tale, now ebbed visibly.

"I'm sorry we couldn't be of more help," his nephew apologized, rising quickly to assist his uncle, "but I must get my uncle home now. If there is anything else we can do for you, please don't hesitate to call."

Samille's father stirred and spoke for the first time since the old man had begun to speak.

"You've been extremely helpful, both of you. We're most grateful. Before you go, there is one more question. The first Samille, the captain's wife—do you recall her mother's family name?"

"No," old Mr. Banks shook his head weakly, "no, I can't recall it. Well, Oliver?"

Young Mr. Banks gave his arm to his uncle and they made their farewells.

Once more ensconced in the parlor of the house on Divisadero Street, Samuel and his friend curiously examined Samille's necklace. It was a thin jade rectangle, approximately two inches long, an inch and a half wide, and barely a quarter-inch thick. A hole had been drilled in one end through which the gold cord had been passed. The cord appeared to have been a continuous wire, with no obvious linkages. Ingeniously crafted, it had worn through at one point and thus broken when Samille had caught her fingers in it.

"The old mandarin, as the elder Mr. Banks called him, gave this to the first Samille, who passed it on to her daughter—your grandmother, who gave it in turn to Françoise, your mother."

"Who gave it to me... on our voyage to Singapore," Samille finished for Michael as he recited the passage of the necklace from one generation to the next. "Mother said I was old enough to have it, as *Grandmère* had given it to her when she was my age."

"It's a peculiar type of ornament, wouldn't you say, Samuel?" Michael O'Grady ran his fingers over the surface of the polished thin stone. "I say, do you have a piece of paper and a stick of charcoal handy from your drawings, my dear?"

Baffled, Samille fetched the items from the study and watched curiously as the rotund Irishman placed the paper over the jade tablet and rubbed gently over the paper with her charcoal.

Samille gasped in astonishment. The unmistakable outline of a dragon's head emerged beneath Michael's fingers, one startling like the drawing her grandfather had created.

"I never really looked at it, not in all these years I've worn it. I suppose because of the circumstances," Samille held the necklace wonderingly in her hand, "but I often touched it, clutched it for comfort sometimes. And I must have felt the figure. My fingers recognized the shape. All those dreams of a green dragon!"

Soon Lee appeared in the doorway.

"Professor, telephone call for you."

Samuel Langley was gone only a moment.

"That was Oliver Banks," he informed Samille and Michael. "A resourceful man. It occurred to him that the firm might have some papers in storage that would provide an answer to my question.

"Samille Winslow's mother was born into the House of Chuang."

"Wei-chu!" Michael and Samille cried in unison.

"Yes." Her father seated himself, raked a hand through his hair. "We've discovered the green dragon—a tangible link to Wei-chu—and the secret the House of Chuang passed from generation to generation. But Banks was right. By itself, the necklace certainly doesn't constitute a treasure. Surely its sentimental value wouldn't drive Wei-chu to such acts of desperation. It must be a clue. But a clue to what? What can it mean?"

"I can think of one person who may be able to tell us, Father." Samille spoke slowly, painfully. Beads of perspiration stood out on her brow. If there was one thing she had never thought to do in her life, it was to willingly suggest she return to Singapore.

"Yen-shu." Michael supplied the name. "The old apothecary in Singapore."

"Yes, Michael."

"No, Samille," her father's voice was hoarse. He understood all too well what was in her mind. "You can't. It's too dangerous for you to return to Singapore!"

Samille went quickly to him, grasped his hands with hers.

"You aren't thinking clearly, Father. There's no risk at all to me. Wei-chu's men could have easily kidnapped me instead of Aunt Jane and Lennie. Wei-chu knows something of the green dragon, but it's obvious he's as frustrated as we are. He can't use the clue any more than we can at this point.

"We can't afford to waste any time, Father, in case he changes his mind and decides he can do better than us at finding the treasure. Then he'd have no need of hostages."

Professor Langley flinched at the brutal honesty of her logic. At last he sighed and met her eyes.

"Let me wire Nathanial Hawkins first, please, Samille. He could speak to Yen-shu for us, and then if necessary, make arrangements for us in Singapore."

He raised a brow at his daughter, and then looked to Michael, who acquiesced with a terse nod.

The burly editor of the *Straits' Times* responded the same evening with a wire of his own: *Have alerted my network. Will attempt to discover whereabouts of hostages. Yen-shu no longer in Singapore. Stop. Further requests? Stop. Nathanial Hawkins.*

Two pairs of green eyes regarded her gravely. Samille stared at the portrait of her mother and grandmother and reached out a tentative finger to trace the line of her mother's neck. The thin gold line nearly obscured by the heavy braid was not an artifice of the artist but a representation of reality, she recognized now. Françoise had worn the necklace in the portrait. Had worn it, in fact, until the day she took it off and placed it around her daughter's neck to distract her from their frightening voyage. Equally clearly, Françoise had not known what it meant to Wei-chu Chuang.

Yen-shu, she faced the thought squarely, must have seen the necklace on any number of occasions. He must have known, too, what it meant and who she was, and, later, why Wei-chu wanted her. But, equally certain, Wei-chu hadn't known she had the necklace. The tong leader must have suspected she could speak when he had commanded Yen-shu to relinquish her, hoping he could force the secret from her.145

Her master, Samille saw clearly now, had known of the green dragon. She recalled his whispered words to her the night she had spoken to him of her plans to leave Singapore. Yet, he had not given her up to his powerful kinsman and had not divulged the secret of the green dragon. Why?

"I'm going to China, Father."

Samille turned about as she spoke to face her father, who put down the book on Chinese history and legends through which he'd been leafing.

"Yen-shu always meant to return to his village in China one day, Father. He must have done so."

As her father said nothing, Samille crossed the room to him, leaned both palms upon his desk and pleaded with him, her low-pitched voice intense.

"I can't sit here and do nothing, Father! You must see that. Mr. Hawkins is an influential and resourceful man." Studiously, she avoided mentioning Benjamin, "but he's not in San Francisco. He's in Singapore. You can't begin to imagine Wei-chu's power there. Aunt Jane and Lennie could be anywhere in the city from his ship chandlery store in the city proper to his villa on the Serangoon Road, or anywhere in the South China Seas, for that matter.

"Yen-shu is our last hope to solve this riddle, Father, and there's no one left to find him except you and I. You know as well as I do Michael has his mind set on joining Benjamin's uncle."

Professor Langley tapped a page in the book before him.

"This is an interesting book, Samille. Were you aware the Chinese believe jade has magical powers? Royalty often had fabulous trinkets and carvings done in jade."

As Samille gaped at her father in dismay, he covered her hand with his in a powerful grip.

"Yes, my dearest daughter, I heard every word you said. I think it best, Samille, if I accompany Michael to Singapore. He's holding himself together on sheer nerves at the moment, but it cannot last.

"You, on the other hand, will be accompanied to China by Soon Lee. I understand he spent several years in Peking and its environs as a child. He speaks the local dialects, knows the countryside, its people, and its customs. He's fairly certain he can locate Yen-shu's village since a branch of the family is established here in San Francisco. They've given him the names of several villages where the old man may be found.

"If you fail to locate your former master within a month of your arrival, then you must wire us immediately and come to us in Singapore. If all else fails, we will simply go to Wei-chu, give him the necklace, and throw ourselves on his mercy."

"Oh Father!" Samille attempted a smile, but could not summon one. "I do so love you, Father, with all my heart."

He patted her hand gently.

"I know you do, my dear." He hesitated. "But, if anything should happen to me—hush!" He held up a hand reprovingly as she shook her head in vehement denial, "you mustn't shut yourself away from life—away from loving, Samille. Promise me!"

Tears swimming in her eyes, she replied huskily.

"I promise."

"Then you'd better pack now, dear. We leave in two days' time for Yokohama. There you and Soon Lee and Michael and I shall go our separate ways."

Samille packed quickly. She would need a few conventional dresses, shirtwaists, and skirts for travel, but at the bottom of her small trunk she packed her coolie trousers and tunics, her slippers, and her broad-brimmed hat. Once they began their search for Yen-shu in the countryside, she would travel more easily as a Chinese peasant rather than as a foreign white woman. Her task complete, she sat on her bed and covered her eyes with her hands.

Her father was so wise and worldly in many ways, but he had not lived among the Chinese for all those long years. He could not guess that Wei-chu simply would not accept failure on their part. If she should fail in her quest to find this mysterious treasure, they would never see her aunt or Lennie again. If only Benjamin—! She halted her line of thought abruptly, biting her lip. She was on her own this time. She and Soon Lee would have to manage. She offered up a prayer then, a prayer to her mother and grandmother, to the first Samille—that their love would guide her in her hour of need. Please, God, she prayed, let me be in time.

Chapter 10

At the light tap on her back, Samille slowly lifted her face from the mud of the ditch into which she and Soon Lee had scrambled what seemed ages ago, but must surely have been no more than a quarter of an hour earlier. The riders were gone. Samille clambered out of the ditch behind Soon Lee, who led her away from the road into the sparse cover offered by a few pines and boulders. Her companion dropped to the ground. Samille drank thirstily from a canteen carried concealed under her jacket, and then passed it to Soon Lee with a tired grimace.

"We rest, Missy Sam. Sleep."

Stretching out on the ground next to Soon Lee, Samille rested as ordered but found she was too exhausted for her mind to give in to the need for sleep. Two weeks' ago, they'd disembarked at the port of Taku and traveled thence to Tientsin and on to Peking with a growing sense of uneasiness and apprehension. It was pathetically apparent a state of economic and political chaos afflicted China. Only Samille's insistence that she was on her way to join relatives in the foreign legation at Peking kept several well-meaning British officers at the port of Weihaiwei from sending her back to Shanghai and on to Yokohama, instead of on to Taku and entry into China.

Once in Peking, she'd contacted a French government official who had known her father during their years in Paris. Monsieur Brevart, a widower, was expecting them and reluctantly allowed her to store her trunk in his lodgings after his repeated attempts to dissuade Samille from her course of action failed. For two days, Soon Lee secured supplies and met with his own contacts, narrowing the focus of their search to a scattering of villages to the south and west of Peking. Samille spent those two days limbering her body, partly to physically prepare for the rigors of the road, and partly to take her mind from the enormity of the task which faced them.

Had her old master returned to China? Could they find his village? And, most importantly, would he be able to help them? Samille tried not to think of time slipping away, of her Aunt Jane and Lennie captives and frightened in Singapore. In the third cold dawn, two rough Chinese peasants crept from the city and blended into the early morning traffic heading south.

As Monsieur Brevart so forceful pointed out, the countryside was no place for a foreigner to be caught these days. Bands of fierce young men roved the provinces beyond the Imperial City. Violently xenophobic and anti-Christian, they formed the core of the *I Ho Chuan*—the 'Righteous Harmony Fists' or Boxers, whose name was taken from the boxing-like dance they performed to gain spiritual powers which they believed would protect them from harm. A Boxers' uprising had occurred in the past year, and it was clear as Samille and Soon Lee made their way from village to village that the Boxers' power had not been quelled in the countryside.

Conspicuously, Soon Lee wore the red headband of the rebels and had provided Samille with a once brightly colored, oversized jacket flaunting the fading character for courage on the back. On those occasions when they were not able to avoid contact with other travelers, he explained her as his elder brother, dimwitted from a head wound sustained in the previous year's uprising. Her head wrapped in a dirty turban and her face streaked with grime, Samille would screech inarticulately at such times and brandish a stick with a red rag tied to it like a sword.

Soon Lee would restrain her and repeat he was taking his elder brother home to his father's village. Luckily for them, only twice had they been put to the test. Both times, after loud guffaws and much encouragement, the bands of Boxers moved on, leaving them sick with relief but unmolested.

Easing her shoulder against the rocky ground, Samille thought with regret of the straw pallet that had been her bed the night before. They had visited a total of four villages now with no sign of Yen-shu or anyone with any knowledge of him. Although he said little, Samille was aware it was only her determination keeping Soon Lee searching. He was increasingly afraid for her and would have willingly returned with all speed to Peking. One more village remained of those suggested by Soon Lee's contacts—a day's walk from their present location. She guessed they were roughly eighty miles from the capital, their route taking them steadily south and west of the city. She forced her eyes closed against the wan, chill daylight. They must find Yen-shu. They must not fail. They must not.

Following the River Wei, they traveled another three hours after their rest until nightfall, taking refuge in a shallow cave. Dried beef brought from San Francisco and hard bread made an unpalatable, but necessarily cold supper, for they'd agreed it was best not to light a fire. The countryside held other dangers, among them brigands who would not be swayed by a red headband and an imaginary sword. The pistol, lying close to hand by Soon Lee, was real enough, although Samille fervently hoped they would have no need of it.

Cold and stiff after a morning repeat of their evening meal, Soon Lee and Samille set off for the village of Shang Tsao well within Shansi Province. By mutual, unspoken consent, they kept a pace bespeaking a peculiar sense of urgency that had driven them since they woke. At midday, they barely slowed for their noon meal. Well before sundown they came within sight of Shang Tsao. Having met no threatening bands of Boxers or brigands along the road, they'd made good time, and yet, if anything, the taut feeling of imminent disaster was heightened, not lessened by the emptiness of the landscape. Samille's head sang with an interior, frenzied refrain of 'hurry... hurry... hurry' before it was too late. Too late for what? Or for whom? She quickened her pace to a near-trot to keep up with Soon Lee.

Samille put a hand on her companion's arm as they threaded their way between walled compounds to the hard-packed earth of the central village plaza.

"Soon Lee," she whispered nervously, "where is everyone? Why are the fields and lanes deserted?"

Soon Lee looked around and shrugged, but made no other answer. They rounded the corner of another walled compound and stopped at the edge of the village plaza. Three gray-bearded men huddled together in the center of the space, arguing loudly with many gestures at an ox. Soon Lee took Samille's arm and pulled her along beside him, her head cast down, her stick trailing in the dirt as they approached the tableau. The elders' argument broke off at the sight of the two newcomers. Politely, Soon Lee bowed and began the lengthy process of establishing their identities and seeking information about Yen-shu. Their story was that Soon Lee was hoping the old apothecary's medicine could cure his elder brother.

Head bowed throughout the interchange, Samille held her stick and stood at attention, outwardly docile and patient, beside the younger man. No one attempted to speak to her, so apparently their story was accepted. Where, she wondered as she waited for Soon Lee to finish, were the young men of the village? A thunderous impatience to be off filled her. Almost as if he felt the same driving need, Soon Lee grasped her sleeve once more and tugged her in the direction of a small compound on the edge of the plaza. One old man guided them, the other two resuming their quarrel with a fresh, shrill vigor.

Looking about surreptitiously as they entered the main dwelling of the compound, Samille noted the charcoal brazier blazing in the dim room into which they were ushered. Perhaps their host felt the chill in his old bones. The man clapped his hands loudly. A young girl scurried into the chamber, a wailing child in her arms. The old man spoke sharply to her. She bent immediately to place the infant into a basket. The young mother produced a plaything to divert the baby's attention, for it ceased to cry. The girl darted frequent glances from large dark eyes from the old man—perhaps her father-in-law—to the infant as she prepared tea for them. Thin wrists extended from her sleeves as she set a tray laden with cups before them. The old man gestured once more and his daughter-in-law went out quickly with only a backward glance at the basket where the baby still fussed intermittently.

Soon Lee questioned their host. The elder replied at length. Samille looked around to find the baby restlessly sleeping, its toy forgotten. The old Chinese man shook his head sharply, negatively, and repeated the gesture. He called out querulously. A moment passed. He rose agitatedly and with much bowing and gesturing, left the chamber. Soon Lee turned to Samille, speaking quickly and quietly.

"Missy Sam, Kwai-Lin full of fear. He say *I Ho Chuan* stir up the young men of Shang Tsao. Much trouble. He say we go back."

"What about Yen-shu?" she insisted. "Has he any knowledge of such a one?"

Soon Lee shook his head.

"It is strange, Missy Sam. He will not say yes or no. He say only we must go back. He will shelter us and feed us tonight, but tomorrow we must leave here."

Troubled, Samille thought over his words.

"Try again to find out about Yen-shu, Soon Lee. We must know! Tell the old one if he will tell us, we will do as he says."

"I try, Missy Sam."

Kwai-Lin's high-pitched quavering voice could be heard through the doorway. A whimper came from the basket. Samille padded over to the infant. Bright, solemn eyes met her own. Gently smiling, she retrieved the child's plaything. A square of paper tied with a red string, it rattled as she dangled it before the baby. Her hand froze. Curiously, she brought the packet to her nose and sniffed it. Quickly she opened it, certain of what she would find. She knew this mixture—had ground the ingredients to prepare it many times under her master's watchful eye. Mothers swore by it to soothe the pain of a teething child.

"Soon Lee!" she hissed. "Look at this!"

Kwai-Lin shuffled in, his daughter-in-law trailing behind him with an armful of firewood. The old man's angry chattering ceased abruptly as he caught sight of the packet in Soon Lee's hand. Then a spate of Chinese burst from him. Over and over he repeated something. At length, Soon Lee turned to Samille, his expression bleak.

Her heart sank. He bowed to Kwai-Lin and led Samille from the chamber. Once outside in the courtyard, he drew her to one side and spoke urgently.

"Kwai-Lin say, Missy Sam, there is such a one as we seek in Shang Jiao Cun, the village south of here in the flowering valley. But, he say we not only persons seeking Yen-shu. He say two-three weeks ago, a young foreign devil came asking for the apothecary. He go to Shang Jiao Cun. But, much trouble follow. The *I Ho Chuan* hear of this foreigner and they come some days ago to Shang Jiao Cun to kill him—to kill him and the old man who welcomed the foreigner into his house.

"And this is where the young men of Shang Tsao are. They go to see the foreign-devil be killed. Kwai-Lin say we must not go near the village. We will be killed if we try to interfere. He does not want Yen-shu killed—the apothecary has helped his grandson, but Kwai-Lin cannot help us. He cannot stand before the Boxers."

Samille lifted fear-filled emerald eyes to Soon Lee.

"Who else would come seeking Yen-shu? Wei-chu wouldn't send a foreigner." A memory came back to her, of a terrace in the moonlight and Benjamin telling her he had an old friend to look up. Her heart constricted.

"Benjamin?" she whispered, horror filling her face.

"I fear so, Missy Sam."

Peering cautiously through a cleft in the rocks behind which she and Soon Lee had taken cover, Samille observed the lay-out of the village below them. As the old grandfather Kwai-Lin had told Soon Lee, Shang Jiao Cun spread out on the plain before the gentle southern slope of Mount Li—one of the small, isolated hills common to the region. Harvested millet fields radiated around the environs of the village, crisscrossed by a network of irrigation ditches and levees banking the River Wei.

Soon Lee touched Samille's arm. In the northernmost quadrant of Shang Jiao Cun, a ragtail mob lounged before an imposing, gated compound. From the height of their vantage point, they could see into the interior of the compound. No one stirred within, and the mob outside made no effort to attack as they watched.

"Missy Sam," Soon Lee gestured at the scene below, "maybe there is a way to reach the compound."

Together they slithered down from their perch. Soon Lee sat back on his heels, and, taking up a stick, outlined his plan in the dirt. A shiver touched her spine. Tersely, Samille nodded her agreement, and then curled up into a ball. Soon Lee would watch the scene below and wake her later so he might rest and she watch, taking turns until the night came on. It just might work, she reflected. Her young companion had proven over and over again on this trip his quick intelligence, his ability to think fast and forestall trouble. With his uncomplaining endurance and quiet humor—he often entertained her in their evenings by telling her wicked stories about the forays of tourists into San Francisco's Chinatown—he had set an example she found herself hard put to meet. Back home in San Francisco, she wondered, to what purpose would he direct his intelligence and energy once he was free from this quixotic pursuit? As a Chinese, she realized shamefully, his options were limited. Maybe her father could sponsor further study if Soon Lee wished? If, she thought grimly, she was once more reunited with her father. No! She must not allow herself to be defeated by her own lack of faith. Determinedly, she closed her eyes, willing sleep to still her mind's turmoil.

Following Soon Lee's lead, Samille fastened her bundle around her neck, and then, keeping as low a profile as possible, eased over the side and into an irrigation ditch. The cold, thick mud sucked at her feet as she inched forward in Soon Lee's wake. The ditch they'd entered ran just north of the village of Shang Jiao Cun. With any luck at all, they would be able to travel beyond the beleaguered compound and approach it from the opposite direction. Undoubtedly, the Boxers would have a man patrolling the perimeter of the compound, but she and Soon Lee would just have to deal with such an obstacle if and when it presented itself. One foot dragged free of the muck, and then the other. Samille found their slow progress nerve-wracking, but it gave her a point of concentration. Why did the *I Ho Chuan* wait? Why hadn't they breached the defenses of one elderly man and his foreign companion?

There, she could see the bobbing of lights ahead. They were quite close now to the village. Soon they would be beyond it, when they could leave the obscurity and protection of the ditch to make their final approach to her old master's compound.

Samille caught the sound of the first bare scrape of a boot against the ground and flattened herself even further into a patch of shadow—fear sour in her throat. The single man on patrol carried a torch, and by its light, she had a quick glimpse of a brawny figure. A soft thud reached her. Cautiously, she lifted her head, jumped up, and sprinted to where Soon Lee bent over the patrol's unconscious form. Binding the man's hands and feet with their red strips of cloth, they gagged him for good measure and dragged his unresisting body into the shadows.

With an agile leap, Soon Lee clung precariously to the wall for a heart-stopping moment, and then he swarmed up it in less time than it took his companion to find her first toehold. Draped across the top, the young Chinese leaned over and grasped Samille's upper arm as she painfully sought to pull herself up. He hauled her over the top and dropped her inside the compound. Samille fell heavily onto hard-packed earth with an involuntary grunt, Soon Lee landing like a cat on all fours beside her. Keeping low, they ran single-file across the open, darkened courtyard to the main door of the compound. Samille looked at Soon Lee. She could just make out his features. He rapped softly on the wooden door as Samille called in a low voice.

"Yen-shu? Open the door!"

Silence. Louder, a hint of desperation clouding her voice.

"Yen-shu? Benjamin? Let us in. Quickly, it's the Sparrow. I've come with Soon Lee."

The door opened inward suddenly and Samille toppled inside, Soon Lee sliding in beside her as the door was closed equally swiftly. Two strong hands lifted her to her knees. In the weak light of a flickering candle flame, Samille looked up into the startled azure eyes of Benjamin T. Greaves.

Somehow, without being aware of moving, she was on her feet and in a stranglehold of arms, hers about Benjamin and his arms crushing her to him for a fierce, breathless moment, and then he set her on her feet again.

"Thank heavens you've come, Sparrow! Perhaps you can save him, if only for the Boxers to finish!"

Benjamin's strained, grim voice shattered the bemusement which had settled over her—partly from the chill pervading her bones and seemingly her brain, and partly from the sheer overwhelming joy of finding Benjamin alive.

"Yen-shu?" The name of her old master escaped her with a painful gasp. "He's hurt?"

Benjamin rubbed a weary hand through his hair and across his eyes.

"I wish to God I could say yes, Sparrow!"

"Benjamin! What do you mean?"

He was already turning away from the doorway and moving down a hallway.

"Honorable Yen-shu very sick, Missy Sam." Soon Lee materialized at her side.

"Where is he?"

Shaking off her weariness, Samille addressed the question to both men. Benjamin stepped back a pace.

"He's just through here."

Quickly, he led them farther down the hall to a room where a carefully-banked fire glowed. In the dancing firelight, Samille could just make out a tiny, shrunken form beneath a blanket. Her heart constricted. Lying with his eyes closed, Yen-shu's labored breaths barely stirred his covering. Kneeling beside him, she gently laid her palm against his cheek. The skin was so dry and hot she felt it would surely crack beneath her hand. He moved restlessly at her slight touch. Sick at heart, she joined Benjamin and Soon Lee by the fire.

"How long has he been like this, Benjamin?"

"He was coughing, weakened, when I came a week ago. I've been feeding him, then the fever began two days' ago. At first it simply drained his energy, but late this morning he became delirious. He hasn't spoken since this afternoon.

"I haven't known what to do." He brushed the fine blond hair back from his forehead in an oddly defeated, helpless gesture. "All his herbs and medicines are here, Sparrow, but I'm ignorant of their use and Yen-shu was too weak to direct me."

Samille took his cold hand in hers.

"Show me," she demanded.

Benjamin directed them to a small chamber down the hallway and adjacent to the kitchen. Closing her eyes for a moment, so transported did she feel at the sight of those neat rows of jars and roots and herbs, she felt she might open her eyes to find herself once more in the Singapore of her childhood. Samille breathed deeply.

"How can we help?" Benjamin, at her side, sounded eager and hopeful as she moved slowly along the shelves, choosing as she went.

"Grind these, Benjamin, one bunch at a time, very fine." She handed him a bunch of herbs. As he hesitated, she took in his drawn features.

"When did you last eat, love?"

Benjamin shook his head, one hesitant finger rubbing at his mustache.

"There was some rice—sometime yesterday, I think."

She glanced meaningfully at Soon Lee.

"I see what I can find, Missy Sam."

"Thank you, Soon Lee. Now these," she added some roots to the pile of material on the worktable before Benjamin, "chop coarsely, please."

Methodically, she assembled scales, mortars, pestles, and cloth, concentrating fiercely to conjure up those long-ago years, those days when Yen-shu demonstrated, and then watched hawk-like over her shoulder. Something was missing... yes! There, on the lower shelf. She ground a generous teaspoon of dried petals and added them to her mixture.

"Do you have hot water, Benjamin?" At his nod, she took up her precious cloth packet. "We'll steep this and see if we can get the tea down Yen-shu. If he takes enough.... If I've remembered correctly—oh, Benjamin!" Her fear overwhelmed her.

Benjamin put his arm about her shoulders in wordless encouragement, and she nodded.

"This should bring the fever down if we aren't too late."

A kettle was steaming on the brazier in Yen-shu's bedchamber. Within minutes, she held a cup of the strong, potent brew before her elderly master's sere lips as Benjamin cradled his weakened body gently. On their third try, his throat worked convulsively and he swallowed. Encouraged, they tried again and again until a scant half of the cup was downed. Benjamin eased the old man onto the bed, carefully covering him, and then took Samille's hand and led her in search of Soon Lee.

They found him in the kitchen, ladling soup into bowls. Covered steamer baskets gave off enticing aromas. Seated before the hearth, they ate ravenously as the hot food revived them. At length, Samille set aside her chopsticks and her bowl.

"I must check on Yen-shu and see if he can take more tea. Then, Benjamin, you'd better fill us in on the situation here."

He gave her a wry grin and rubbed the shadowed stubble of his chin.

"As you wish."

The old man still burned with fever, but this time she and Benjamin managed to get a full cup of tea down him. Yen-shu seemed less restless as they made him comfortable once more and moved away to the fire. His eyes fluttered open, but he did not try to speak. Benjamin fed a little coal into the brazier, sat down and eased his back against the wall, looking from Samille to Soon Lee.

"To be succinct, my dear, I came looking for Yen-shu after I left San Francisco. I felt certain he must know more of this puzzle than he'd confided to us. After all, as Wei-chu's cousin, it seemed likely he would simply have given you up as ordered.

"But, he risked his life and Sakai's to get you away from Wei-chu. This was my urgent business in Singapore, Samille." A ghostly grin flashed across his features and Samille was glad the firelight did not give away her blush. She was certain he was remembering the words she'd flung at him the night he'd told her he was returning to Singapore to find an old friend. Benjamin continued. "When I got back to Singapore, Yen-shu was gone. It took a while through Uncle Nate's contacts to find out where he might be in China.

"Once I was reasonably certain I could find him, I caught a steamer and made my way here. I made steady progress, except for the week I lost backtracking thanks to an old gentleman in the neighboring village of Shang Tsao. He sent me back toward Peking before I figured out he'd tried to keep me from continuing southward. I turned around and made directly for the next village south of Shang Tsao. I found Yen-shu here in Shang Jiao Cun. My arrival," he announced drily, raising one fine brow, "did not go unnoticed. Apparently, the local Boxers have decided to make an example of me and of poor old Yen-shu as well, for harboring a foreigner."

"Why haven't they mounted an assault on the compound? Soon Lee and I saw a mob of men outside the gate. Soon Lee took care of the Boxer who was patrolling your perimeter."

"I'm not entirely certain, my Sparrow. Yen-shu was weak when I came, but when we were first informed an attack was imminent, Yen-shu sent his apprentice into the village to say Yen-shu would summon a demon to awaken the dragon if the Boxers attacked. Then he had me carry him into the courtyard and strike a gong there while he shouted something in Chinese. A summoning spell, he told me.

"I think the effort overtaxed his failing strength, but it seems to have worked for the moment. Most of the Boxers appear to be local boys. But Wang, Yen-shu's apprentice, tells me there are strangers among them who have sent for reinforcements."

Samille and Soon Lee exchanged a quick glance. Benjamin looked from one to the other.

"It can't have been good news bringing you here so precipitously to me, Sparrow. And I see my tale of a dragon does not surprise either of you. Have you solved the mystery? Or has there been yet another catastrophe? Your father?" Alarm rang in his voice.

"Not my father, Benjamin. Wei-chu has taken Aunt Jane and Lennie hostage in exchange for the Green Dragon's treasure."

Carefully, she pulled her necklace on its mended golden cord free of her tunic and shared with Benjamin all that had happened since his departure from San Francisco.

"Yen-shu must hold the key. He referred to the green dragon before I left Singapore for America. I didn't understand at the time, I thought he probably meant Wei-chu's power." She glanced helplessly at her former master. To have come so far and still be thwarted in learning the truth of this strange matter! "If only, God willing, we can save him from both the fever and the Boxers!"

"How long," Soon Lee interposed, "does Wang say until more *I Ho Chuan* come to Shang Jiao Cun?"

"No more than a days' time. I'm afraid," Benjamin's sardonic blue eyes flared, "your ingenious method of arrival will not also see us to safety. To try and carry Yen-shu through an irrigation ditch would surely hasten his end. Let's hope we can think of another plan. Now, I suggest we take turns resting and dosing Yen-shu with his tea."

Shortly before daybreak, Samille woke sharply, aware she'd slept longer than was her intent. Benjamin stirred at Yen-shu's bed side.

"Yen-shu?" She sat up anxiously. Benjamin held up a hand.

"Soon Lee and I took care of him, Sparrow. He's resting easier."

Bending over the fragile old body of her master, Samille laid her palm to his forehead and reached quickly for his wrist, where she felt for his pulse. At length she replaced his hand under his blankets and turned away blindly, weeping silently. Benjamin's arms came around her across the old man's narrow bed.

"The fever's gone! I think he'll live." Relief choked her, and Benjamin's arms tightened. He rose unsteadily, guiding her across the chamber to the brazier's warmth. Brushing the long dark hair away from her eyes, he looked into a face that shone with relief and happiness and something else. His eyes widened and a pulse beat rapidly in his throat. Her own heartbeat quickened. Whatever he saw, felt leap between them, Benjamin pulled her roughly into his arms and claimed her for a kiss that seared their searching lips, their fast-held bodies, touching their souls with wonder and release.

Samille's knees gave as Benjamin lifted his head at last and time moved forward once more. With a throaty, uneven laugh, he sat and pulled her close. Her head tucked against the warm hollow of his neck and shoulder, he stroked the sleek dark head and murmured soft, incoherent expressions of love while she found herself able only to sigh, "Oh, Benjamin!" like one besotted and to hold him closer, if possible, until they lapsed into silence and were content to simply hold one another. At length he stirred and shifted her weight slightly as she raised her head to face him.

"Bejesus, my love! You scared the wits from me when you were only seventeen! I think I was already half in love with you then, but too stupid to understand."

"Hush!" she commanded. "You thought I had a school-girl's crush, but on my last night in Singapore, Benjamin, when you named yourself my friend... a shiver went through me. It was as if a shadow-play flashed before my eyes—showing me you would always be my friend—and more!"

He stopped her words, stealing a kiss from the corner of her mouth.

"I love you, Samille. More than life itself, but," he flashed a lopsided grin, "I'm hoping it won't come to that! Let's pray Yen-shu wakes by morning. He seems to feel there is hope. He kept mumbling about the dragon protecting her own. Let's hope he's right!"

Two hours later, when the morning sun lifted clear of the horizon, Yen-shu opened feeble eyes and attempted to sit up. Samille gently forced his shoulders back onto the pillows. His eyes widened at the sight of her. A ghost of a smile touched his face.

"Sparrow has done well."

Samille could barely catch the reedy whisper and bowed her folded hands.

"I had a most worthy teacher, Master." Soon Lee passed her a cup of steaming, fragrant broth. "You must eat now, Master, then rest."

By late afternoon, they had repeated their efforts over and over as the wizened old man slept and woke hourly. His dark eyes shone with intelligence once more and he managed to take an herbal measure Samille prepared to relieve his rasping breath and to clear his chest. After his last meal, Yen-shu motioned for them to come closer. Dark eyes swept the three arrayed about his bed—Samille, Benjamin, and Soon Lee. But before he could speak, the sound of soft padding footsteps reached them.

Soon Lee was on his feet with a swiftness that astonished Samille, instantly wary, but Benjamin stayed him with a firm hand on the younger man's arm. A boy of about twelve years of age, slight and wiry with quick black eyes stepped into the bedchamber. He bowed perfunctorily at the tall American, blinked in surprise at the sight of Soon Lee and Samille, and then came forward rapidly to Yen-shu's side.

"Master Wu, they are coming. More *I Ho Chuan*. By nightfall they will join their comrades here in Shang Jiao Cun to attack this compound."

Yen-shu lifted a thin hand to stroke the boy's bowed head.

"Thank you, young Master Wang. Now you must go to your grandfather in Shang Tsao and be an obedient son in his house."

A tremor ran through the boy. He lifted a tear-streaked face to the old man.

"I wish to stay, Master. Please do not send me away."

Yen-shu pointed a shaky finger at the boy.

"You must obey, Master Wang. You have been an excellent student, and you have acquired some small knowledge and skill. It must not be lost. Go. If it is permitted, I will once more be your master and watch your knowledge grow. Do you understand?"

Young Wang nodded miserably.

"Yes, Master. I hear and I will obey."

He bowed deeply to old Yen-shu, then to Benjamin, turned blindly and was gone as quickly as he'd come.

Yen-shu sighed, closed his eyes, and then opened them to beckon Samille, Benjamin, and Soon Lee forward.

"Closer. I am an old, tired man, and there is much to say." His bright eyes swept across them.

"You, Sparrow," his cracked voice faded. Yen-shu cleared his throat, took a sip of the tea that Soon Lee held to his lips, and continued, "you wear the sign of the Green Dragon." She lifted the jade tablet from its hiding place, slipped the cord from her neck, and placed it in the old apothecary's hand, closing his fingers about it.

"She has slept for hundreds upon hundreds of centuries, her secret guarded generation after generation by our family. The oldest daughter of each generation has worn her emblem." The old man's eyes closed and he fell silent.

"Whose emblem, Master?" Samille queried softly. The dark eyes opened.

"The Princess Dai—royal consort to a prince and ruler of all China two thousand years ago! She is the dragon princess and she will save her own."

Again, the thin, tired voice rasped to a halt. His sharp glance took in their bewildered faces. Only Soon Lee nodded.

"You shall see, my Sparrow. These are not the ramblings of a sick old man. We must rest until nightfall, and then I will reveal to you how the Green Dragon will guide us to freedom and safety.

"I will sleep, now." His eyes drooped and shut. His breathing slowed, steadied. He slept.

Chapter 11

Samille secured her packets of herbs carefully in Benjamin's knapsack. Her former master's insistence that the dragon princess would save them, on the face of it, seemed sheer folly, but his faith bespoke all doubts. In the event he did know of a way out of the compound and the village, he would have need of his remedies. Taking up her bundle, she met Soon Lee coming from the living quarters with a similar bundle of food, and joined Benjamin in the old man's sleeping chamber.

Impassively, the wizened, aged face of Yen-shu took in the pistol stuck in Soon Lee's sash, the rifle slung with a bedroll over Benjamin's shoulder, to Samille at Benjamin's side.

"Take up a lantern, each of you," he ordered.

Soon Lee knelt and lit three lanterns, passing two to his companions. The old Chinese apothecary nodded his satisfaction.

"We go."

Benjamin stooped over the bed and scooped up Yen-shu's featherweight body, wrapped the blanket securely about the old man, and stood easily.

"To the courtyard," the thin voice directed them, and once there, Yen-shu pointed to a disused well with its covering trellis rickety-looking, but surprisingly strong as Soon Lee leaned over the brim. A turgid gleam far below reflected his light.

"We go down," Yen-shu informed them. "Before the water, you will find a ledge. At the ledge, this side of the well, you will find bricks—not stone—bricks not mortared. Push them inside. They give onto a tunnel."

In the lantern light, Samille and Benjamin exchanged doubtful looks. Soon Lee handed his lantern to Samille and lowered himself even as the old man finished speaking. As Samille peered over the edge, holding the light for Soon Lee, she could see a series of rusty iron rungs set into the well wall.

Anxiously watching Soon Lee's descent, Samille gripped the trellis and held her lantern wide. In the dim shadows she could scarcely see Soon Lee's descending figure. Then she heard him grunt and caught the splash of something going into the water. Beside her, Benjamin tensed. Moments later, Soon Lee's head, considerably dirtier than when he'd started down the well shaft, appeared. His dark eyes glowed in the lantern light.

"The way is clear, honorable Grandfather."

Benjamin lay down his fragile bundle.

"There's rope in one of the outlying buildings. We'll rig a seat for Yen-shu. I'll lower him to you, Soon Lee, and then send down Samille. I'll undo the rope and come down last."

Soon Lee nodded, and Benjamin went in search of rope.

"It is a narrow way, Missy Sam," Soon Lee called softly up the well shaft. "I think roof may have fallen in part way. I did not go very far. But, air seems funny. Old, Missy. Tunnel very, very old."

Benjamin materialized out of the gloom, clutching a crisp length of half-inch diameter rope. Quickly, he looped the rope below Yen-shu's knees, then under his arms, creating a harness with the blanket folded to protect the old man's thin, brittle bones. As he worked, he caught Samille's green eyes wide in the lantern light. A faint grin played about his mouth.

"Ready?" Securing the rope to the well head, he picked up Yen-shu and dropped him gently over the coping, slowly paying out the rope to keep it from twining about and bumping the elderly apothecary against the stone wall of the well shaft. "Good," Benjamin nodded as Soon Lee reached up to grab Yen-shu and maneuver the precious bundle into the tunnel opening. "We'd better make tracks. Over the wall, my darling. I heard a great deal of activity beyond the gates. I've a feeling reinforcements have arrived sooner than expected."

Samille spared a rapid glance about. Their furtive activities had left very little trace about the well. Some disturbed dust on the trellis and coping were the only evidence. But, who would notice? Who would bother with an abandoned well in the frenzied search for the foreign devil?

A moment later she was on her way down, gingerly, because of the lantern. Halfway down, she passed her lantern to Soon Lee, and then reached up to take the light from Benjamin, who promptly slid over the coping to descend behind her. She felt for the next rung and met instead solid stone. A hand closed about her wrist and Soon Lee was guiding her into the opening he had made.

"This way, Missy Sam."

"Yes," she whispered, mindful of the sounds coming from above—faint shouts and pounding reached her. Then Benjamin's arm was about her as he clambered through the broken well wall behind her. As soon as he was in, he and Soon Lee set to restoring the wall of bricks as best they could. A gap was present where some of the bricks had fallen into the well, but there was nothing in the tunnel to use to stop up the hole. Soon Lee picked up a lantern and moved away down the tunnel, followed by Benjamin with Yen-shu. Samille, carrying the other lanterns, trailed behind her companions.

Dust clogged the narrow confines of the tunnel, dancing in the flickering light of the lanterns and swirling about them as they passed. Consisting of earthen walls shored up with timbers, the tunnel barely cleared Benjamin's head and constrained them to travel in single file. No sound reached them except for the rasping of their own breathing as they wended their way further into the dank, cold darkness. Samille strained her ears for any betraying sound of pursuit, but nothing came, and she concentrated on keeping her footing, on the reassuring sight of Benjamin's back in front of her—anything to block out the claustrophobic thought of this ancient tunnel caving in and entombing them alive far beneath the ground. Soon Lee was right—the air seemed queerly dead in the tunnel. Uneasily she eyed her lantern. The flame burned steadily; the flickering should have reassured her. The air might not be fresh, but the supply appeared constant. Where, she wondered uneasily, was this tunnel leading them?

A cough wracked Yen-shu after they'd advanced along the tunnel for some twenty minutes, Samille estimated. Benjamin halted as the coughing continued, calling softly to Soon Lee.

"I've covered his face, Samille, but the dust...," he shrugged, dropped to his knees and lowered Yen-shu gently to the tunnel floor. "Water, please."

Samille pulled a water bottle from Benjamin's knapsack and held it before her old master. Yen-shu drank deeply, slowly, and cleared his throat.

"Thank you, Sparrow." He gestured weakly at the tunnel. "The well wall collapsed once, long, long time ago. Our ancestors found this tunnel when they repaired the well wall. For these many generations now, we have guarded this way into the Dragon Princess's tomb."

Samille spoke thoughtfully.

"If this is so, honorable Grandfather, how is it the emblem of the Green Dragon Princess came into the hands of my family? And what of Wei-chu, who does not know this, but seeks even now the treasure of the Green

Dragon? He has taken my father's sister and a young friend hostage, Grandfather, that I should bring him this treasure to ransom their well-being."

Yen-shu bowed his head. When he lifted it, grief and shame and anger weighed his features.

"Our grandfather, Sparrow, had a younger brother who listened as their father lay dying and passed the secret to his eldest daughter and to our grandfather, who was the eldest son. The daughter went as a wife to a wealthy merchant in Peking, where her daughter married a seafaring captain. Our grandfather and his younger brother remained in Shang Jiao Cun. The younger brother's presence was discovered listening as his father lay dying, and thus he heard only that a sign of the Green Dragon's favor was held in sacred trust.

"From that time forward, he sought to possess the secret—"

"—and after him," Samille interrupted with cold certainty, "his own son, Wei-chu."

"Yes."

"And you, Yen-shu," she continued, "you knew the sign of the Green Dragon because you are the eldest son of an eldest son. And that is why you took me in when I took shelter in your doorway."

The old man nodded.

"It is so. You, my Sparrow, are the last living daughter of the eldest daughter." He reached out a hand to touch her cheek gently. "But I did not discover this until after you had been with us some days and Saki show me the necklace you wore. We had already decided, my Sparrow, to keep you with us."

Tears sparkled in her eyes, and Samille clasped his hand in hers.

"I 've been a most fortunate child. And I'm honored to call you Grandfather, Master Yen-shu."

"Shh!"

Benjamin's arms tightened around the old apothecary. Soon Lee squeezed past Benjamin, past Samille, and slipped back through the tunnel. Several tense moments later, he returned and shrugged.

"All is silent, Master Greaves. Some earth has fallen in our passing. We must not linger." He raised a brow. Yen-shu tugged his scarf once more over his nostrils, Benjamin picked up his light weight, and they moved off at a fast clip down the tunnel. Literally down, Samille noted. The tunnel perceptibly descended as they traveled farther along it. Small sounds seemed scattered, amplified by the darkness beyond their flickering lanterns, by their hurry, by the eerie unreality of their situation.

Samille tried not to think of pursuit, or of rats, or bats, or any other creatures roaming this dead way into the heart of the earth. She lost all track of time in their endless, desperate plunging descent. What if there were no way out? What if the tunnel roof crumbled behind them and they could not turn back? Panic rose, choking her, blinding her, and she lurched against Benjamin, nearly dropping her lantern as he came to an abrupt halt.

When she raised her eyes, her heart convulsed. A fall of earth blocked the way ahead. She sank to her knees in wordless despair.

"Closer, please," Yen-shu ordered and Soon Lee held a lantern to the wall of earth. "Here," Yen-shu pointed to Soon Lee, "dig, please."

Carefully setting his lantern down to shed light on his work space, Soon Lee dug into the soft earth with the point of his knife. It fell away easily. Several minutes later, his knife struck a stone. After he cleared the dirt away from it, Yen-shu arrested his hand when he would have pulled the stone free.

"Clear on either side, please."

Puzzled, the young man worked on one side while Benjamin laid down his bundle and took up the task on the other side. More stones were uncovered loose within the fall of dirt. The old Chinese man grunted.

"It is a roof fall—ancient disturbance. We can make a way to go through. Rest one at a time, eat and drink now. Soil loose. It not take long to break through to other side. Not far now."

He lay back limply on his blankets. Groaning, Samille put aside her lantern, and knelt by the dirt.

"I'll go first."

Sweaty with fatigue, Samille watched Benjamin's arm engulfed to the armpit. He spoke without stopping, breathless and eager.

"We've done it. A few more minutes and we're through!"

"We must make only a small hole," Yen-shu spoke up suddenly, firmly, "and it must be stopped up again from the other side. When we are ready, Sparrow, you must enter first."

"Yes, Grandfather."

Pushing the knapsack and her shoulders through the enlarged hole, Samille was vaguely aware of a sense of space opening around her—as though the tunnel were much larger here. Quickly she reached back for her lantern and turned.

"Samille? Sam!"

At the urgent call behind her, Samille tore her bewildered, awed gaze from the scene before her and stuck her face into the gap to find Benjamin's anxious features silhouetted on the other side. She opened her mouth, gestured helplessly, and turned away again.

"Soon Lee, your turn. Quickly!"

Samille heard the slithering of soil marking the young man's arrival, then a soft grunt from Yen-shu as Soon Lee took him from Benjamin's arms, and then the swift intake of breath from Benjamin. He took three long steps past her and held his lantern high.

Before them, in a vast silent chamber, row upon row of warriors marched into the distance, frozen in time, in space, in the yellow glare of lamplight—lit now as they had not been for century upon century. Far in the distance, older roof-falls half-covered even more figures. Wordlessly, Benjamin whistled and turned back to his companions. With Soon Lee, he chinked their opening from the tunnel with rocks, packing dirt about the rocks until Yen-shu nodded brusquely. Once more they took up their burdens, Benjamin carrying Yen-shu, and moved with wonder down a corridor between two rows of figures.

Upon closer inspection, Samille saw the soldiers were life-sized terracotta statues. And here! She stopped in amazement. Four small, sturdy horses pulled a chariot! So much were they like their long-dead counterparts, four sets of ears might have flicked forward and dark eyes gleamed as her breath came out in a gasp. The charioteer still stood, one hand extended to hold reins rotted ages ago; yet traces of green paint remained on his long jacket which had once been topped by bright red armor. Light purple trousers with green puttees met reddish-black shoes. A turban covered his head while black pupils stared sightlessly ahead. Eyebrows and a beard finished his face.

Yen-shu spoke quietly; his face reverent and grave in the shadowed light.

"Before us stretches the emperor's army protecting the Dragon Princess in death even as her warriors protected her during her lifetime. These are the foot soldiers and charioteers of the cavalry. It is said, before this emperor's reign, all who served the royal house went into death to serve them still, but two thousand years ago, the Dragon Princess was enlightened and would not have the lives of her people taken. It was decreed that each should follow her in spirit. Thus, an image of each was created." He gestured about them.

Soon Lee looked from one figure to another with awe.

"It is so, Grandfather. See, each face is different. Can this be so for all?"

As far as Samille could see, the figures stretched away before them. Benjamin pointed to a nearby figure wearing fancy armor and an elaborately braided, knotted hairstyle.

"An officer?" he guessed, and, as Yen-shu nodded, "cavalry, yes. See, there, they carry weapons for close-quarter combat. Swords and those?"

"*Jin gou*," Soon Lee supplied. "A crescent knife, designed with double blades to thrust and hook one's opponent."

Samille shuddered, remembering the small curved rice knives of the Malay sailors. The *jin gou* looked much more deadly. She moved closer to Benjamin.

"Grandfather," she began diffidently, "this is a great treasure, make no mistake, but surely it is impossible that Wei-chu would accept one of these statues, even if we could safely take a warrior from this place."

Yen-shu pointed with a shaky finger down the corridor ahead of them.

"We must go on, Sparrow, and enter the royal palace of the dead. Perhaps the Dragon Princess will hear our pleas and give us a token to ransom two fragile lives."

"Yes, Grandfather," Samille whispered, involuntarily glancing ahead of them down the long, darkness-enshrouded corridor between warriors. In the eerie silence she could almost feel a palpable force of intelligence and will emanating from the princess, as if she were well aware of the intruders. If a doorway to the outside world opened before them at that moment, she would have turned her back on it, so firmly was the need driving her to go forward, step after unwilling step.

As they moved on, faster now, Samille threw one furtive glance backwards, and then frowned. Had there been a flicker of movement behind them? She watched steadily for a long moment. The ranks of soldiers stared back unblinkingly. They were extremely lifelike. She shrugged. Fear was causing her to imagine things. Unable to completely dispel the shudder of unease creeping up her spine, she set off rapidly to catch up with the others.

Side corridors opened periodically from the one which they traversed, gaping dark holes, uninviting and filled with more troops—some engulfed by roof-falls, heads and limbs bizarrely visible in the rubble. Time seemed skewed down here. They might have been walking two thousand years into the past. Stumbling along in the wake of Benjamin and Yen-shu, Samille felt overwhelmed by the weight of the royal power manifested all about them. How many workers, for how many years had they labored to create these figures, and dig the massive tomb complex? Would they ever reach an end to this army?

As if in answer to her unspoken question, the foot soldiers gave way to a company of kneeling archers, crossbows deployed at ready. Ahead, Soon Lee hailed them, his voice cracking with excitement. The corridor in which they stood wound through a vast gate and disappeared. Samille craned her neck, but could not see the top of the massive walls to either side of the gate even when Benjamin held his lantern aloft. They entered the gate into the inner compound. Here, as elsewhere, the vagaries of time and man had caused a partial collapsing of the wall and roof of the tomb structures.

"Incredible!"

Samille's astonished gaze met Benjamin's. Yen-shu's sharp eyes softened.

"It is but part of the royal gardens. See—there is a seated soldier with a bird. And there," he explained, "the kneeling figure who feeds the deer. The royal palace would have had many such private parks for the pleasure of the princess."

Soon Lee started around another fall of earth, and then stepped back abruptly, his lantern held high with a shaking hand. Before them rose two towering bronze chariots with horses, flanking another gate set into an inner wall.

"They are the vehicles for the ghosts of the royal family," Yen-shu's thin voice barely penetrated the gloom. Only Benjamin seemed to suffer no nervous imaginings at the forbidding sight of the immense figures. With a last, stupefied glance, they passed between those fierce guardians and entered the first of a series of antechambers—chambers with brass rings from which silken drapes had once hung. Down the center of each chamber, lining the corridor, two rows of stiff warriors commanded their attention, bronze spears held at their sides. Samille counted sixty-four of the imperial guards by the time they stood before the final set of bronze doors.

"Wait!"

Samille put a trembling hand on Benjamin's back. Soon Lee rejoined them, eyes narrowed, his lips pursed. She bit her lip, her pupils wide in the flickering shadows playing across the tomb walls. Like the *dalang's* shadow-play, she had the sense they were but puppets upon some grand, eternal stage—a stage controlled by the long-sleeping presence stirring even now on the other side of those doors. A deep, chilling foreboding gripped her. She did not want to awaken the Green Dragon!

"I can't!" She whispered, "Please, Yen-shu...." Agitatedly Samille looked from Benjamin's alert, azure eyes, his features concerned, the mobile mouth and its blond mustache stilled, to the steady, unfathomable twin pools of intelligence marking the elderly apothecary's eyes, pleading for understanding.

"I can't disturb her rest. I can't!" Tears brimmed over. Screwing her eyes closed, she sniffed ineffectually, and then felt Benjamin's gentle arms gather her rigid, cold body into his comforting, warm embrace.

"Ah, but we can."

Samille stiffened, whirling about in Benjamin's arms.

Three armed men faced them—all Chinese and none that she recognized. All wore the red sign of the *I Ho Chuan*. The central figure, a short, rotund figure with a thin queue and thinner beard, indicated the tableau before him with his pistol and spat out an order. A second man, this one taller than the leader and younger with a smooth chin, stepped cautiously around Benjamin and motioned jerkily for the rifle. The third man, smaller and more wiry than his companions, pulled nervously at a wispy beard as Benjamin reluctantly released Samille and eased the weapon from his shoulder. The man in charge smiled coldly.

"Most wise, Foreign Devil. Now you, Miss. Open jacket wide so we may be assured no weapon lies concealed within."

Samille did as she was ordered, willing herself not to glance behind them.

"Most fortunate." The leader of the three stepped forward into the lamplight with his companion. His pale face gleamed with an unhealthy pallor save where the vivid slashing of his right cheek had left a red, puckered scar. His eyes were mere insolent slits. Dressed in dusty trousers and tunic, his red Boxer's badge was tied about his left arm. He gestured quickly once more. As he raised his hand, his sleeve fell back. Benjamin's fingers dug sharply into Samille's arms as the tattoo of a green dragon came into view. The man's eyes nearly disappeared in his amusement as he caught her slight, involuntary movement.

"Yes. We are to be feared far more than the *I Ho Chuan*!" He fairly spat the words out in contempt. "I am Ji Chou. We come to claim treasure for the leader of the Tong of the Green Dragon—Wei-Chu Chuang!"

Ji Chou's voice rose excitedly.

"You," his minions prodded Benjamin, "take up your burden. And you, English miss, open the gates to the Green Dragon's tomb!"

Warily, Samille turned as Benjamin stooped to gather up a silent, watchful Yen-shu. Her spirits lifted. Soon Lee was nowhere to be seen. Had he entered the tomb ahead of them? The doors before her sagged open. He could have easily slipped through. She put her hands to the heavy door and pushed, praying silently that Wei-chu's henchmen would not notice the third lantern and deduce that their party was short one member.

Within the tomb chamber, objects gleamed and were lost in the pale light of her single lantern. Huge pines and cypresses formed the walls and rafters of the room. Through the thin soles of her boots, she felt the hard brick floor, no longer simple packed earth. The ceiling bore reed and bamboo mats; how something so fragile had survived countless centuries, she could not guess, but there was a feeling here of power—immense and long-dormant, but now stirring.

Stumbling forward, she saw the sharp greenish patina of bronze vessels, here the dull gleam of gold reflected the light, and, there, iron tripods tilted crazily. Elaborate ornaments of gold, silver, and jade—brooches and paperweights and daggers and necklaces among other treasures—glinted among piles and piles of exquisite black-lacquered vases and pottery urns.

Dishes and cups, still bearing stains of the food and wine which had once filled them, sat upon fragile remnants of silken textiles. The tomb was enormous. Samille guessed wildly that thousands of objects filled the chamber. Her booted toes struck some object sent skimming across the bricks. With dismay she saw the bones of horses which had fallen within the shafts of the chariot they'd pulled in life. Her people had followed her in spirit, replicated in earthenware statues, but apparently the animals closest to her had suffered their lives for their imperial mistress. Beyond the horses, the bones of another small animal—perhaps a dog—caught the edge of her glance. She stopped, feeling sickened. What would greet her eyes as she moved further into the tomb?

A quick jab startled her into motion; from the corner of her eye one of Ji Chou's underlings reached out to prod her forward. Fastidiously stepping over the sprawling bones of yet another horse, Samille worked her way between staggering piles of funerary objects. The amount of precious metals among these gifts was mind-boggling—surely more than enough to make Wei-chu wealthy beyond his wildest imaginings.

Benjamin's indrawn breath sounded behind her. Too busy watching where her feet were going, he had seen before her what lay upon a stone catafalque. Carefully laid out with her arms at her sides, the Dragon Princess wore a suit of green armor. *Jade was thought to prevent decay....* Dimly, her father's musings echoed in her mind. Thousands upon thousands of thin jade wafers had been meticulously sewn together with gold thread to complete the imperial princess's eternal armor. Samille's hand went to her throat. The source of her necklace was obvious. The suit had gently collapsed in two thousand years, the flesh of the dead princess long withered away.

Yet, the weight of a terrible, breathless majesty filled the vast chamber. The hair stood up on Samille's arms. The princess had lain undisturbed, with only a single slender clue to her existence hoarded and guarded from generation to generation. Did Wei-chu believe the Dragon Princess would relinquish her long sleep gracefully?

Samille turned back to their captors. Ji Chou's eyes had widened with astonishment and greed. He spoke rapidly to his accomplices. One man held his gun on Benjamin and Yen-shu, motioning for her to move closer. She did so, noticing only then, as Ji Chou bent avidly near the body of the princess, the personal offerings heaped about the princess. Pearls lay threaded through loops of finely wrought gold necklaces. The ivory spines of fans caught strands of jade beads and other precious and semi-precious stones among tattered silken ribs. Amber, lapis lazuli, and garnets winked in the rays of the lantern set down by the third Chinese tong member.

Yen-shu coughed. Ji Chou's sharp glance raked the old man. The coughing shook the apothecary's slight body.

"May I give him water, Ji Chou?" Benjamin asked tersely. At the man's distracted nod of assent, Benjamin knelt on one knee and settled Yen-shu on the brick floor beside Samille. She drew out her canteen and bent toward them. As Yen-shu drank, Benjamin's hand closed about the leg of an iron tripod. Their guard's eyes shifted with increasing rapidity between his captives to his comrades—increasingly lingering upon the latter. The other two men were intent upon their looting, muttering soft grunts and cries as they reached for one treasure after another.

Benjamin lunged at their guard, thrusting the plundered tripod into the man's thin face.

"Run, Samille!" His hand in the small of her back propelled her forward with such force he nearly sent her sprawling as he snatched their guard's pistol and grabbed for Yen-shu. Ji Chou exclaimed. The other tong member reached for his own weapon as he straightened abruptly, taking aim at Benjamin's retreating back. Samille, looking back with horror, tripped.

"Benjamin!"

Her cry of terror was arrested by the sight of a lithe figure catapulting from the shadows. Like a cat, Soon Lee landed before Benjamin's assailant, twisted, and struck out before his target could recover and defend himself. The man doubled over, the haft of a *jin gou* blade gleaming in his stomach. Soon Lee broke from the man, leaping after Samille. His hand shot out to stabilize her flight.

"Run, Missy Sam!"

Samille ran, dimly aware of Ji Chou and his remaining comrade in furious pursuit as Soon Lee pounded behind her and they hurled themselves through the wide-gaping tomb doors. The whine of a bullet sang near her head. Ducking instinctively away, she dove into a side-chamber, Soon Lee on her heels. Wei-chu's men reached the tomb entrance. Ji Chou shoved his companion and gestured angrily, clearly torn between giving chase and the treasure yet to be plundered.

The other man had just as clearly not forgotten the two men—at least one of them armed—who now lay hidden in the vast maze of rooms which surrounded the central tomb. Obstinately, he refused to leave the shelter of the tomb doors. Ji Chou gestured for the man to stand guard at the tomb entrance. As long as Ji Chou's man stood guard, they were trapped. Soon Lee's silent exploration had already confirmed the small room in which they had taken cover exited only in the clear view of the tomb's entrance.

When Samille pointed equally silently at Soon Lee's pistol, he shook his head and indicated the earthen roof over their heads. Grimly, she returned her attention to the tableau before her. They would wait. Uneasily, his Mongol features pinched with caution, Ji Chou's man held his post at the doors to the tomb and faced the antechambers. A sudden clanging noise rang throughout the halls as if one of the imperial guards must have toppled over—or sprung to life. The guard jumped, eyes rolling, and fired wildly down the central corridor. Ji Chou appeared a minute later, angrily cuffing his accomplice. The man spat out a reply.

Palms against the wall, Samille felt a tremor. An echo from the fallen statue? The Mongol staggered back a step, clear of the doors. Ji Chou followed, pulling his own gun. They fired at the same instant, Ji Chou's bullet taking the smaller man directly in the neck. Blood spurted wildly. The second bullet went wide. The sight of the blood blurred Samille's vision—the horror of the Malay mutiny welled up before her eyes. She heard the thunderous crashing of waves against the side of the ship, the screams of the Chief Mate and the Second Officer as the Malays slashed at them. Then she became aware of someone shaking her. Her terror was so great she could not move to fend them off.

"Missy! Missy Sam! We go now!"

Soon Lee. It was Soon Lee beside her. Samille freed her face from her hands. Before her, where the great doors had stood, dirt still settled from a gaping hole in the roof. The dead man was mercifully covered. Of Ji Chou, there was no sign. Benjamin emerged from the central passageway.

Samille ran to him and flung her arms about him. He held her tightly for a moment, and as one they turned bleak faces upon the blocked entrance to the tomb. Benjamin's sharp eyes roamed the ceiling thoughtfully. He let go of Samille and strode over to the mound of dirt, one finger absently stroking his mustache. She recognized his look of intense concentration, but even Benjamin couldn't dig through the mound of rubble.

"It was a trap, my sweet."

Her startled gaze re-evaluated the hole torn in the ceiling. Save for the ragged edges of the bamboo mats, it formed a neat rectangle—far too regular to have been a random section when all about it the roof still held. She said as much to the motionless figures beside her.

"Don't be too sure about the rest of this roof holding, Sparrow. I suggest we beat a rapid retreat." Those azure eyes met hers squarely. "Don't worry, darling. We'll think of something to appease Wei-chu. We still have the jade token. We can always offer that and a map to Wei-chu. He'll have to provide his own shovels!" He kicked at a clod of dirt. "Let's grab Yen-shu and get out of here! I left him back there, out of harm's way."

"Wait!"

Soon Lee darted forward and squatted at Benjamin's side. Sickened, Samille saw a dislodged clod had revealed a clenched fist. By the careful manicure, it belonged to Ji Chou. Gently, Soon Lee eased the dead man's fist open and pried a pouch from the dead man's grasp. He stood and shook part of the pouch's contents onto Benjamin's outstretched palm. Matched black pearls glimmered in the wan lantern's gleam. Dumbfounded, the three eyed one another, and then Benjamin carefully poured the lustrous, magnificent jewels back into the pouch. Soon Lee spoke, his voice hushed and reverent.

"The Dragon Princess did not forsake you, Missy Sam, in your moment of need!"

Benjamin let out a hiss, one part disbelief and one part sheer relief.

"She certainly did not! Come on, let's collect Yen-shu. He says there's another tunnel—one the workers used who built this tomb—not far from where we are. It will take us to the outside world. Let's get out of here before the Dragon Princess changes her mind!"

Chapter 12

Twelve days later, the *Shanghai Rose* cut her engines as she nosed into a berth along a pier in the Roads. Wrapped in the past, Samille stood on deck and let the frantic activity wash over her in a wave of familiarity. She might never have left this raging city of lions.

A hand steadied her as a disembarking passenger bumped her. Benjamin's face wore a look of concern, his fair hair flying in the breeze, his blue eyes alert and lively. She'd forgotten, in their own manic rush back to Peking and on to Singapore, that he would be coming home. Could she come back to this city to live? She brushed the thought away brusquely and joined the flow of passengers now thronging the gangplank. She hadn't been asked to stay, had she?

Yen-shu, once safely recovered in the tomb from behind a statue of an imperial guard, had directed them down a narrow side passageway. Twisting through further ranks of broken and buried terracotta warriors, the passageway had eventually brought them out on the side of the hill, as promised. Twice they'd had to stop to dig their way through roof-falls, and it had been daylight before they reached fresh air. Surveying the landscape before them, Yen-shu had directed them well away from Shang Jiao Cun. Threading their way through the low hills dotting the flat landscape, Samille had given one last glance behind her to the hill which covered the tomb of the Princess Dai. And then, stumbling, her gaze narrowed speculatively, she eyed the other low hills. Yen-shu, as if he read her thoughts, nodded once. Samille said nothing, her mind overcome with awe.

She came back to the present with a start as Benjamin hailed a rickshaw and directed the driver to her father's hotel. It hadn't been possible, not knowing if other tong members might be on the watch, for them to wire Professor Langley or Nathanial Hawkins from Peking. As for notifying Wei-chu Chuang, Benjamin observed grimly they stood a better chance of freeing their hostages if he, Samille, and Soon Lee remained alive to do so.

Silent in the confines of the rickshaw cab, she sought Benjamin's hand and hoped Soon Lee, who'd traveled separately from them on the *Shanghai Rose* steamer, would have no difficulty reaching Min Lee at the Emperor's Lotus restaurant. The Green Dragon's ransom had been relegated to a money belt secured about Benjamin's trim waist. As soon as they could meet with her father and Michael O'Grady at the hotel, they would notify Nathanial Hawkins of their arrival in Singapore.

Once they knew how matters stood in the city, they would decide upon the proper approach to make to Wei-chu. Yen-shu, reluctantly left behind in Shang Tsao with his overjoyed young apprentice, had repeatedly urged them not to trust his cousin's word. For the treasure of the Green Dragon, he told them somberly, Wei-chu would kill with no more compunction than if he were ridding himself of roaches for Raffles' penny bounty.

The rickshaw driver dropped them at the corner of Esplanade and High Street in front of the Courthouse. Across the way, Samille saw the old *Hotel de l'Esperance* was now the *Hotel de l'Europe*. Entering the hotel, however, Professor Langley and Michael were nowhere to be found. A discreet inquiry at the desk by Benjamin turned up inexplicable news—the two American gentlemen had gone up the Malay Peninsula three days earlier to tour a tin-mining operation. Nathanial Hawkins, when they telephoned the *Straits' Times*, had left word for his nephew to the effect he was seeing to business matters in Macau and would return to Singapore by mid-week.

Taking rooms in the hotel, Samille met Benjamin for an early supper on the terrace facing the hotel gardens. Fidgeting restlessly as the waiter served their food, Samille bit back her worries. Even Soon Lee had failed to report back to them. As soon as the waiter bowed himself away, Samille turned to Benjamin.

"I don't like this!" Startling Benjamin from his reverie, she reiterated her misgivings, fear and uncertainty shadowing her pale face beneath its cloud of thick dark hair.

"Nor do I, my Sparrow," Benjamin agreed, "but what do you suggest we do? I begin to feel faintly ridiculous, having arrived triumphant only to find our co-conspirators playing tourist as if nothing out of the ordinary concerned them. But," his eyes narrowed thoughtfully, "Uncle Nate rarely goes to Macau—he's got a perfectly competent staff there. I wonder what the old fox is up to?"

"Benjamin... what if?" Samille's throat closed on the rest of her thought. Hastily, her companion clasped her fingers in his own warm grasp.

"Don't even think it! Something's afoot, I can feel it. No," he continued reassuringly, "I don't believe Wei-chu has somehow spirited your father, Michael O'Grady, my uncle, and Soon Lee away." He shook her hand gently. "You give the man far too much credit. Why don't we sit tight until Uncle Nate returns from Macau, and then we'll approach Wei-chu?"

"If," Samille added with a calm she did not feel, "he hasn't already contacted us by then. I'm glad, my dearest," she lowered her voice as Benjamin's grasp tightened, "we made a deposit in the hotel safe.

"But," her neck straightened and deep green eyes sought her dinner companion's gaze, "do you really think, Benjamin, I can calmly wait to see if my father walks in the door unharmed? Besides, I can't endure the thought of Aunt Jane and Lennie being held by that monster for a single day longer!" She shuddered and drew her shawl more closely about her shoulders. Benjamin sighed and signaled their waiter for more wine.

"I was afraid you'd see it like this, Sparrow. My god, you're willing to beard the dragon in his den?" His free hand smoothed a corner of his moustache as his blue eyes flared briefly. "Very well. Tomorrow morning, then, let us retrieve a single token from the safe and pay a visit to Wei-chu. Let's be prudent, though, shall we, and call upon him at his ship chandlery store at Battery Road and Flint Street, isn't it? We can walk there after breakfast.

"Let's just hope," he added with a slight frown, "that Soon Lee turns up before then. And now," he changed the subject, his azure eyes sparkling, "I propose we finish our meal and take a short turn in the gardens before an early night."

Arm in arm they paced sedately along the moonlit paths, Samille seeing, like a wraith from her past, a memory of a young unhappy girl filled with pain and longing dancing in those shadows. Remembering, too, how a stranger's voice had been rough with concern, yet his touch gentle. She glanced up from beneath her lashes to find Benjamin staring at those same shadows. Her mouth curved into a tender smile. She halted.

"Thank you, Benjamin," she whispered, amusement catching in her throat. He shook her arm lightly.

"It's about time, young miss. That bush left wicked reminders of my noble efforts on your behalf."

His hands came up to smooth the soft, thick mass of black hair framing the deep-lashed eyes sparkling like liquid moonlight, the full mouth tinged with amusement. He bent his head slightly, brushed his mouth against her sweetly responsive lips like one drunk on the joy of her touch, then pulled her closer—or did she pull him closer?—for a breathless series of kisses that left her heart—or was it his?—beating an erratic tattoo against her chest. She stole one last kiss and looked up, her face strangely grave, her eyes wide and earnest.

"Thank you, Benjamin."

He rubbed his thumb along the nape of her slender neck.

"I think, my love, you already thanked me."

Slowly, reluctantly, he began to retrace their meandering steps back to the lights of the hotel verandah.

"No, Benjamin," Samille's words came softly, but distinctly, "thank you for loving me, for risking your life in China for the ungrateful wretch you left behind in California, but most of all, thank you for what you did tonight."

He stopped on the path and faced her, grinning broadly.

"Is that a hint, my love, my turtledove, my Sparrow? If so, I'm more than happy to oblige again."

He puckered his lips exaggeratedly. Samille planted a quick kiss against them, and was almost sidetracked from what she meant to say.

"You know very well what I intended." She drew back a little breathlessly from his tempting mouth, its owner's moustache twitching with amusement. "Any other man would have told me not to worry my pretty little head, to leave it to him to deal with. I love you, Benjamin T. Greaves, with all my heart!"

The amusement faded from his face. He kissed the knuckles of the hand he held. Then a brow lifted and his eyes danced again.

"It's not your heart that interests me at the moment." He gathered her close for a brief, hard embrace. "Come along, Sparrow. Let's put you to bed before I forget myself."

Samille brushed her hair vigorously, loosely braided it, and slipped into bed, putting out the light as she did so. A small line creased her brow. For a few precious moments in Benjamin's arms, she had been able to forget her aunt's and Lennie's peril, her fears for her father and Michael held in momentary abeyance. She knew all too well Wei-chu Chuang held the power to kill rather than release his hostages as promised. They were playing a dangerous game with no way to predict the outcome.

And what of Benjamin? Her gaze brushed the dimly visible connecting door leading to his room. He'd insisted he have the room next to hers. What would she do if he asked her to stay in Singapore? Although, her brow knotted again, he hadn't exactly declared undying love for her, had he, out there in the moonlight? Her gaze widened as the connecting door swung silently open into Benjamin's room. A tanned forehead, tousled fair hair falling over it, appeared at knee level. She raised herself onto an elbow in her bed and began to giggle. In the light from the adjoining room, she could just make out Benjamin's smug grin.

"Benjamin T. Greaves!" Mock accusation filled her voice. "You picked that lock!"

He stood, displaying a long hairpin.

"Damned right, my lovely." He grinned happily, and she laughed outright. "I most certainly did. I'll lock it come morning, Samille, to preserve your reputation, but for the night, you only have to stir in your sleep and I'll be at your side. Now," he inquired hopefully, bouncing slightly on the balls of his feet, "shall I tuck you in?"

"No, thank you, Benjamin," she murmured demurely. "Good-night, my love." She lay down on her side once more, facing the door between the rooms.

With a two-fingered salute, Benjamin retired to his room, leaving the connecting door ajar. Shortly thereafter, his light was extinguished and the faint squeaking of the bed reached her as he settled himself for the night.

The topiary figures wavered in the shifting moonlight. Stylized bears, peacocks, and an entire aviary took on life. Round and round the figures danced and fluttered about her, coming closer and closer. Faster and faster their dancing swirled until the dark figures blurred, merging into a writhing, coiled mass of green that reared a sharp-fanged face before her.

Paralyzed with terror, her screams died in her throat.

Ever more tightly, the scaled coils twisted about her.

"Samille! Sam, darling!"

Her eyes opened into the light. Uncomprehendingly, the muscled bands surrounding her were not green.

"Samille, wake up!"

At last her frenzied brain lost its hold on the nightmarish images gripping her, and she twisted about to burrow closer into Benjamin's comforting arms. He stroked the dark hair which had escaped its braid and cascaded wildly about her shoulders until her shivering stilled. For a long moment she said nothing, then in a halting whisper, she described the vivid, menacing dream.

"Sh-h!" A gentle finger caressed her cheek. "Put it from your mind, my love. We've come too far to fail, and besides, the Green Dragon is on our side, remember?" He raised her chin and kissed the tip of her nose. "Now, let's get you tucked in for what's left of this night."

He suited his actions to his words. Her unblinking gaze never left his face; then, as his stood, she sat up and grabbed his hand.

"Please stay, Benjamin!" she pleaded. "Will you talk to me until I sleep? It's still there, the nightmare, behind my eyes. Please?"

His fingers turned in hers, encasing hers in his own firm, strong touch. Steady blue eyes warmed her even as his lips brushed the back of her hand.

"Of course, Sparrow," he agreed softly, his voice infinitely gentle.

Stretching himself on top of the coverlet, he pulled her trembling form closer as he turned off the light. She felt his lips in the briefest kiss against her temple.

"How would you like to hear the story of my life, hmm?" Without waiting for a reply, his measured words continued. "I was born on a small farm in northern Ohio, my love, where I ran as wild as the bald eagles on the shores of Lake Erie until I was about twelve years old. My father was killed that winter when one of his Percherons stumbled on the ice and crushed him. He died instantly.

"My mother took me to San Francisco, then, to live with her brother Nathanial, his wife Sarah, and their three daughters—my cousins Susannah, Lilly, and Miranda."

"San Francisco?" A muffled note of surprise escaped her.

"Yes, my dear. San Francisco is my home town. Uncle Nate worked for various newspapers there—moving up from gopher to copy editor to editor. After my cousins were all married and Aunt Sarah passed away, Uncle went out to Singapore at the urging of a friend and fellow editor. Oh, about fifteen years ago now.

"I more or less followed in his footsteps, having no inclination to return to my roots as a farmer. I like writing more than editing, and when my mother's heart gave out on her, I took myself off to Singapore to visit Uncle Nate. He was persuaded of my talents and took me on as a reporter."

"Do you... do you ever miss your old life, Benjamin?" Samille's unguarded, hesitant voice must have touched a chord, for his embrace tightened momentarily.

"Not really." He felt the slight, unmistakable stiffening of her body. "You see, I was a fairly lazy fellow in those days, Samille—drifting from job to job, through a series of casual encounters, watching the antics of my fellow human beings as mere amusing grist for my pen.

"I'm afraid you would have found that young man frivolous and callow, my Sparrow."

"And in Singapore?" she prompted sleepily.

"I grew up in Singapore," came the low answer. "Here I learned to care about the people behind my stories. To be objective doesn't have to mean being aloof or sarcastic. Lord knows why Uncle Nate ever took a chance on me! But, he always was a crafty old dog!"

"Mmm...." Beneath Benjamin's encircling arm, Samille relaxed. He felt the even rise and fall of her breathing. She'd fallen asleep before ever he reached the end of his tale. Serve him right, he mocked himself. Nathanial Hawkins had pointed out more than once he tended to wordiness.

Gray light barely lifted the night's warm gloom from her hotel room and the hour when Samille opened sleep-drenched eyes and felt the unaccustomed weight next to her. Carefully, she eased herself about to watch Benjamin as he slept. He'd spent the rest of the night here, beside her, to comfort her in case her sleep was disturbed once more. Yet, she'd slept deeply and trustingly, secure in his very presence—comfortable with his body snug beside her own as if long years of companionship lay between them. Society would be shocked at his presence, but she found she cared not a whit.

Stilled for once, his fine pale hair fanned forward to frame his strong-willed face, relaxed only as he slept. What had he called himself last night? Callow? Never, she told herself and suddenly her heart constricted. She wanted fiercely for two sleep-weighted lids to rise, revealing those intelligent azure eyes, the mobile mouth to be roused. Her breath caught in a quick gasp. She could not endure his presence so close yet so far away. Her hand slid beneath the heavy silk of his robe, across the chest, to tighten involuntarily at his waist as twin pools of blue regarded her without a hint of surprise stirring in those sensual, glittering depths.

"Samille...."

The soft expulsion of breath upon her lips teased her as he whispered her name, then his body tautened against her.

"What? Sh-h!" he cautioned under his breath.

The sound reached her even as Benjamin rose from the bed and padded cautiously to his room. A soft scratching, as if a breeze scraped the merest twig against the shuttered windows. It came again. Snatching up her robe from the chair beside her bed, Samille fled after the disappearing figure of Benjamin. Stealthily, he made his way along the wall to the double set of French windows overlooking a small verandah above the hotel gardens. As he paused for a moment at his bedside, Samille watched as he lifted a revolver from the drawer of his bedside table. Judiciously approaching the windows from the side, he lifted the catch and pulled the shutter open a slit. A shadow slumped into the room. With a half-choked cry of recognition, Samille leapt forward as Benjamin lowered his revolver and knelt by Soon Lee's sagging form.

Dutifully sitting still with a cold cloth pressed to the livid bruises on his cheek, Soon Lee plunged into his tale, but softly, as if he feared the very walls were listening.

"I find my way to the *Emperor's Lotus* restaurant, Missy Sam, and ask to speak with Min Lee. A server tells me to follow him and I do so, to an alley where three men ask me not so nicely why I come looking for Min Lee. When I do not answer, they ask once more.

"At last, a small man step from shadows. 'Enough,' he says to them. 'I am Min Lee. Why do you come here? How do I know you are who you say?' I tell him, Missy Sam, you and Master Greaves have come to ransom back young Miss Eleanor and Mistress Gooden."

Soon Lee turned his one good eye to them.

"They take me blindfolded, this way and that along the waterways. We go by boat some ways until finally my blindfold is removed. And who should I see," he clutched at Samille's arm in his excitement—although even then, he pitched his voice low, "but Miss Eleanor with Professor O'Grady and your honorable father."

"What?!" Samille and Benjamin exclaimed as one.

"I speak the truth, Missy Sam! Your old friend, Penang, she see one day young English miss with blonde curls. She know Green Dragon tong; she know Min Lee look for such a miss. So she contact Min Lee and he tell Mister Hawkins."

"Who contacted the professors," Benjamin finished for him.

"Yes!" Eagerly, Soon Lee nodded and turned to him. "Penang say young miss guarded in a warehouse near the Roads. Min Lee and the others plan—your father, Missy

Sam, and Professor O'Grady pretend to go to the interior of the peninsula. Mister Hawkins pretend to go to Macau.

"But instead, they go to steal away missing daughter with Min Lee's help. They distract guards with small fire in opium bales and take daughter out in a wheelbarrow. Then they all hide."

"Why, Soon Lee?" Samille asked him, her bewilderment plain to read. "Where is Aunt Jane? Why they are hiding?"

Soon Lee's eager face crumpled.

"Most sorry, Missy Sam. Miss Eleanor say that Wei-chu's people separate her from Mistress Gooden once they arrive in Singapore. The tong moved Miss Eleanor every so often. First she was in a house in the country—a fine house, then in a hut, and once in an attic. In house-boats on the canals, and finally in the warehouse.

"One time, she think she heard—in the room next to her—your aunt's voice protesting, but she—Miss Eleanor—had no chance to look into this room before she was moved once more."

"So," Benjamin summed up, "Lennie is trying to recon-struct her movements. The others have been lying low both to help search for Jane and to deceive Wei-chu into believing Lennie escaped on her own. That close, Soon Lee?"

"Yes, Master Greaves. Most correct."

"Where is my father, Soon Lee? Can you take us to him?"

The younger man shook his head before she finished.

"No, Missy Sam. Your father say must not lead the fox to the nest." He exchanged a quick, oblique glance with Benjamin.

Samille clasped her hands into fists. "Then we must go immediately to Wei-chu and bargain for my aunt's release."

"No." Again, a darting glance to Benjamin. "Missy Sam, Professor Langley suggest you contact Wei-chu Chuang by message and wait at the hotel for a reply."

"Why shouldn't we approach him directly?" Stubbornly, Samille pressed her point. "Why waste time sitting around here running messages back and forth?"

"Min Lee and professors think they know where Mistress Gooden is located, Missy Sam. If you distract Wei-chu's attention, then perhaps they can free her without you ever having to face tong leader."

"I see." Benjamin's succinct and clipped comment clearly showed his agreement.

"Well, I don't agree!" Samille flared, facing her two companions with rising color in her cheeks. "What if they can't reach Aunt Jane? What if Wei-chu has her moved to a new location in the wake of Lennie's escape? What if he brings her with him to meet us?" At the silence which met this outpouring, she insisted, "Well?"

Soon Lee shrugged, a tiny sigh escaping him.

"He will not, Missy Sam." Helplessly, he looked at Benjamin as if for aid.

"What news are you keeping from us, Soon Lee?"

"Mistress Gooden has been kept at the bungalow on the Serangoon Road."

"But surely not!" Samille exclaimed in disbelief. "Wei-chu would never risk keeping her there! He often entertains foreign guests at his home. How could he take a chance Aunt Jane might manage to make contact with someone? She's a very resourceful person!"

Benjamin might have guessed what was to come, for he moved unobtrusively to Samille's side and rested his hands on her shoulders as she ceased her restless pacing and sank down in bewilderment on the end of Benjamin's bed.

"Wei-chu has no need to fear her. He has quieted her with the drug opium. She is only rarely aware of herself or her surroundings. And then, only to be drugged again," Soon Lee broke off bleakly.

"Oh, dear God, no!" Samille's anguished whisper tore at her self-control. "Benjamin," she tried agitatedly to rise, "we must go at once! Let me up, I must dress. Benjamin!"

Iron hands held her until the fight went out of her, and she buried her face in her hands, sobs wracking her slender body. Gently, Benjamin pulled her hands away from her face as he knelt beside her, his voice fiercely determined.

"We will free her, Sparrow. Uncle Nate and your father wouldn't prevent us from going to Jane's aid if they weren't confident of success." He tilted her chin up and brushed away her tears with his thumb. "Ours will be the most important task, my dear. If we are to save her now, we must skillfully misdirect Wei-chu Chuang's attention away from his hostage to his desire to claim the Green Dragon's treasure.

"Come," he put his arm about her and helped her stand. "Let's put you back to bed. We must not let anything seem to be amiss. Remember," he walked her into her room and guided her to her bed, "we aren't supposed to know Lennie is safe, nor that your aunt's condition is critical."

Turning her face away from the day, Samille slid into bed and closed her eyes obediently. She would not sleep, but best not to add to Benjamin's and Soon Lee's worries.

Much to her surprise, Samille dozed and woke to find sunshine held at bay behind the wooden shutters of her windows. With day, too, her despair was checked by a heavy calm. She would wait only so long, then she would go to Wei-chu alone, if necessary. If he had done this to Aunt Jane, clearly he had not planned to ever free her. But, to acquire the treasure of the Princess Dai, he might be persuaded to give her up.

The tong leader would relish, too, she acknowledged with a chill, the opportunity to avenge himself for her long-ago escape from his clutches. Now, she must dress and find Benjamin. Perhaps, the hope blossomed within her, Aunt Jane's escape had already been affected with the efforts of Min Lee, her father, and the others. But as she dressed, she knew in her heart it was not so. With a cold certainty, she knew she would meet Wei-chu Chuang before this day ended.

Pulling a fresh chemise from her trunk, she slipped her hand deeper and felt the reassuring folds of her old tunic and trousers from those long-ago days when the Sparrow had roamed the streets of Singapore for her master. Beneath these, she knew, lay her slippers. A footstep sounded from Benjamin's room, and then a soft tap came at the connecting door.

"Just a moment, Benjamin."

The verandah lay swathed in shadows in the early afternoon. Samille sipped her iced lemonade, her green eyes fixed on her companion as Benjamin paced slowly back and forth. Then he turned and the strain of waiting was evident in the tightness about his eyes and mouth. He came to her.

"You're bearing up wonderfully well, my dear. I'm sure Soon Lee will return soon. I think I'll just check the desk one more time for messages." He patted her hand and was gone.

A message had been sent to Wei-chu's ship chandlery store when Samille had come down for breakfast at ten o'clock. Within the hour the reply had come—directing them to meet the tong leader at his Serangoon Road bungalow at four o'clock in the afternoon. While they had hoped he would be drawn into the city, Benjamin reasoned their nemesis would not be expecting a move against him and their co-conspirators still had a chance of success.

Consulting her watch, Samille saw it was shortly before three o'clock. She finished her lemonade and began to gather her gloves and fan. Without looking up, she knew no word from her father had awaited them at the hotel front desk. She raised her eyes to meet Benjamin's.

"There's time still, Sparrow. Don't give up hope!"

She permitted a small frown to crease her forehead.

"I think I'll go up to my room and lie down, Benjamin. This waiting...." She let her voice trail off. "You'll wake me when it's time?"

Benjamin took her arm.

"Of course, Samille." He squeezed her elbow. "I'll see you to your room; lock your door behind me, Sparrow. I'll tap like this," he beat a light tattoo against her door as he opened it and deposited her within, "when I have news." He brushed his lips across her forehead, his moustache tickling the soft skin. She resisted the impulse to gather him to her for a last embrace. If her plan did not succeed, it did not bear thinking about!

"Rest, my dear." The door closed behind him. Samille locked it and stood listening as his footsteps moved away.

Crossing to her trunk, she stripped away her blouse and skirt as she went, dropping them upon the floor as she drew out her coolie costume. Her hat, unfortunately, had been left in China at the end of their desperate adventure there. She thought quickly and improvised a turban from one of her cotton scarves. Once in the bazaar, a few *woman-doits*—the Malay term for British coinage—would buy her a wide-brimmed hat and a ride down the Serangoon Road. Taking up pen and paper, she thought hard for a moment and then prepared a note for

Wei-chu. It was unlikely she'd be admitted on her own in her current disguise.

After reconnoitering the hallway, she slipped out of her room and made for the servants' stairs, one hand at her throat. Monsieur Castellyns, the current manager of the *Hotel de l'Europe*, most certainly would not give a Chinese urchin access to the valuables secured by a guest in the hotel safe. Therefore, she would have to trust her jade pendant, along with her explanation of its significance, would be enough to convince Wei-chu that she in fact had the knowledge he had sought for so long.

The imposing gates shut before her were of wrought iron. Two dragons were intertwined at the top of each gate. Approaching the gated entrance to Wei-chu's bungalow, Samille wordlessly held out her note to one of the guards who strode forward, gesturing angrily at her to move along. He was not, she was glad to see, Chin hui. Still, it took all her will to keep her knees from buckling as he handed the note off to his partner, who took it and disappeared down the long, winding drive to the bungalow proper.

The guard was back within minutes, swinging the gates ajar to admit her. Once inside, he set off at a trot down the drive, Samille scrambling to keep up.

Wei-chu Chuang was taking tea on a verandah. The man was small and tending more to fat than she remembered from her days in Singapore. Wearing Western dress, the tong leader's starched white collar pinched a rolling chin. A thin, carefully clipped moustache accentuated a mouth cruel even in repose. Against his broad, flat cheeks, his eyes were hard, bright slits—totally absorbed at the moment in the laden tea-tray before him.

At last the double-ringed fingers of his right hand dipped. His maidservant—a young woman, her painted doll's face strikingly blank of expression—served him with the cakes he indicated. His hand flicked at a second cup. The young woman took up the sterling silver teapot and poured a second cup of tea. Only then did his eyes lift from the tea table. He waved away the servant, who disappeared with a rustle of silks into the bungalow.

"Please sit, Miss Langley."

Pushing back her coolie hat, Samille took the chair across from him, determined not to show her fear of this man. She would be a fool not to be afraid of him—both he and she knew this—but controlling her fear might give her an edge. She held the upper hand at least for the moment. If he killed her, the knowledge for which he hungered would be beyond his grasp. She forced herself to meet the merciless intelligence in the gaze with which he raked her. A certain contempt altered the set of his mouth. Clearly, the Green Dragon tong leader felt himself to be in absolute control of the present situation.

"I have the information which you seek, Wei-chu Chuang. It will be yours upon the release of your hostages." Samille forced a calmness she did not feel into her voice. The man sitting across from her must not suspect she knew one of his hostages had already been liberated from his grasp.

Wei-chu's eyes widened slightly. A harsh rumble of amusement wheezed out past his collar.

"You dare bargain with the Dragon, Miss Langley?" His sausage fingers deftly palmed a sugar cube. The massive fist closed about it. His mouth twisted with a false smile, then he finished his cake, fastidiously brushing crumbs from his shirt cuff.

"You are a stupid female, Miss Langley." He dismissed her attempt to bargain bluntly. "I will have the treasure from you with or without your consent. Do you understand? Your very presence here will lead the others to you—to attempt your rescue. They too will die. Then the secret will be mine and mine alone."

Samille's stomach lurched.

"They will not be so foolish, Wei-chu. I have come here to free my aunt and the girl. To give you that which you wish. A simple exchange. If you do not allow us safe conduct, then my father and his friends will bring the British authorities here with them. They will not walk into your house unarmed." Pray she was right!

Again, rasping laughter shook him.

"The British Consulate is a dear friend, Miss Langley. He will not believe such a tale as your friends will tell." Scorn dripped from his words, yet she had the tiniest impression of worry as his eyes looked quickly away from hers. The British Consulate might indeed dine at Wei-chu's Serangoon Road bungalow, but no British official survived long in Singapore without understanding something of the way tongs worked. The whispers about Wei-chu Chuang would have reached the man's ears. He continued, "What proof can they offer?"

When she made no answer, he clapped his hands once, sharply. Chin hui appeared with a second man. Their leader gave them a series of commands in Chinese, and then picked up his cup.

"There are one or two matters to which I must attend before we speak again. Take her away."

He waved a hand, much as though she was an annoying gnat to be dispatched. The men grasped her arms; she went without a struggle, her mind working frantically as she studiously avoided the unholy gleam of anticipation on Chin Hui's face. He, too, it seemed, was remembering when she had escaped his clutches once before.

Propelled along between the men, Samille was taken to the rear of the bungalow. In spite of its name, the house was a huge, rambling mansion built in the colonial style. They took her up a narrow flight of stairs and along a dark hall to a small, airless room. Shoved unceremoniously into the room, she heard a bolt clang into place behind her as the door was shut.

With outstretched arms, she fumbled her way into the room. Her fingers encountered something yielding. Head-high or taller, all around her she could feel stacked bales. Soon Lee's words came back to her: Lennie's escape had been engineered with a fire in bales of opium. Apparently, business was booming if Wei-chu must use his home for storage as well. Feeling with her hands, Samille sat down with her back to a bale, keeping the line of light marking the doorjamb to her left.

Fighting panic, she tried to think through her predicament. First, her threat had meant something to Wei-chu. Why did he wait to question her? Surely, he was not yet certain Lennie's freedom had in fact been contrived by the Americans. For all he knew, Professor Langley and Nathanial Hawkins might even now be camped in the British consulate offices. On the other hand, how could the tong leader be certain Benjamin did not possess other proof of Wei-chu's actions—such as the treasure and his—Wei-chu's—note for them to meet here at the bungalow? Unless—she swallowed painfully. If Wei-chu had taken Benjamin? Had killed him already? Oh, what a fool she was! Benjamin had been right; their safety lay in staying together. She closed her eyes wearily as despair hit like nausea, thick and clammy in her throat.

No! She opened her eyes and struggled against panic. Benjamin was not stupid. He would not be easy to take. Her eyes narrowed. She strained them against the dusty gloom in the locked room where she was imprisoned. It seemed lighter, more diffuse around the edges of those bales. Curious, she put her shoulder to a bale. It gave. She looked back at the door. The bales didn't weigh enough to bar entry into her prison, but enough of them might considerably delay the entry of her captors. With renewed vigor, she set to work, methodically shoving and stacking the bales in front of the door.

As she shifted the bales, the gloom perceptibly lightened behind her. At last, perhaps an hour later, a shuttered window was revealed in the wall opposite the door. A closer investigation and several broken fingernails succeeded in parting the window's shutters by the barest inch. Gratefully, she sucked at the fresh air and waning light admitted through the crack, choking on the heat and renewed dust her earlier efforts had stirred up in the room.

At length, she roused from her stupor to take note of the strip of view revealed below as day deepened into dusk. The storeroom overlooked the rear of the bungalow—its fabled gardens spread out below her. The topiary figures of her nightmare mocked her. The peacock might have spread its wings and screamed. It screamed again. Samille pressed her eye more closely to the crack. A live peacock fluttered just within sight, perched on the absurd pagoda-summerhouse in the center of the topiary garden. What—or who—had disturbed it?

Footsteps. On stone. She tried to look down, but a narrow ledge blocked her limited view. Frantically, she put her ear to the shutter.

"Most sorry, Mr. Chuang... lot of unnecessary bother...."

"I insist, sir! The house and gardens must be searched!"

Samille's heart lurched with a painful thump against her chest. Benjamin! And with help!

"...dear fellow... drug addict...."

The distaste of that utterance left no doubt as to the officer's allegiance. Wei-chu was denying nothing, saying nothing, his very silence as an influential and powerful figure in the community speaking for him. Futilely, Samille cast a glance about her. Her throat was so dry and choked with dust that no sound came as she tried to croak out Benjamin's name. Her frantic hand clutched her throat. The scarf! Her erstwhile turban remained wrapped around her neck. Why hadn't she thought to pull it over her nose and mouth?

Jerking it unsteadily from her neck, she felt the tug of her pendant and rapidly removed it. Grimly tying it to the scarf with the golden thread, she pushed the shutters as far apart as she could. With any luck at all, the jade rectangle would act as a weight to the flimsy fabric of the scarf, and, since the jade wafer's mates all lay buried in northern China, Benjamin would have no difficulty recognizing it.

Carefully, she put her ear to the crack, barely able to hear for the pounding of her heart. Yes! The weight of a body as someone shifted their stance on the terrace reached her. Now! She pushed the fabric through the crack in the shutters, the jade clearing the narrow stone ledge and dragging the scarf free to plummet over the edge.

"I say!"

"No, you don't, Chuang!" Benjamin's rough voice. "What's this? Samille! She's here, Litton! This belongs to her!"

Rapid exclamations sounded, running footsteps, a muffled curse.

"Greaves, are you all right?"

Benjamin! Samille lurched to her feet. She'd outfoxed herself. Doggedly, she set to work tearing down her barricade. Moments later, Benjamin's anxious cries reached her from the hallway.

"Sparrow? Where are you?"

The knob of her door rattled. Despairingly, she tried to force his name from her parched lips, and then scrambled onto the remaining bales and beat at the door with her fists. The footsteps were retreating. Tears streamed down her dirt-streaked face. She pounded furiously at the door.

"Here, Greaves! Stand clear inside!" A voice bellowed.

Samille half-rolled, half-fell from her perch. The door shook violently, then burst inward, pushing the bales atop her. Benjamin reached her before she regained her feet, lifting her in an embrace that nearly strangled both of them.

Inspector Litton, tall and lanky with a drooping black moustache, reappeared on the terrace where Samille greedily drank the glass of water poured by a beefy sergeant, whose grin at the sight of her in her tunic and trousers and dust-streaked face faded as Benjamin eyed him sharply. Chin hui, one side of his face swelling agreeably, she saw as they gained the verandah, had been secured to a pillar with handcuffs.

"Chuang's gotten clean away, Greaves. I suggest—."

"He'll go to the *Hotel de l'Europe*," Samille interrupted, addressing the inspector and Benjamin, gripping the latter's jacket front. "He's defeated and he knows it, Benjamin. He won't leave Singapore without taking his revenge—someone must pay for his disgrace!"

Bleakly, Benjamin faced the white-faced British officer. "How quickly can we get to the hotel from here?"

"Quickly enough," Inspector Litton considered, pulling thoughtfully on his long chin, "but there's no need to worry. My men have orders to stand guard at the hotel. They're on their way now. Chuang won't dare go there. He'll be trying to get off the island. You'll see."

Samille's grip tightened wordlessly.

"Nevertheless," Benjamin's arm came around her shoulders, "we insist."

Inspector Litton shrugged.

"As you wish, Mr. Greaves. McElroy, escort this gentleman and, er, lady to the *Hotel de l'Europe* at once."

Dusk deepened as they rode back into the city. The onset of twilight had always been her favorite time of the day in Singapore, but now she barely noticed the way the oncoming night obscured the tawdry outskirts of the old lion, the way the cool night breezes stirred, the way the soft lights transformed the tropical flowers and trees into a perfumed mass wafting sweet enticing scents across the avenues. She clung tightly to Benjamin's arm, sitting on the edge of her seat as shadows filled the city—shadows massing as if from some *dalang* master's shadow play where evil sallied forth to combat the dragon and the princess.

At last, the lights of the hotel lobby spilled from the multiple sets of French doors thrown open to the night air. Inside, the lobby appeared deserted. Hurling herself from the rickshaw, Samille crossed the street without regard for traffic. Benjamin took her arm as he caught up with her at the hotel entrance. As they started up the steps to the lobby, the low whine and purr of the ornate lift reached them. Voices, laughter. Nathanial Hawkins' booming tones. Michael O'Grady's light-hearted reply. Litton must have called the hotel from the bungalow. The doors of the lift slid open. Professor Langley stepped out first.

Samille tripped in her haste to reach her father as they climbed the last step. Benjamin steadied her as she broke her fall with a palm. She half-turned to thank Benjamin as he bent to help her. Out of the corner of her eye, she caught a movement. What? Near the banked ferns grouped by a pillar in the lobby. Out of the shadowy corner, an arm raised—knife in hand! Wei-chu!

A voice screamed. Samille froze. It was her voice! She was aware of her father's startled head jerking about and a savage angry growl erupting from the shadows where Wei-chu crouched. Nathanial Hawkins' bull voice roared like an echo of that growl. Then, a lithe, lean phantom streaked into the light and bounded with a roar and snarl toward the open lobby doors and freedom of the night. A tiger!

Samille fell, pushed to the ground with Benjamin's weight shielding her. Long afterwards, she swore the great cat's fur brushed them both as it leaped clear in a smooth stretch of orange and black striped limbs, disappearing into the Lion City.

Chapter 13

The fine morning mist had lifted. Samille shaded her eyes against the glare of the sun. Someone was building on her hideaway! She picked up her skirts and started to climb up the path, rucksack secure on her shoulder. Lennie had shooed her from the house on Divisadero Street earlier in the day. Rather irritably, Samille had given in when Lennie's exhortation to get some fresh air was echoed by her father. The clearing on Telegraph Hill was still her favorite spot for retreat from the world of schoolwork and to think, although there hadn't been time to take advantage of it since her return to San Francisco.

Prudently picking her way along the path, Samille shuddered. It was nearly summer now, nearly June—months since she'd stood over Wei-chu Chuang's crumpled body, his face and chest shredded by the tiger's slashing claws in the lobby of the *Hotel de l'Europe*. Nathanial Hawkins thought it had been a female, lean and hungry, lured into the gardens at dusk by the smell of food from the kitchens. She'd have been stalking Wei-chu as he crouched in the shadows unaware, waiting an opportunity to exact his revenge. Her scream must have startled the tigress. Wei-chu had died instantly, his neck crushed.

Samille paused to adjust her knapsack, and reflected as she climbed once more. Aunt Jane had already been rescued when she'd staged her ill-advised visit to Wei-chu. Sick from the drug and ashamed, Jane Langley Gooden hadn't been cooperative with her rescuers, delaying their arrival at the hotel. Absently, Samille shooed a honeybee from her path. Her aunt had been pitifully thin. Professor Langley had insisted upon an immediate return to the United States, where Doctor Adams could be relied upon to look after her with care and discretion. Because of her physical condition, it had been necessary to build up Jane's strength before attempting the voyage home. In the meantime, the British authorities questioned them exhaustively concerning their connection to Wei-chu's activities.

They rented a small villa for privacy and her father engaged a local staff to see to their needs, but it was a month before her aunt's recovery was judged sufficient to take her home. Samille's heart twisted every time she held those bone-thin hands, talking to her aunt—reassuring her over and over that they did not despise her and that she would get well and be free of the drug. Their company took turns sitting with her, so she never felt shunned or abandoned. Even Nathanial Hawkins came regularly, wheeling Jane out onto the verandah for a bit of fresh air and reading to her from his favorite works, such as *Much Ado About Nothing*. His Dogberry did him much credit, and, moreover, elicited the first real laugh from Jane.

Stopping abruptly on the path, Samille caught her breath. This next section of the climb was tricky, filled with loose pebbles to turn an unwary ankle. As tricky as her memories. Sighing, memories of those days came flooding back. Memories of Benjamin. Benjamin, walking stiffly beside her as she boarded the steamer for America. His eyes smoldering, shadowed, flaring as his thoughts matched the turmoil of her own. He had a future in Singapore, his work was there, and she could not abandon Aunt Jane, even if, a small voice reminded her, he had asked her to stay. Which he hadn't.

"Don't tremble so, my Sparrow," he'd whispered at the last possible moment. "This is not good-bye!"

Her straw hat fell back as she wiped her brow. When they reached San Francisco, her father had promptly engaged a full-time nurse/companion to take charge of Aunt Jane's recovery, and Bridgett O'Hanratty swept into the household with an unbiased professional air which did wonders for Aunt Jane's state of mind. Bridgett tended Jane as if she simply suffered from an illness of any other sort, making Jane feel much less a burden to her family.

Ho Lee, meanwhile, still ran the household with very little need of assistance from Samille. She missed Soon Lee's presence, but, true to his word, Professor Langley and Michael O'Grady had sponsored the young man as a student at the University of California, where he'd quietly been accepted in the engineering program. His share of the pearls had helped to pave his way. Nowadays, Samille frequently encountered him in the library as she finished her own program.

The spoils from the Green Dragon's treasure had been divided with the O'Gradys as well, Michael putting his share into trust for Lennie. Part of the Langley's share was being put to use for Aunt Jane's needs, while the rest, over Samille's vigorous protests that her mother's inheritance was sufficient for her needs, was put into trust for her. A share of the pearls had been left with Yen-shu, and another with Nathanial Hawkins when Benjamin flatly refused to take a portion.

As for her future, Samille mused as she climbed nearer to the clearing, Professor Maybeck was encouraging her to go on to Europe for further study, but she'd decided against such a step. For one thing, Aunt Jane was not completely on her feet again. In addition, Julia Morgan had intimated that a place might be found for Samille in a local architectural firm if she'd care to apprentice in San Francisco. Those last school projects she'd completed for Professor Maybeck had caught the eye of one of Julia's associates.

The edge of the clearing came into sight. Samille's breath caught as she bit her lip over the unaccustomed exertion. Go on, admit it, she chastised herself. There was, of course, another reason she did not want to go to Europe. Benjamin's letters had been sporadic, but lengthy and lively accounts of his days, filled with reassuring expressions of his continued affection for her. Her lips curved reminiscently, her hand patting her skirt pocket.

This last one had been especially fervent. Who knew, the next one might.... Her thought was lost in astonishment.

Sited in the center of the clearing, the frame of a house rose before her, nearly complete, nestling in the protected heart of the clearing and angled to take full advantage of the views of the city and San Francisco Bay, of the play of light and shadow as day progressed across her old refuge. A tiled roof was taking shape under the cheerful shouts of the construction crew.

Her mouth open, Samille walked slowly along the rough drive. A workman gave her a friendly salute and a smile. Behind her, gravel crunched and a firm hand steadied her as she stepped back to avoid two burly workmen with a ladder between them.

"Does the reality measure up to your vision, my love?"

Whirling about, Samille found herself facing a pair of eyes the color of windswept waves, alight with humor and excitement. Flinging her arms about his neck, she kissed Benjamin unrestrainedly, releasing him only when the good-natured catcalls and whistles of the workmen brought her back to her senses. Grinning as her cheeks flamed, Benjamin tucked her hand into the crook of his arm and escorted her on a tour of the site.

"I don't understand," Samille swung about to face him. "When did you arrive, Benjamin? What...." her voice faltered, "what are you doing here?"

"I arrived last night, Samille. And I arranged with Lennie to lure you from the house. That young woman will go far in life, I do believe!" he added irreverently.

"As for what I am doing here, Miss Samille Beauvoir Langley, I have the pleasure to announce that I am the newly acquired prize writer of a shrewd San Francisco city editor, Virginia Barstow of the *Bulletin*."

"But, but," Samille stammered in confusion, "what about Uncle Nathanial? What about your job at the *Straits Times*?"

"'Uncle Nathanial'?" Benjamin repeated. "What a nice ring, coming from you, my dear. I approve." He kissed her other hand, which he had somehow gotten hold of as their progress halted. "Uncle Nate has retired, Samille. He's come home to San Francisco. My cousins Susannah, Lilly, and Miranda—not to mention their husbands and assorted offspring—are delighted. Also, it seems," he added, dropping his light tone in wonder, "he's quite taken with your aunt. They've been frequent correspondents, didn't you know?"

"Aunt Jane and Uncle Nathanial?" Samille's startled green eyes met those clear blue ones.

"I take it you approve, Sparrow?"

"Why, yes, yes, of course," she declared, smiling at the thought of gruff Nathanial Hawkins and Aunt Jane together. He had already shown himself to be a good friend and support to her aunt—to them all—she couldn't think of anything that would make her happier than to see Aunt Jane happy again.

"And the house?" Benjamin's voice was unexpectedly hesitant, uncertain.

"It's mine, isn't it, Benjamin?" she said softly. "I mean, my plans. Here, taking shape!"

Benjamin's mustache twitched as he grinned broadly.

"Of course! Courtesy of your dragon ancestress, my love. A wedding gift from Uncle Nate. I wanted only the best for my Singapore sparrow. For my bride... if you'll do me the honor?" He cocked an anxious brow at her, and Samille saw the doubt lingering in his eyes.

Conscious of an overwhelming desire to giddily pirouette about the clearing, Samille threw back her head with a bursting shout of triumphant laughter. Demurely linking her arm through Benjamin's, she shot a glance at him.

"Didn't you know, Benjamin love, all the time I drew those plans, I wore your image in my heart? Every line, every plane is infused with my love for you. Our children," she added softly for his ears only, "will grow up surrounded by our love!"

Benjamin halted. Above them, a rousing chorus of cheers greeted the sealing of their confession, their promise, and this time, it was Benjamin who broke their kiss and sighed, staring out over the bay.

"Yes, my darling, as many children as you want, as long as I get one dark-haired daughter with green eyes."

And so he did—not one, but three—all in good time.